THE MOTHERLAND SAGA

The Epic Novel of Turkey

VOLUME ONE

LEGACY

1897-1917

THE MOTHERLAND SAGA

The Epic Novel of Turkey

VOLUME ONE

LEGACY

1897-1917

HUGO N. GERSTL

PANGÆA

PUBLISHING GROUP

LEGACY: 1897 – 1917
Volume One - The Motherland Saga
The Epic Novel of Turkey

Copyright © 2019 Hugo N. Gerstl
www.HugoGerstl.com

ISBN 978-1-950134-20-5
Pangæa Publishing Group
www.PangaeaPublishing.com

Cover image: *Istanbul twilight © Daniel Boiteau, Dreamstime.com*
Inside images: *Border © Antsvgdal, Dreamstime.com*

Cover design and typesetting by
DesignPeaks@gmail.com

For information contact:

PANGÆA PUBLISHING GROUP
25579 Carmel Knolls Drive
Carmel, CA 93923
Telephone: 831-624-3508/831-649-0668
Fax: 831-649-8007
Email: info@pangaeapublishing.com

To Nazan Fulat Gürgün, the very first person I met when I first came to work in Ankara so many years ago – and a wonderful friend to this day, to Dick & Claire Gorman, my closest friends since our Air Force days in Arizona and Turkey

AND, OF COURSE, FOR LORRAINE

HUGO N. GERSTL

THE MOTHERLAND SAGA
The Epic Novel of Turkey

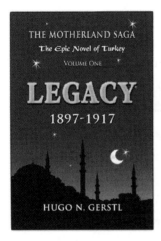
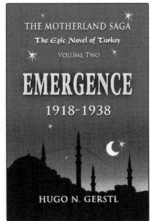
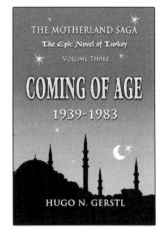

Do not miss them on your shelf!

*For Hugo N. Gerstl's complete novels list and descriptions,
go to www.HugoGerstl.com*

PANGÆA PUBLISHING GROUP
25579 Carmel Knolls Drive
Carmel, CA 93923
Email: info@pangaeapublishing.com

PROLOGUE

Today Turkey stands once again at the center of the world.

Wealthy Russians, Iranians, Arabs, and Europeans scurry to buy multimillion dollar *yalıs* – mansions on the Bosphorous in Istanbul, one of the coolest, most "happening" cities in the world.

The days of begging to become a member of EU are over. The EU now needs Turkey more than Turkey needs the European Union. Turkey is the dominant player in the Middle East – a stable, solid democracy which has left the once iron fist of the military with ten broken fingers. But recently there have been problems as the Islamists and Secularists battle for the history of the country.

As Turkey has turned increasingly Islamist, the days of the strategic alliance and unbreakable friendship with Israel seems to have hit a serious bump in the road, which may finally be smoothing out ... for now. And Recep Tayyip Erdoğan's increasingly authoritarian Islamist rule has started to show the first serious backlash in over a decade.

Everywhere the stores are filled with every modern product the world has to offer. Once thought of as a third world country, today's Turkey is very much first world, an economic force which must be reckoned with.

Yes, today Turkey stands once again at the center of the world.

But not so long ago, it wasn't that way at all…

PART ONE:

TURHAN 1897–1912

1

The mottled brown hawk circled slowly over the dun-colored hills, its eye alert for prey, as it flew toward the setting sun. Before it lay the sluggish Euphrates. Behind it, beyond its view, another river, the Tigris, descended from distant mountains. A single telegraph wire, strung on a row of wooden poles, stretched along a dirt road as far as the raptor's eye could see, the only scar across the vast landscape.

Usually the outskirts of the village provided ample fare: field mice, a rabbit, sometimes, if the hawk were lucky, a very young lamb. Today the fields were empty.

The hawk flew over the squat, thatched-roofed mud huts, and the stone minarets of the village's two mosques. On the outskirts of the village, a tall spire, attached to a white, wooden building, rose as high as the minarets. The great bird dipped for an instant toward a large, noisy crowd of people, then rose sharply into the sky, wheeled about, and headed east, toward the high mountains.

The village was observing *Kurban Bayram*, the holiday com-memorating the patriarch Ibrahim's aborted sacrifice of his son Ishak thousands of years ago. Every Turk who could afford to do so, and many who couldn't, bought and slaughtered a lamb on this day each year, distributing portions of its meat to the *truly* poor.

Near the central square a small, slender Turkish boy with black hair, dark eyes, and tawny complexion held his grandfather's hand tightly. Everywhere he looked, the village's dusty paths were filled with crowds of men and herds of sheep. The gamy odor of animals mingled with the pungent smell of unwashed human bodies. The raised voices and bawling, jittery animals made him nervous, but he forced himself to be brave. After all, Grandfather had allowed him to wear long pantaloons and a turban for the first time. He dare not disgrace the older man. The boy was four years old.

Bülent the harness maker turned to his grandson with a cheerful wink and said, "Well, Turhan, what do you think, should we buy the white one or the gray?"

Turhan pointed to a small, white lamb, a portion of its fleece dyed blue, a symbol of the occasion.

"A very wise choice, young master," the shepherd said, fawning over the boy. "Clearly Allah would approve the sacrifice of this whitest of lambs. Now, good sir," he said, turning to the tall, bearded man who held Turhan's hand, "since it pleases the youngster, I'll give you my best price, ten *kurush*."

At that moment a rooster, strutting amidst the crowd, crowed incongruously. Grandfather laughed good-naturedly. "Excuse an ignorant old man, shepherd *effendi*, but whatever that rooster may think, this is the end of the day. Most villagers have already purchased the best lambs. This scraggly fellow is worth no more than two *kurush*."

"Allah! Would you bargain for blessings on this of all days? I'd sooner give this perfect lamb to the imam, the priest, for nothing. But I won't embarrass you in front of your boy at this holiest time of the year. I will sacrifice my pride, and let you have him for eight kurush."

"Four."

"How dare you suggest such a thing?" the shepherd wailed. "I spend my lonely life in the fields, day after miserable day, caring for flocks as did Ishak himself. Would you deprive me of my only means of livelihood? The Prophet's shame! Steal from me if you must, but allow me seven kurush so I might purchase a bowl with which to beg on the streets."

"By the looks of your sheep and your belly you spend most of your 'miserable day' sleeping in the shade of an olive tree," the harness maker said, chuckling. "But I feel particularly charitable today. Five."

"Six, Effendi?"

"Done," Grandfather said. He handed his grandson the rope which secured the lamb. Turhan puffed his chest out with pride as he led the tethered, bleating animal to the alley in front of their home. Grandmother, in her finest clothing, her face partly veiled, saw man and boy coming from several yards away.

"Bülent!" she called. "What a wonderful lamb you and Turhan have purchased! Come quickly! Everything's ready." She handed her husband a glass of *ayran* – the wonderfully cooling drink of yogurt mixed with water – and a kitchen knife.

Several neighborhood children gathered round as Grandfather sharpened the knife which he'd used for this very purpose for forty years. He knew it was kindest to the sacrificial animal if the blade were razor sharp. After he recited the appropriate prayer and thanked Allah for the privilege, Grandfather held up the creature's head. With one deft, clean motion, he drew the blade across the lamb's throat. A gush of blood spurted into the alley, joining a small rivulet formed by sacrifices farther up the way. The little animal collapsed, shuddering in its death throes. Grandfather proceeded to dress the newly slaughtered lamb, pausing at intervals, to drink from the large glass of *ayran*.

Turhan gazed admiringly at Grandfather. How he wanted to be like this wonderful, strong man!

Turhan had never met his mother. He knew only vaguely of her existence. Bülent's daughter Lâle, uncontrollable from her youngest days, had flaunted her budding, sensual beauty to a troop of the sultan's soldiers passing through the village. One night, when her parents were asleep, she quietly left the house, met two girl friends, and stole away to the hills beyond the village. There, several men enjoyed her body. In time, she gave birth to a baby boy. Within days of the child's birth, Lâle ran off to Diyarbakır, the provincial capital, leaving the boy to be raised by his grandparents.

Bülent, who'd fathered no sons, considered this a belated blessing and determined to raise the child, whom he named Turhan, as his own. From the first, a loving bond grew between Turhan and his grandfather. The man took the boy with him to the coffee house, where he would bounce the youngster on his knee and sing old Turkish folk songs to him for hours on end.

Although Bülent could neither read nor write, he impressed upon his grandson the need for education. "No matter whether you're a harness maker, a shepherd, or the provincial governor," Grandfather said, "knowledge is the key that unlocks the door to everything."

By the time Turhan was nine, he'd learned simple readings from the *Koran,* and rudimentary knowledge of the Arabic letters used to write the Ottoman alphabet. The village tailor, who earned a few extra *kurush* each month as a teacher, knew no more than that, so Bülent found an educated, eighteen-year-old Armenian boy and hired him to continue Turhan's lessons. Bülent's coffee house cronies were unanimous in their objections.

"How dare you hire a *Christian* to teach a Turkish lad?"

"Next thing you know, he'll become a Jesus-person. Let the boy become a farmer or merchant. Teach him your trade, Bülent."

"My friends," the harness maker replied. "If the sultan's government can't provide education for its citizens, that's the state's problem. If they can't find someone to teach my boy, that's *my* problem. If the Armenian can teach Turhan to read and write, I trust enough in my grandson's character to believe he'll know right from wrong when it comes to other matters."

Four hundred people lived in the village. There were no streets, only dirt paths set up in an irregular pattern radiating from the central square. The Turkish majority, two hundred fifty people, lived closest to the hub. Greek and Armenian minorities lived on the other side of a small, muddy stream, which usually dried up halfway through the hot, dry summers.

Shadran Vartunian, Turhan's tutor, came from the village's poorest quarter. His home was no different from the hovels around it, a mud hut consisting of two rooms with a packed earth floor, which housed seven people.

Shadran's father had worked for the nearby military garrison until, crippled with arthritis, he could no longer sew buttons on soldiers' tunics, nor shine officers' shoes each day. Shadran was just under six feet in height, taller than most men in the village. His hair was the color of light sand. He had clear, wide-set blue eyes.

The family had sacrificed what little they had to send Shadran to the Armenian high school, a three hour walk away in the next village. For years, Shadran rose before dawn six days a week to attend classes. He trudged home at night and arrived well after the sun had gone down. He worked at as many jobs as he could find – pitching hay, cleaning streets, whatever would bring in a few *kurush*. When his family expressed dismay that their son would demean himself by teaching a loathsome Muslim, Shadran reminded them that Father had worked for the Turkish military. The family should take whatever he could earn, no matter where the money came from.

Initially there was a natural wariness between Turhan and Shadran. Each had been warned that the other came from a filthy, backward race. The Ottomans in the *kahve hane*, the coffee house, told Turhan in no uncertain terms that he was to learn reading and writing from the Armenian, but otherwise avoid the older boy. Above all, he must not discuss anything of substance with the Christian, lest Turhan's mind be poisoned and he give away secrets – he was never told what these 'secrets' were – to this infidel.

Shadran's neighbors, in turn, pitied the handsome, young Armenian who was forced to be a money-slave to the heathen Turks, barbarians who'd ridden into Armenia from the plains beyond the Indus River, and stolen the land of their forefathers. They told Shadran to avoid any but the most minimal contact with Turhan.

Nevertheless, during the next two years, a bond grew between Turhan and Shadran. Although Turhan was much younger than Shadran, the boy was so bright and eager to please that Shadran soon accepted him as a younger brother. Turhan idolized his teacher.

"Why do you work so hard, Shadran?" Turhan asked one day.

"First, of course, to help my family. But I hope, with the help of Christ Jesus, to attend university one day."

"What's 'university?'"

"A huge, wonderful school, in Constantinople – your people call it Istanbul – the *Müderrise*, where there are so many books you could never read them all in your lifetime. You study to be a doctor, a lawyer, or anything you'd like to be. Sometimes, when you graduate, you become so famous you can go to a different country. Turhan, if I tell you a secret, will you promise to keep it to yourself?"

"Word of honor," the smaller boy said, solemnly.

"Anatolia is no place for an Armenian to live. Some day, I'm going to leave this village. When I do, I'll never return." Turhan's face fell.

"Don't worry. By the time I leave, you'll be grown up. You, too, must see the world beyond. You're a Turk, so you'll be safe enough in the Ottoman Empire. Do you know where I really want to go?"

"No"

"America." He pronounced the word slowly, with reverence. There was a faraway look in his eye. "America," he said, more softly, as though the word itself was as sweet as *lokum*, the sticky Turkish candy.

"Where's that?"

"Far away. Over a body of water almost too huge to imagine. It takes months to get there. They say that anyone who works hard enough can become wealthy in America, that no one ever goes hungry there, and that a man can practice any religion he chooses."

2

Early morning the day before Easter, a dozen mounted Turkish soldiers thundered through the streets of Diyarbakır, the provincial capital, slightly more than two days' travel from Turhan's village. The governor was in session with his privy council. A crowd had gathered outside his residence. The atmosphere was ominous.

Two officers dismounted in front of government house. Behaving with the arrogance their German military instructors in Istanbul had taught them would impress the peasants, they strode up to the front door. The provincial governor, flanked on either side by his councilors, acknowledged their smart salute with a curt nod. One of the officers handed him a document.

The governor searched through his coat pockets, found his spectacles, put them on, and unfolded the paper. The two soldiers, their faces impassive, remained standing at attention. The administrator turned to his councilors, and then announced to the assembled crowd, "This message from the Minister of the Interior came over the telegraph less than an hour ago: 'Esteemed *Vali!* His gracious and glorious majesty,

Abdül Hamid the Resplendent, sends greetings. At this season, the scurrilous, cowardly Armenian community, which has scorned the Prophet's Word while enjoying the sultans' hospitality for a thousand years, is preparing for its annual Christian Easter Festival. Historically, this ungrateful and obstinate minority has used this so-called 'religious' holiday as a time for insurrection and testing our national patience. This year is no exception.'"

A man coughed. The councilors shuffled about, nervously. The governor continued.

"'Only yesterday, Allah-the-Merciful be praised, we uncovered a major conspiracy of Armenian revolutionaries seeking to overthrow the duly constituted government.'"

There was a loud sigh. The officers turned sharply and glared at the townspeople, looking for the source of the sound. Not finding it, they remained facing the populace in stony silence.

The administrator read on. "'We believe it to be the Sultan's will, Allah grant him long life, that officials throughout the Empire take immediate, definitive action to preserve the sanctity and honor of the Turkish people. Let the word go out to every village, in every province. We will not tolerate such treason. We must teach these subject people a lesson they will not soon forget."

At the same time, in the provincial military fortress outside Turhan's village, the garrison commander, a burly colonel with olive-colored skin, finished reading the same telegram. "Allah!" he said, wearily, to himself. "Let them do their own dirty work! I will not send my troops!"

A young officer rushed in, interrupting his reverie. "Colonel, Sir. They've found dog feces smeared on the *mimber*, the pulpit of the village mosque, just south of here."

Within minutes of the time the garrison commander received word of the desecration, a throng of furious men gathered noisily inside the mosque. An *imam*, the priest, walked among them with a water bucket and rags. He washed the dried animal droppings from the pulpit. Throughout the village, word spread quickly. The Turkish community seethed.

What work there was in the village was ordinarily completed by mid-morning. Women spent the rest of the time before the noon meal haggling in the village's vegetable stalls for potatoes, cabbage, turnips, and greens, to throw into the ever-simmering iron kettle at home. On market days, they bargained for a bolt of cloth, sturdy needles, and thread. The women spent several afternoons each week with their friends, sewing shirts, *shalvar*, the baggy pantaloons worn by Ottoman women since time beyond knowledge, blouses, and scarves, while they awaited the clang of the brass bell over the bakery door and the fresh, sweet aroma which announced that the evening's bread was ready.

There was no social interchange between sexes. Aside from dinner, which was served shortly after noon, men spent most of their day at the coffee house, the *real* center of their lives. Here they alleviated life's hardships and boredom. They played endless rounds of backgammon, shared news and gossip, told and listened to stories for the thousandth time, and enjoyed a glass of tea or a water pipe. Despite the apparent somnolence of the place, news was conveyed as quickly as though the sultan's telegram had been sent directly to the *kahve hane*.

That afternoon, conversation was heated. "So once again God's Shadow on Earth gives us leave to slaughter more lambs," Bülent said, disgusted. "This time Armenians. Tomorrow Greeks."

"Caution, Bülent," his friend Mahmud advised. "One can never tell when the sultan's spies are about."

"Does it matter?" asked the harness maker, bitterly. "How long can we go on pretending to accept this senseless destruction? Abdül Hamid locks himself in the Yildiz Palace, granting Europeans everything they want. The daughter of the *muhtar*, the community's headman, is raped in the village square in front of fifty witnesses. With the approval of Allah's earthly representative, the guilty Frenchman leaves town untouched, and the grateful French lend our Sultan a little more money. Helpless people suffer for our shame. Have you ever noticed that bloodletting is always encouraged around the time of a religious or national holiday?" All eyes in the coffee house were on him. He stopped, took a long sip of *chay*, the strong, smoky-flavored tea, then muttered, "Don't expect me to take part in it. I slaughter lambs as the Prophet commands, on *Kurban Bayram*. Another human being's blood will not be on my hands."

Mahmud addressed his friend quietly. "Bülent, even as you speak, our people notice things that disturb them. Your grandson's companion, Shadran, is nine years the boy's senior and a grown man. His father, the Armenian pig, is a known socialist revolutionary. Never mind he's an invalid. They're all alike. They smile at you and curse you behind your back."

"All his life, I've taught the boy that human beings are created equal. I won't mock my word by showing him our prejudices."

"Mind Bülent, you make no friends in the Turkish community by condoning such a relationship. I'd watch my home were I you."

"Is that a threat?"

"No, but one day you may need a favor from our provincial governor or the garrison commandant. It never hurts to exercise discretion."

"I'll remember that," Bülent said sourly.

"Do, my friend, for your own good."

Their conversation was interrupted as a man burst through the door. "Come quickly!" he shouted. "They're stacking firewood down at the Armenian church. Those damned Christians will finally learn their lesson tonight."

The coffee house emptied. Mahmud turned to Bülent. "Well?" he asked. "Are you coming?"

"Certainly not," Bülent replied. "I must see to the 'safety of my own home.'"

Early that morning, Shadran and Turhan had departed the village and gone to the hills to quarry stones. Shadran, hoping to augment his family's meager income, had borrowed mining tools, a tired old horse, and a creaky cart from his uncle. Each spring meant fresh construction. If parents had a new baby, they needed another room. If a wall had been flooded out during the winter, it needed shoring up. The *agha*, the district's richest man, invariably wanted fresh stones to line his garden.

Now, happily exhausted, they finished loading stones into the wagon.

"I don't know about you, Turhan, but I'm going to lie here and rest for an hour before we start back down toward the village," Shadran said.

"I think I'll climb to the top of the ridge and survey my kingdom."

"Go ahead, my young prince," Shadran said, executing a mock bow. "By your leave, I'll simply take a nap."

When he got to the top of the stone ridge, a hundred feet higher than their rock quarry, Turhan looked over the countryside toward the village. This was surely the loveliest time of the year. In two months, the blasting summer sun would bake the ground to the hardness of stone. But for now, a gentle, cooling breeze tempered the sun's heat, and there were small, puffy clouds here and there, contrasting with the deep blue of the sky. Although the crest of hill where Turhan stood was sere and rocky, a carpet of young, green grass, interwoven with gold and red flowers, covered the flanks of the foothills below. Sheep fed quietly and contentedly in these pastures, the silence interrupted only occasionally by the panicked bleating of a new-born lamb which had momentarily become separated from its mother.

A narrow ribbon of road cut across well-tended fields, green with early growth, toward the village, some three miles distant. There were no women working this late in the day. Their planting, hoeing, and tending started before the sun came up each morning. They were invariably finished in time to allow them to prepare the mid-day meal for their menfolk and children.

The finest land in the area, sheltered from the afternoon sun by gentle slopes, was owned by the *Agha*, the squire of the area. The village's Ottoman inhabitants farmed the fertile flatland fields between the foothills and the village.

Turhan could make out the two minarets and the church steeple, but the village's smaller buildings were blurred and indistinguishable. The Greeks and Armenians, he knew, had a much more difficult time raising crops, for to them was left the rocky, poorly watered soil on the other side of the village.

Turhan turned his gaze in the opposite direction. The road coursed through barren wilderness and low, rocky hills until, just at the horizon line, he could barely make out patches of greenish-brown, the outlying fields of another village.

When he returned to the quarry, Shadran had just finished harnessing the horse to the wagon. The ancient nag could not have carried the weight up an incline, but the road back to the village was downhill all the way. "Praise Allah!" Turhan said. Shadran crossed himself.

They'd gotten halfway to the village when they saw a column of Turkish soldiers blocking the road. "Damn!" muttered Shadran. "The whole day's work for nothing. We'll probably lose the horse and wagon as well."

The commanding officer raised his hand for them to stop. He inspected the aged horse, the decrepit wagon. Shadran, hunched his shoulders, bowed his head, and mumbled, "Rocks, Sir, nothing more."

"Sivri!" the commander called. "See if we can use any of this junk for the fort." The sergeant glanced cursorily at the loaded wagon, then summoned several of his troops.

"Major, *Effendi*," Turhan said, "Why do you want to harm a good man who's only trying to help supply our village?"

The officer stepped forward, glaring. "Who might you be, little nit?"

"Turhan, grandson of Bülent the harness maker, Sir."

"I see. Is the filthy Armenian your servant?"

"No, Sir. He's my friend."

"Your friend? Since when does a Turk cavort with inferior vermin?"

"He's not inferior, Sir, he's just like you and me."

Turhan's voice halted as the commander sharply cracked a short whip. Its tip grazed his mouth, stunning him. Turhan wiped the back of his hand across his lips. He looked down and saw blood.

"Listen, insolent puppy. I don't need such garbage from you. Another word and your relatives will find your body in some ditch between here and your miserable village, understand?"

The boy gazed at the officer in shocked silence.

"I said '*understand?*'"

"Y… yes, sir," the boy stammered, blushing deeply.

"Now, my young spokesman," the officer snarled, "if you have such great love for the Armenian, why are you so cruel to the old horse, which is at least his equal? Eh?"

The boy remained mute. From the corner of his eye, he observed the troops. The soldiers varied in years from Shadran's age to a large, fat man who looked older than Grandfather. Their uniforms were dusty. Many had buttons missing. Although the commander's boots were polished to a coal-black sheen, those of the soldiers looked as if they'd been buffed with rocks. Together, the forces seemed incredibly large, cruel, and menacing.

"Men," the Captain addressed his soldiers. "Are there any among you who think this poor beast does not deserve to be treated as well as the Armenian?"

No one raised a hand.

"Very well, then. See how the poor horse suffers under the cruel load she's made to bear for the profit of these vicious taskmasters. Can any of you think of a way to make her happier?"

There was a chorus of sarcastic comments.

"Tie the Christian to the yoke. Let the horse ride on the seat."

"Tether them together. They deserve one another."

"See if the Armenian stud can give the old girl some real pleasure," a particularly coarse, fat man remarked.

"Enough!" barked the major. "The most humane way to ease the poor old mare is to unload the weight she carries."

The men started tossing rocks out of the wagon, quickly, carelessly, breaking several as they did so, clearly enjoying their bully's game.

"Shall we cut the horse loose and overturn the wagon, Sir?" one of the men shouted.

"I don't see why n…" The officer froze in mid sentence as the garrison commander's adjutant rode up and saluted.

"Major Ismet, Colonel's orders. All men report to the post immediately. They expect serious problems in the villages."

"Is it that urgent we can't have a little innocent fun, Nader?"

"Sorry, Ismet, those are my orders."

After the soldiers departed, Turhan and Shadran looked sadly at the ruination of their day's work. Turhan started to pick up the stones that had not been pulverized. "Shadran," he said, "perhaps we should stay up in the hills tonight."

"I can't," Shadran replied. "If the soldiers were called back to their station in such a hurry, it means trouble. My family will need all the help they can get. I must return home."

The pitiful trio passed half a dozen small, sturdily-built farmhouses before they came to northern outskirts of the village, an hour later. Just before the main bridge leading into the village, the dirt and small stones of the country road were covered over by a thin, uneven veneer of tar. Over the bridge, the village's main thoroughfare was cobblestoned. Dusty paths led from the street to villagers' homes. The *Eski Camii*, the larger of the two mosques in the village, was located on the main street, two hundred yards beyond the bridge, abutting Market Square.

As the three weary travelers approached the plaza, an Armenian boy, Turhan's age, ran toward them. "Shadran!" he shouted. "Father says you must go to the church immediately!"

"I must sell these stones first."

"What do I tell him?"

"Precisely that. Get back to the sanctuary! Hurry!"

After Shadran had sold most of the load, a middle-aged man came up and whispered to Turhan, "Our house is on the outskirts. We could hide your friend until things cool down."

"He'd never allow that," Turhan replied.

"It's the same with all Greeks and Armenians. One day they'll be gone, him sooner than most. Probably won't survive 'til Easter."

"Turhan," a shrill female voice called. "Your grandfather says you're to come home this instant." The boy looked at his friend. Shadran motioned him to go.

"What will you do, Shadran?"

"I'm going to the *Lion's Throat.*"

"What?" Turhan asked, amazed. He'd heard that despite the Muslim prohibition against drinking wine, the *taverna* just outside the village limits prospered from those who regularly bent the Prophet's injunctions. "Why there, of all places?"

"To drink with those who'd cut off my balls."

"For God's sake, why?"

"Because it makes me happy to do so!"

3

Turhan's grandfather rocked him gently as he would a small child.

"But Shadran's no different from me, *Baba*. Why can't we all just live our own lives?"

"The world isn't a fair place, boy. I can't answer why the Creator put Armenians and Greeks here, nor why Turks hate them so much. We live in a tortured land, in a troubled time. Each year, the motherland becomes smaller, food becomes more scarce."

"Why don't they move away?"

"To where? The Armenians haven't had their own land for nine hundred years. The Greeks belong here in Anatolia as much as we do. Where would they get the means to move? Parts of Greece are poorer than our own land. Christians lived here many centuries before the Prophet revealed Allah to our people. I'm told that many days to the west, they built places of worship in stone caves and decorated the caves with paintings. When they were hunted down by Arabs, they built cities underground."

Despite his misery, Turhan was fascinated. He tried to picture the fantastic places Grandfather described. Then his mind returned to the present. "*Baba,* can't we do anything to make things better for them?"

27

"Nothing. My friends are angry with me because I refuse to join the bloodletting. We must stay inside and wait it out. Now, it's time for you to go to sleep for the night."

Turhan went to his room. An hour later, he stuffed pillows under the covers. If Grandfather looked in, he would think the boy was sleeping. He opened the window and quietly slipped out of the house, into the chill evening air.

A standing village joke was that the only difference between the local garbage dump and the "Lion's Throat" was that the dump smelled better. The taverna's packed earth floor was filled with porters, drovers, criminals, servants, the lowest of the low. The place stank of stale *raki,* urine, harsh cigarettes, and sweat. More smoke than light emanated from the cheap oil pots at every table.

A large, lumpy woman with a frowzy moustache and fat, hairy legs, sat on a raised platform, surrounded by two guitarists, a drummer, and a half-drunk *saz* player. She bellowed songs of unrequited love in a shrill voice, louder and more irritating than the four instrumentalists combined. No one danced on the small wooden floor in front of them.

Turhan searched for his friend. He found the Armenian drinking alone at a table. Shadran looked derisively at the crowd, then spat on the dirt floor. "The cesspools of Anatolia have been emptied!" He laughed bitterly.

The music ended. Turhan watched silently. Shadran stood up and walked toward the platform where the vocalist was seated. He tossed a few coins at the woman's feet. The musicians started to play again. He stepped onto the plank floor and began a sinuous, slow, dance, weaving, snapping his fingers in rhythm to the music.

The Armenian lost himself in the spirit of his movements, clapping his hands for the band to play faster. Two men came up to the orchestra and spoke to the woman. The music stopped. All eyes in the place turned to Shadran. The woman looked down at the coins, then kicked them off the platform. There was a strained, tight moment of silence, followed by shouts in the distance. Shadran turned and addressed Turhan. "It's started."

4

Ordinarily, the evening before Easter was a time of great rejoicing for the village's Armenian minority. Not tonight. The terrified Christians sought sanctuary in their church, guarded by their largest and strongest men.

Inside the humble place of worship, women lit candles. The light from these tapers cast faint, eerie shadows across everything in the church. Mothers held their frightened children close to their breasts. Ascetic faces of saints and martyrs, painted hundreds of years before on dark icons that hung on every wall, looked silently down on the pathetic scene. The sour odor of nervous sweat and burning candle wax pervaded the stuffy, closed-in room. Prayers and shrill wails filled the air.

Fifty feet from the church, Turhan watched anxiously, as Shadran walked calmly toward the chapel. The Armenian glanced back at the youth and smiled gently. "This is no place for you, Turhan. Things could get ugly."

"I know," the boy replied. "But I must stay. You may need me." It did not occur to him to question how he could conceivably help his friend. All he cared about was that Shadran might be in danger.

A hundred Muslim Ottomans gathered outside the church. They shouted raucous obscenities as they stacked dried branches and twigs against the wooden walls. More Turks walked toward the building, their arms loaded with wood for the growing pile. Half a dozen disheveled soldiers, led by a huge, sloppy sergeant, helped stack the fuel.

Turhan knew this cat-and-mouse game occurred periodically. It was a battle of nerves. Invariably, the government sent soldiers to insure that things never got totally out of hand.

Suddenly, an elderly Turk shouted, "Death to the Christian pigs!" and threw a lighted torch on the woodpile. The Ottoman soldiers looked expectantly at their commander. The fire smoldered. Smoke started to rise. The sergeant hesitated a moment, then said, "Shit, it's nothing but a wooden church. They can put up a new one when it's over."

Torches arced toward the building. Turks threw more wood on the pyre. Flames licked at the wooden structure. There was a sharp, concussive *crr-ack* as a dry log burst with a sound louder than rifle fire. Turhan coughed in hacking gulps, as he breathed in acrid smoke. He heard the shrill scream of women and children from inside the church as the Armenians realized the building was burning. One wall of the church had caught fire. Desperate Armenians inside started to batter windows with anything they could find. Turhan realized they were doing the worst thing possible. Smoke poured into the interior of the burning edifice. The Armenians' screams turned to choked gasps.

The Muslims outside took up the chant, "Death to the pigs! Death to the pigs!" There was an abrupt shattering of glass. With an agonized scream, a small girl, her long black hair ablaze, leapt from the building. As she hit the open air, fire ignited her dress. Within moments, she was a writhing pillar of flame. Turhan stood transfixed, helplessly doing nothing, nauseated by the sweet smell of the child's searing flesh.

Before Shadran reached the church, several Turks blocked the church's front door, barring the Armenians' exit. Flames ate away at two sides of the building. There was an explosion like a cannon shot. The roof caught fire. Bedlam erupted as the Armenians found they had no means of escape.

"Turhan, the door!" Shadran shouted. Before anyone could stop him, Shadran smashed the commanding sergeant's nose with his closed fist, then drew a small knife from his belt and slashed the man's throat. An instant later, he grabbed the dead man's pistol and fired three shots into the nearest soldier. The front door of the church was momentarily left unguarded. Turhan rushed forward and yanked it open. Armenians, some covered with flaming cinders, burst out of the burning building.

A dozen Turks covered Shadran like ants on a crumb of honeyed bread. Through smoke-glazed eyes, Turhan saw others butchering helpless Armenian men, women, and children, indiscriminately. Suddenly a group of the attackers turned on Turhan. "There's the turncoat who opened the door and let them escape! Let's teach the little bastard a lesson!"

Turhan bolted, hysterical, and started to run, but he had waited too long. Within moments, his legs were knocked out from under him. Massive arms pinioned him and dragged him back toward the church. He flailed, bit skin wherever he could find it, scratched and gouged anything soft with his nails. A great open palm slapped him across the face, harder than he'd ever been hit in his life. He felt an incredible wave of pain.

As he blinked through tears, Turhan saw that the church was now completely ablaze. The mob had strung up half a dozen Armenians, Shadran among them, to wooden posts they'd thrown up during the melee. His arms and legs bound, Turhan was thrown to the ground at Shadran's feet. A huge brute of a man crushed him under one heavy foot, as one would an insect. He looked down at Turhan with contempt. "Far be it from me to keep such good friends apart," he said, viciously. "Blood brothers are you?"

Shadran glared at Turhan's gross, sweaty tormentor, raised his head, and spat in the man's face. The enraged Turk muttered, "All right, goat turd. If it's blood brothers you want to be, blood brothers you shall be. You filthy Jesus-lover, I'll make a Christian symbol of you!"

He took a rusted, short-handled knife from its scabbard, and slashed it horizontally across Shadran's throat, severing the jugular. While the Armenian gurgled in his death throes, the Turkish soldier pulled the knife in a downward motion, from Shadran's forehead to his groin, slashing him open in the shape of a cross.

"Don't kill the other one!" someone shouted. "He's a Turk. We could get into trouble."

"I won't. I'll let the governor deal with the little bastard."

Turhan felt a gush of warm liquid and raised his eyes. Shadran's blood streamed onto his head and face. He gagged as Shadran's body, relieved of muscular control, voided its bowels. The smell of feces mingled with that of sour sweat, half-digested food, and death. Shadran's intestines and organs, cut loose by the soldier's knife, dropped onto Turhan's head, and tumbled into the dust where he lay. Turhan screamed until he felt himself being kicked in the face. Then, mercifully, he fainted.

In the prison yard, twenty desperate, frightened Armenians sat on the ground amidst blood, vomit and excrement. Turhan sat among them, holding Shadran's peasant cap. A boot nudged him.

"Up, little pigshit Armenian lover! They want you inside."

Turhan felt himself half-lifted, half-dragged to a side entrance of the governor's district office. The guard held a wooden club above his head, and muttered, "Not a word, understand?"

The boy nodded meekly. The guard shoved him into the building. Turhan found himself in a small holding cell. There was a narrow, screened opening, through which he could see the governor's office, a large, square room. Grandfather sat in a chair, opposite the administrator, looking submissive, shrunken. The governor, a rotund, greasy-looking man of sixty, sat at a massive, walnut desk.

The two men spoke in hushed tones. A boy brought in *limon cologne* – a small jar filled with water-diluted lemon juice. Each man sprinkled some on his hands, face and neck. The lemon water did not camouflage the stench of fear that permeated the place. "Once these unfortunate matters start, they must run their course," the governor began. "It's so regrettable the Christians had to start these troubles. With Allah's help, I fervently hope all men, even Armenians, may live in harmony one day." He sighed dramatically.

"Wisely said, Excellency," Grandfather responded, fidgeting.

The governor smiled gently. "Don't worry, my friend. They'll bring him shortly. A shame one of our honorable Turkish boys somehow got mixed in with the real criminals. Dreadful. Dreadful."

"I'm so grateful to you, Excellency."

"No problem at all, my friend. I like you, Bülent, Effendi. Your fine, upstanding reputation has preceded you."

Grandfather looked as if he did not for a moment believe this. If anything, the governor's spies, present everywhere, knew exactly where he stood on the issues. Nevertheless, he must endure the administrator's indignities. "In my insignificant village, we all know of Your Excellency's reputation for justice and mercy," he said humbly.

"Indeed, I'm pleased to hear that. I make almost no money here. You realize that, Effendi. I am only here for the service I can render my subjects."

At the mention of money, Grandfather reached into his pocket. "And we are all so very grateful, Your Excellency."

"A man can only try his best," the governor continued silkily. "And I *do* help my people in any way I can, Bülent, Effendi. Would you not agree?"

Grandfather nodded.

"You are a harness maker? I'm told your work is of the finest quality and that you've prospered in your village. They say there's a waiting line for your excellent craftsmanship."

"With your help, and that of Allah, I survive, Your Honor."

"That makes me happy, Bülent, Effendi. Very happy indeed."

There was a rustle at the cell door. Turhan felt the iron grip of the guard's hand on his upper arm, propelling him into the governor's office. Grandfather's face turned ashen. The governor smiled benignly and extended his right hand. As if on cue, Grandfather rose from the hard, straight-backed wooden chair in which he'd been sitting. His hand came out of his pocket. As he bent over to kiss the governor's hand, grandfather pressed several Ottoman bills into it. The two men resumed their seats.

Turhan caught a glimpse of himself in a large mirror on the office wall. His eyes were black, swollen nearly shut. His hair was matted and greasy, pasted to his head. He was pale. His clothes were caked with an accumulation of dried black matter. He gathered from the wrinkled noses of both men, that his stench must be overpowering.

"Now we must at all costs protect the young man," the governor said. "Of course, he cannot stay in the village. He would almost certainly be subjected to retribution at the hands of Greek or Armenian thugs. I think it best that he move to the city where he can be under my protection."

Grandfather gasped at this unexpected turn of events. Turhan bit down hard on his lower lip. He said nothing.

"Is there anyone with whom the lad could live?" the governor went on smoothly. "I believe his mother resides in our provincial capital, does she not?" His smile was benevolent. Grandfather looked as though he'd swallowed a live snake. "Yes indeed," the governor continued. "I think it would be best for all concerned if he were safely away from the village for a while."

"How long, Highness?" asked grandfather, his voice hoarse.

"That will depend on how things go. Let's just say the boy's stay will be indefinite, but not necessarily permanent."

He smiled at the two supplicants and clapped his hands. A servant entered with a tray of refreshments. At the governor's signal, he offered steaming glasses of tea to Bülent and Turhan. The governor proposed a toast. Grandfather, who appeared humiliated, begged his leave. "My friend," beamed the administrator. "You wouldn't dream of offending your host, would you?"

The harness maker, managing a forced smile, choked down the drink. Within a quarter hour, the two were dismissed. Turhan's body was a mass of pain and stiffness. Only now did he grasp the magnitude of what had happened. His closest friend had been slaughtered for no reason at all, except he was Armenian and had tried to defend his community. Grandfather had been forced to cower before a greasy, bald-headed little man who, with a few carelessly dropped words, had torn the family apart and condemned him to an unknown, but dreaded, fate.

Grandfather had taught Turhan that Allah was good. If this were so, how could the all-knowing God allow such things to happen to him, to Grandfather, to Shadran? How could Allah give power to such men as soldiers, prison guards, the governor? If there was an Allah, there must be justice. There must be a way for the weak, those whose faces were pushed in the dirt every day of their lives, those who had to grovel before those small, evil men in power, to balance the scales of justice.

"I swear by Allah I won't forget this," Turhan said with grim determination. "I'll get even for this. I swear I will show that good men can win."

Grandfather said nothing. His face was tight. Behind them, Turhan heard the governor welcome another supplicant, an elderly, frightened-looking Armenian. Turhan had seen the man sitting with his hat in his hands, a few moments before.

"Ah, Pan Harabedian, my friend," they heard the governor say. "It is my pleasure to be of aid to *all* my subjects. Please, please come in. I am at your disposal. Of course I will try to be of any assistance I can."

5

In Istanbul, many miles and a world away, His Imperial and August Majesty, Allah's Shadow on earth dwelt in the sumptuous Yildiz Palace, in the most magnificent city in the world. Abdül Hamid, the dour, reactionary old man, who'd sat on the Tulip Throne for thirty-two years, scoffed at whispered suggestions that the Empire he ruled with an iron hand was crumbling. One need only look at a map of the Eastern Mediterranean – an Ottoman lake – to give the lie to the prattle spread by idiotic European doomsayers. True there'd been some losses in the past century: Algeria, Tunisia, Egypt, the northern Balkan Peninsula, and parts of Russia were no longer part of the Empire. And Allah-cursed Greece had declared its so-called "independence."

But the entire Middle East, from Syria to the Persian Gulf and down into the Hijaz was still firmly in Ottoman hands. The African lands of Tripolitania and Cyrenaica still swore allegiance to the Empire.

Life had been easier when Abdül Hamid had first ascended the Tulip Throne. Reformists had deposed Abdülaziz, the weakling who'd ruled from 1861 until 1871. Then Murad, who'd replaced Abdülaziz had gone insane after only three months on the throne, and the reform-minded minister, Midhat Pasha, had paved the way for Abdül Hamid's elevation to Sultan.

Midhat Pasha, that old fool, had believed that Abdül Hamid seriously intended to abide by the so-called "representative" parliament. Abdül Hamid had shown him a thing or two. Within a year of the Sultan's ascendancy, Midhat Pasha had been dismissed and murdered, and the parliament disbanded. For the next quarter century there'd been no more foolish talk of "reform."

Abdül Hamid had never cared much for Dolmabahche, that outrageously ugly monstrosity of a European "palace," built by Abdülmecid some fifty years before. The damned thing, which had replaced Topkapi as the Sultan's residence after four hundred years, was an overstuffed eyesore in the middle of *European* Istanbul. If only the money squandered on that ridiculous fiasco had been used to modernize the Ottoman military machine... But it was too late to look back on what had been.

Nowadays, Abdül Hamid didn't wander far from his own Yildiz Palace across the Bosphorous. Rather, he enjoyed the view of his capital from the windows of the jewel-like castle. The *yalts* – sumptuous summer homes of the very rich – lined the European and Asiatic shores of the strait which separated the Black Sea from the Sea of Marmara. Modern buildings climbed the hills of the capital, a sure sign of healthy progress. How dare anyone say that his was the capital of a decaying Islamic superpower?

Several miles away from the Sultan's residence, across the Bosphorous and south of the Golden Horn, spread *Turkish* Istanbul, which some called "the Queen City of the World" and more called "the Whore of the Ages." Just as the whole of Istanbul was a world away from Turhan's village, so was the old quarter of Stamboul, just over the Galata Bridge, a universe away from Pera and Galata, the city's European enclave.

From the *Yeni Mosque*, which was not "new" at all, at the southern end of the bridge, Stamboul crawled gaudily up its seven hills, through streets and alleys congested with humanity day and night, to the ever more grandiloquent, ostentatious mosques at the top of each hill. *Aya Sophia* and *Sultanahmet*, which Europeans insisted on calling the "Blue" Mosque, *Süleimaniye*, the exquisite treasure built by Sinan, the greatest Ottoman architect of all time, and the *Fatih, Beyazit* and *Selim* mosques. Day and night there was the noise of the marketplace, the silence of the mosques, vast wealth, and the desperate poverty of hopeless immigrants who'd come to the capital in search of fortune.

A peddler hawking old shoes pushed a rheumy hand-cart along one of the narrow, filthy alleyways that crawled through the old quarter of the city. The muffled moans of a boy of eleven issued from a dilapidated shack fronting on the alley. The peddler had heard such sounds before, more times than he cared to remember. They didn't affect him. Coughing up phlegm, he spat a wad of it toward the nearest curb and moved his cart farther up the alley.

Inside the shack, the boy, Abbas, tried to stifle the scream he felt would burst from him as he raised his arms to fend off the blows to his face.

"I'll teach you to talk back, you little shit!" Ahmet snarled. "Is that how you speak to your father, huh, you little worm? Who do you think you are, one of those fancy Jews with a shop in the Grand Bazaar? An Armenian overlord? The Greek scum that lords it over me every day? Take that!" He kicked the boy viciously in the shins. As the youth fell and rolled into a fetal position, the man continued to kick him in the stomach, the legs, the ribs.

Abbas felt a crack and a searing pain as one of his father's heavy boots caught him just below the chest. He could no longer hold back. He screamed out, his reserve broken. He gasped for air, unable to pull in enough to cry out again.

"Allah damned Jews!" the man spat, turning away from his sobbing son. "They own everything. They run everything. I break my back hauling their loads halfway across the city and kiss their rear ends for what? The lousy *kurush* they give me for an hour's work? Not enough money to buy bread for my own children. I'm sick and tired of it! I'll be dead in a year and what'll they do then? I'll tell you what they'll do. They'll hire another *hamal* and work him 'til he dies as well." The man stopped his tirade long enough to guzzle a drink from a cheap bottle of *raki*. He belched loudly, and walked out of the room without a backward glance at his son, who lay there with two broken ribs, his eyes puffed shut, moaning incoherently.

Soon enough, the man was snoring in a drunken stupor. It was like that almost every evening. Ahmet led a bitter life. A *hamal* – a human beast of burden – he occupied the lowest rung on Istanbul's social ladder. He was illiterate, a peasant who'd left his village many years before to make his fortune in the capital. Now he was thirty-five years old, but walked with the crabbed gait of a man twice that age, his back a permanent mass of arthritic pain. Still, he continued to haul more than a hundred pounds of anything he was hired to haul – meat, furniture, fertilizer, it made no difference – several miles at a time for barely enough to purchase bread for his family and *raki* for himself.

Abbas was the youngest of three children. Hamra, his oldest brother, had taken their father's abuse until he'd reached fifteen and towered over Ahmet. One day, six months ago, Father had gone too far and started paddling the back of Hamra's knees with a stick. Hamra had grabbed the stick and cracked it over the old man's skull, stunning him. The other two children prayed silently that their brother had done him in, but, alas, the *hamal's* skull was so thick the wood shattered. Like an enraged bull, Ahmet charged his eldest son. Hamra managed to dodge his father easily. As the older man reached out and lost his balance,

Hamra pushed him down and started kicking at the old man's thick neck.

But Ahmet was as tough and leathery as an ox. He reached out, grabbed his son's ankle and pulled Hamra down. In the ensuing scuffle, Hamra lost three front teeth and his nose was broken before he'd managed to break away and run from the hovel. Abbas had not seen him since.

After Hamra left, there was one less boy to share the vicious cruelties. Bakhar, twelve, had whispered to his brother a week ago that he wasn't going to take their father's "discipline" much longer.

"Where would you go, Bakhar?"

"Doesn't matter. Anything's better than this. Maybe a Jew in the Grand Bazaar would take me on as a worker."

"Don't talk like that! It's thanks to the Jews we have this for a father."

"You really believe that, Abbas? Don't make me vomit. That old bastard would blame Allah Himself for his troubles. He's just an old sot who's still got the strength to beat up on his children."

"But he's still our *father...*"

"Yours maybe. Not mine, Abbas. Come with me when I leave. We wouldn't starve, you know. We could go to the sultan's soup kitchens."

"Bakhar! You can't mean that!"

But Bakhar did mean it. Three days ago he'd gone and now Abbas was the only one left to endure his father's wrath. His mother, Basra, was little more than a silent hulk, who invariably covered her face with a heavy black shroud, even in the house. The quivering, useless cow had never so much as raised her voice on his behalf. He felt no love for the woman. All women were pretty much the same. Weak, ugly, and useless. But he was trapped. He didn't know where Bakhar had gone. He was too young to brave the world alone. He would simply have to endure as best he could.

Abbas harbored great anger toward his father. But he believed in his heart that the old man was right. If it wasn't for the foreigners – the Greeks, the Armenians, the Frenchmen, but most especially the Jews – the family could have been wealthy. Then Father would have been happy. And there'd have been no more beatings.

6

The governor soon forgot all about Turhan. During the week following Easter, he traveled to all parts of his province, for there had been many fires the night of the sultan's telegram. As he said, it was his desire to be of assistance to all his subjects. Shortly after he returned to Diyarbakır, the governor's wife was seen wearing an expensive Russian fur. The administrator did nothing to quell the ensuing gossip. At least now his wife would cease questioning him about his monthly trips to Mosul. Praise Allah she didn't know he'd purchased a similar sable for that delicious Syrian girl.

Turhan was the only Ottoman and by far the youngest of the six in his village who'd been banished to the provincial capital. The sad party, chained together and guarded by three mounted soldiers, marched overland for two days, until they reached the outskirts of Diyarbakır. When the sun rose on the third day, Turhan saw the ancient black, basalt walls that surrounded the city. As soon as they'd arrived in the central plaza, he was unshackled, and found himself facing a tall, gaunt woman with stringy black hair, a dark growth of moustache on her upper lip, and a sallow complexion. "You must be Turhan," she said coldly. "I'm Lâle, your mother. Follow me. Try not to make too much of a nuisance of yourself."

Despite his fear, homesickness, and unease with this strange, garishly dressed woman, who reeked of foul odors like the goats outside Grandfather's home, Turhan was excited by the sights and smells, the noise and bustle of this ancient crossroads. Diyarbakır's center was a large, rectangular plaza. Stalls of all shapes and sizes filled its central market. Jewelers peddled their wares in one part of the marketplace, fishmongers in another, cloth merchants in a third. There were egg sellers and butcher stalls. Everywhere he looked, boys his own age ran through the market selling glasses of tea. A large, stone bakery stood near the plaza, steam rising from its roof. Administrative offices, the courthouse, and inns ringed the central square.

Turhan's mother led him to a poor quarter, crowded with small, ugly mud-brick hovels. The alleyways were narrow. Turhan inhaled the pervasive odors of frying onions, tallow and urine. The dirt-and-cobblestoned streets were surprisingly free of dung. Most horses and mules had burlap or canvas bags fitted over their rear ends. "They save everything here," the woman remarked. "They sell the manure to farmers in surrounding villages."

Lâle's hut had but a single room. Where Grandfather's home had always been neat, swept free of dirt, her place was greasy and smelled rank. Toward the rear of the room was a stone sink that held four small plates and three chipped bowls caked with dried food. In another corner, a lumpy mattress with a grease-stained blanket thrown haphazardly on top lay against the wall. In answer to his querying gaze, Turhan's mother said, "Don't expect Topkapı Palace. The *kurush* don't come easily. You can sleep on the floor until you find some rags to lie on. His gracious worship, the governor, didn't give me much notice you were coming. No one sent me money to take care of you. There's soup in the pot."

"Grandfather gave me some money," Turhan said. "You can have it if you want."

The woman pocketed the coins without bothering to thank him. A grimy black kettle hung over the small fireplace. Turhan gagged as he stuck his finger into the tepid, slimy liquid and licked the sour, rancid-tasting stuff. "I never pretended to be the Sultan's chef," his mother said. Turhan said nothing. "Listen, boy," the woman said harshly. "You may as well know things happen around here that won't please you. I don't make much money cleaning other peoples' houses. Many nights I work right here."

Turhan raised his eyes questioningly.

"Whether you're here or not doesn't make any difference to my 'friends.' Just keep quiet and stay out of the way."

Soon enough, Turhan found out what his mother meant. From time to time, Lâle told her son she was "entertaining company." Different nights, different men. Smelly, greasy, usually drunk on cheap rakı. Often, he fell asleep to the sound of grunting, harsh breathing, and heavy coupling in the other corner of the room. Other nights, the sticky, sweet smell of hashish pervaded the room, and his mother's eyes glazed over. Those times, she would not respond sensibly to anything Turhan asked.

Grandfather came to Diyarbakır three months after Turhan was banished from the village. Turhan met him at the city's edge. The boy was shocked to see how bad the old man looked. Grandfather's once bright eyes were dull, lifeless. He'd become cadaverously thin.

"Grandfather...?"

"Don't say it, boy," the old man croaked, his voice hoarse.

Turhan hugged his *baba*. Grandfather felt so shriveled, so frail. The boy couldn't stop the hot tears from flowing, and didn't try.

"Can't I come back, *baba*? I'll promise the governor anything. I'll lick his boots if need be."

The old man held his grandson at arm's length. Turhan could see the man's rheumy eyes flickering with a fire long banked. "Is that the lesson you've learned, boy? To be ground under the dust like a worm? To have a man spit in your face and pretend it's raining?"

"But *Baba*...?"

"I know," the old man whispered. "I didn't set a very good example, did I? But I believed if I could keep you with me a few more hours, a few more days... Now, those days are not many..."

"*Baba, no*!" Turhan said, a rising urgency in his voice.

"I had to come, boy. Don't you understand? I had to see you one more time. I love you, boy."

Turhan's tears flowed copiously now, and his body shook. "There, there," the old man said, rocking him as gently as he had on that terrible night a lifetime ago.

They sat together, man and boy, on the outskirts of the city for little more than an hour. They said little. Grandfather continued to rock Turhan from time to time. Sometimes he sang the silly little folk songs he'd sung when Turhan was very young. His voice was scratchy, now, and he coughed a lot in between the lines. And at the end, Grandfather hugged the boy for what seemed far too short a time. "Turhan, I will never forget the courage you showed that night. One day you will be a lion who will *eat* the likes of the governor." Shortly afterward, Grandfather took his leave. Turhan watched through his tears as the man walked back toward the village that had been their home. Once a giant among men, he was now a pathetic, stooped figure, who stopped every few moments as ragged coughing savaged his body.

Within a year of Turhan's exile to Diyarbakır, Sultan Abdül Hamid, the Shadow of God on Earth, was unceremoniously deposed. The governor quickly departed the province of Mesopotamia amid reports that substantial sums were missing from the provincial treasury. For several weeks, Turhan waited for the call to return to the village, which never came. Five months after Turhan had last seen Grandfather, he learned that *Baba* had passed away. The doctor said it was cancer. Turhan knew better. It had been cancer of the soul. By the time Turhan heard of Grandfather's death, it was too late to attend the funeral.

Turhan's sorrow now turned to anger. Shadran and Grandfather both dead within the year. His own life turned upside down by the thoughtless wave of an official's hand. Even as he came to accept that this was the way of the world, he determined he would fight back.

7

Turhan's fascination with Diyarbakır outlasted those first weeks. There were hundreds of stone buildings. Wealthy merchants rode in fine carriages, over wide streets. Caravans, headed in every direction, stopped briefly in the provincial capital. Men spent countless days in coffee houses, gossiping, playing backgammon. Kurds, their heavy-flanked horses foaming, pounded over the city's streets, madly galloping to Allah-knew-where. Turhan envied these untamed tribesmen who owed allegiance to no one, who roamed freely wherever they wanted, from Diyarbakır to the very gates of the far-off Persian capital.

Soon, Turhan learned that men from the outlying areas rarely, if ever, moved up the rungs of city society. Most returned to their native villages within a few years, failures. The best they could truthfully say was that they'd lived in their small world's great city. Most lied about why they returned, masking the real reason so they could be heroes to their village cronies. They talked of marvelous carriage rides and shiny black horses, failing to add that only the wealthy rode thus, and that when *they* had ridden at all, it had been in community buckboards, smelling of horse urine and human sweat. The horses which pulled *these* wagons

49

were ancient hacks, fed a combination of stale hay and sawdust which kept them barely alive. Sharp, narrow ribs poked through splotched, unkempt hides of these sway-backed, spavined beasts. Turhan had seen them drop in the streets. Their owners whipped them, even after they'd fallen. When the corpses did not stir after half-an-hour of such abuse, their bodies were dragged off to an unknown destination.

Returning villagers told of magnificent lamb shish-kebab and shashlik, which they'd seen in the city's fabulous restaurants. They did not say that *their* meals had consisted of the same flat bread and goat cheese they'd cursed in Chermik, Antak, or any of the thousand villages spread throughout this part of Turkey.

Life for Turhan was far worse in Diyarbakır than it had been in the village, but he couldn't afford to return home. His meals consisted of overcooked rice and decaying vegetables. Once in a great while, there was thin gruel, with slimy remains of gristly meat. Conversation between Turhan and his mother was non-existent. One evening, she said, "Listen, boy. You've been here nearly a year. I can't afford to feed, house, and clothe you any longer. It's time you earned your keep."

"What do you mean?"

"I work too hard by day, cleaning other peoples' fancy places. I can't steal enough to make it worth my while. Lately I've been too tired to carry on my night work. I could make a much better living for us by doing that kind of work full time."

Turhan felt ill. He was hardly an innocent, but hated still to hear his mother speak so directly of how she made their extra money.

"I can't wander through the marketplace advertising my wares," she continued. "I need an agent. Instead of wasting your time in the marketplace every day, you could be finding work for me."

"Sell my own mother? Have you no shame?" the boy shouted angrily.

The woman slapped him hard across the face. "Don't you *dare* lecture me!" she screamed. "Where do you think I get the money to feed you? You have the run of this city, acting like a nobleman. Have you been to school for one day? Have you done anything, *anything at all*, to show your thanks? Don't tell me how to live! Men use my body, but at least they pay for it! You have the gall to eat my food, and sleep in my home for nothing. You've known since you got here exactly how I earn my living. If you don't want to help me, find another way to earn money or get out!"

Turhan rose to his feet. He threw his soup bowl against the wall, shattering it. "You have no right to ask me to secure business for you," he said grimly. "You said nothing for a year. Now you suggest such an unnatural, ungodly thing? Allah's shame on you! You want to be rid of me? Now you are!" He calmly walked out of his mother's house, vowing never to return.

Turhan soon found he wasn't the only refugee who slept in alleys and under the bridges of the *Dijle* – the Tigris River – which flowed just beyond the city walls. He hunted through garbage containers in back of food stalls. Occasionally, he begged scraps at the end of a market day. Others fought their poverty by petty thievery. Stealing was a way of life in Diyarbakır and early afternoon was the best time. After a heavy lunch of greasy fried foods, shopkeepers were ill-inclined to give chase for the couple of apples that disappeared from their stand.

One afternoon, Turhan saw an opportunity he couldn't resist. There was commotion in the marketplace. A wooden cart laden with bolts of cloth collapsed. The man and woman who owned the wagon, fearing the loss of their merchandise, called out for help. A fat butcher nearby wiped his bloodied hands on a soiled apron and waddled over to help his fellow merchants.

Turhan flashed past the butcher's stall, snatched a lamb loin as he ran, and reversed his direction. Within moments, he hid among a crowd of people watching a puppet show. Still breathless, he secreted the lamb under his loose-fitting clothing. Suddenly, he felt his arm frozen in an iron grip. "Are you certain you want to do that?" a deep, authoritative voice asked. Turhan looked around, terrified. He was staring into the hard face of a market policeman. "Perhaps you and I should walk back to where you were a few moments ago."

The boy trembled as they approached the butcher's stall. Fear of an unknown fate mingled with shame at having betrayed grandfather's teachings, disgrace at having been brought to this low station.

"Good afternoon, Jalal Bey," said the market officer. "You no doubt missed a slab of lamb from your stand when you returned from helping Abdullah and Gül?"

"That's true, Sergeant Enver."

"It was not a dog who seized the meat. Rather a different animal." He shoved the youth toward the butcher. "Do you want to press charges?"

"Hmmm. What do you think, boy?"

Turhan summoned his last shred of dignity and gazed, unblinking, at the fat man. "I believe you should, Sir. I make no excuse for what I did. I was hungry. I stole the meat from you. I'm prepared to take the consequences."

"Do you know what those consequences are?"

"No, sir."

"You're willing to accept them anyway?"

"Yes, Sir. My grandfather taught me that when you do something you know is not right, you must be ready to accept what punishment you deserve."

The butcher looked surprised. This was not the usual response. "Perhaps, Officer, you might release him to my custody. I doubt if he'll run far, will you boy?"

"No, Sir."

"Very well, then. Thank you for performing your job in a most exemplary manner." He handed the officer a large cut of the finest lamb.

"Thank *you,* Jalal Effendi," the policeman replied, gratefully. He departed.

"Who are you, little thief?"

"I'm not a thief, Sir," said Turhan.

"You admit you stole?"

"Yes, Sir."

"Why?"

"I was banished from my village for helping save Armenians when Turkish soldiers burned down their church. The governor sent me here to live with my mother. I left her home because she and I – had a disagreement. I can't remember when I last tasted meat, Sir."

"And you stooped to thievery to do it?"

"What else could I do?"

"You could have found a job selling tea, running errands."

"Effendi, the city boys take every job there is. They protect their territory. If I tried to compete with them, I wouldn't survive 'til next sunrise."

"What's your name, boy?"

"Turhan, Sir."

"Turhan, it's now the late afternoon. Come with me for a short walk. I want to show you something."

Jalal led the boy toward a narrow alley two blocks from the market square. Even before they reached the place, Turhan heard pathetic wails and was sickened by a terrible stench. As he entered the alley, he saw men and women in varying states of mutilation. The least injured held out a stump of what used to be a right hand and begged for food. A woman close by, wearing torn rags that barely covered the scabrous, pustulating sores all over her body, cackled meaningless words at a man with neither arms nor legs, who was propped up in a makeshift wagon.

Turhan wanted to run. Jalal held him firmly in tow. "Beggar's Alley. Some were born that way. Most weren't. The ones with normal bodies but missing hands were convicted of stealing. In this part of the world, thieves have been treated the same since the days of the Prophet. The right hand is cut off at the wrist."

Turhan knew the consequences of such an amputation and shuddered. In the village, men ate from a community pot. Always – *always* – a man dipped into the pot with his right hand, and *only* with his right hand. The left hand was used for wiping oneself after defecation. No man would dream of placing his left hand into food. To do so would sentence him to death by stoning.

"A man without his right hand is automatically branded a thief," Jalal said, "not fit to eat with anyone of honor. He begs, he steals again, or he starves. If he's caught stealing a second time, he loses his other hand. I don't think I need to point out what happens after that."

"Allah bless your footsteps, Effendi," the boy said. "How can I thank you for not condemning me to such a life? Please let me pay you back in any way I can."

"Very well, boy. You can start tomorrow. A week's labor will cure the insult and repay the bounty I gave the policeman. If you prove the fellow I think you are, we'll see about a regular job for you. You may be able to eat meat after all."

8

For the first year that he worked for Jalal, Turhan lived with his employer. During that time, he learned that the butcher was far different from most merchants in the marketplace. For one thing, the man was scrupulously clean. No matter how soiled he appeared at the end of the day, he invariably came to work next morning in a freshly laundered shirt, and his apron was clean and white. He washed his hands, face and arms several times a day in the public fountain that ran outside the nearby mosque, and insisted that Turhan do the same. The youth found it easy to perform this injunction, for Grandfather had always insisted on cleanliness back in the village, and he'd found the filth in his mother's home an abomination.

During the hottest time of day, between the time the sun was at its zenith and late afternoon, Jalal covered his meat with a cloth net so the flies would not get to it.

Jalal was a widower, but he was far from a recluse. As Turhan soon learned, ladies of all stations sought Jalal out. His home was large, well-appointed and situated in one of the city's better quarters. "Just because one works in the marketplace doesn't mean one has to live like a poor man," Jalal told his young charge. "I've been more fortunate than most. For more than twenty years, I've made a good living as a butcher. If you're honest and give people good service and good quality, they'll find their way to your stall."

Turhan's mother hadn't cared a fig whether the youth had been present when she brought home her male "friends." Jalal, although completely candid about his social activities, was far more urbane and diplomatic. He made no attempt to hide the fact that occasionally he brought home a woman.

Within a few weeks after Turhan moved in, Jalal noticed the youth's discomfort around his women friends. The butcher was not only wise in the ways of the world, but had the special gift of good timing. Since he'd raised two sons to manhood, he instinctively knew when a boy needed an adult male to guide his steps. One morning, Jalal suggested that he and Turhan take the day off and go for a walk outside the city.

For the first hour, they walked briskly, speaking hardly a word to one another. The morning was frigid with the nip of oncoming winter. Turhan noticed, not for the first time, that his initial perception of Jalal as a fat man was not entirely accurate. Although Jalal was a trencherman of the first order, he worked as hard as he ate, and the impression of obesity was partly a result of the butcher's huge upper torso and barrel chest. Turhan felt short of breath as he hastened to keep up with the older man. Jalal kept up the pace until they'd breasted the crest of a hill, then bade Turhan halt.

"Enough," he said. "You young people have all the energy in the world. A tired old man like me needs to rest every so often." He grinned at the surprised look on Turhan's face. "Did you think I didn't hear you huffing and puffing?"

"It's not that, Jalal Effendi. I'm surprised you needed to stop at all. I was afraid you'd go on forever."

"No one goes on forever, Turhan. Let's go sit a while and have some tea," he said, pointing to a rustic tea house a hundred yards beyond them.

They'd been sitting for some time when Jalal said, "Remember back on the trail I said that no one goes on forever?"

"Yes, sir."

"No one and nothing."

"What?"

"No one and nothing go on forever."

"What do you mean, Effendi?"

"Anger, bitterness, hatred."

"I don't understand."

"When I first met you, you were frightened, but you had a fierce pride. How long had it been since you'd had a roof over your head?" Turhan blanched. He shuffled uncomfortably in his chair, but said nothing. "A day? Two? Three? A week?"

Turhan mumbled something incomprehensible.

"Do you think I don't know you lived in your mother Lâle's house?"

Turhan, feeling like a cornered animal, glanced left and right, looking for a means of escape. Finding none in the crowded tea house, he averted Jalal's gaze, stiffly staring down at the tulip-shaped glass half-filled with tea.

"Turhan?"

"She's not my mother," the boy mumbled at last.

Jalal waited a long time before he spoke, knowing he must choose his words with care.

"Perhaps, perhaps not. It's not important to me whether she is or not."

"Then why did you bring it up?" Turhan refused to look in the man's eyes.

"We're all born of someone. Do you know anything about why your mother is the way she is?"

"I said she's not my mother."

"Very well. Do you know why Lâle does the things she does?"

This time it was Turhan's turn to sit in silence. Jalal continued. "Turhan, what did you know of your mother before you came to Diyarbakır?"

"Nothing. She was a bad woman. She hurt my *baba* and grandma very much."

"I see."

"And she never once, in all the time I was alive, ever came to the village to see me."

The youth's voice was shaky, but he was starting to talk. Good, thought the older man. *Inshallah*, there will start to be cracks in the stone wall. Turhan continued. "I suppose you know how she treated me when I got here. She was as happy to see me as if I'd been a dead animal."

"Mmmmm," the butcher said.

"What do you mean, 'mmmmm'?"

"How old are you, Turhan?"

"Thirteen. Almost. Why?"

"Have you ever made a mistake in your life? A serious mistake? Done anything you were sorry for?"

The boy thought back guiltily. It had been less than two months. "What does that have to do with my... my mother?"

"Turhan, think for a moment. Where would you have been had I turned you over to the authorities? Don't forget, you'd already been exiled from your village for one act against the government."

"But I was *right*!" Turhan raised his voice to a near-shout. "I tried to save my friend!"

"Right or wrong has nothing to do with it. Morality has nothing to do with it. You defied authority. Once. Do you think that would not have come up had you been tried? Guilty of a violent crime *and* thievery? Just where do you think you'd be today?"

"So you'd throw that up into my face?" Turhan said, angrily. "And I trusted you..."

"Not so fast, my young friend. No one's talking about turning you in." Now would be a time for utmost sensitivity, the butcher thought. He'd be treading on delicate territory.

"Turhan," Jalal said. "It is the province of young people to make mistakes. Have you ever... felt... sensed a sort of funny feeling in the lower part of your body?"

"What are you talking about now?" The boy had abandoned the honorific "*effendi*" in the deepening well of this talk. "I can't understand what you're trying to say."

"Let me be blunt, then, my young friend. When you see a lovely young girl walking through the marketplace, do you ever think about her at night? And when you do, do you find yourself getting hard?" From Turhan's sharp intake of breath, Jalal knew he'd struck home. He continued, more gently. "Turhan, there's no shame in feeling as you do. Believe an old man when I tell you it's as natural as getting up in the morning and needing to urinate. Without such a feeling, life wouldn't go on."

In a direct, but tactful way, Jalal the butcher introduced Turhan to the wonder of life, the way in which one generation gave birth to another. During their talk, they stood up, left the tea house, and continued their walk through the countryside, down to the banks of the Tigris which, at that time of the year, was a sluggish, muddy stream.

"What does that have to do with my mother?" Turhan asked at one point.

"Your mother is no different than any other woman, no different than you or I," Jalal answered. "The 'needs' I told you about start at just about your age. Maybe a little older. Do you know how old your mother was when you were born?"

"No."

"I'd wager she was quite young. Remember I told you earlier that it's the province of the young to make mistakes?"

"You mean *I* was a mistake?" The boy's eyes bulged.

"Maybe not a *mistake*," the older man said, his face crinkling into a smile. "Let's just say an *accident.*" He noticed the boy glance at the ground shamefacedly. "Hey, boy," he said, punching the youth companionably on the shoulder. "You're not in bad company. Half the *world* is here because of such an 'accident.' That's surely no reason for *your* shame. But maybe it's cause for other peoples' shame."

"What do you mean, Effendi?"

"*Society's* shame?"

"You're talking in riddles again."

"Turhan, let's say your mother got those feelings I told you about. Let's say she gave in to those feelings. And let's just say that because of what she did, she had an 'accident.' She lived in a village where any kind of – activity like that – before marriage meant she'd be banned from the village. No second chance. Not even a first chance.

"When the time comes, she has a baby. Now, she can take the baby with her as she leaves her village with her shame. When I tell you a woman alone with a small child has *no* chance – *absolutely none* – to survive in our society, you may well believe it.

"So she has a decision. If she leaves the baby with someone she knows will raise it with love, she knows she is giving that child an opportunity she could never give it. And she knows she can never come back. *Never*. Do you understand what I say, boy?"

Turhan's eyes remained glued to the ground. He felt a choking sensation in his throat as the magnitude of his mother's sacrifice began to dawn on him.

"And so, at the ripe age of sixteen, not much older than you, this girl-woman, little more than a child herself, had to make a decision that would dictate the rest of her life."

"But grandfather..."

"Grandfather, what, boy? Your grandfather was a good man, and I won't dishonor the memory of the dead, but did he ever once make any more effort to come to her, to help his own daughter in her shame than your mother did to you?"

"I don't want to hear this."

"I'm sorry you don't want to hear it, Turhan. But you must. Call it a lesson in man's inhumanity to man if you want. But, as we Turks say, don't say how many gray hairs a man has in his beard until you, yourself, sit in the barber's chair."

It was twilight when they returned to Diyarbakır. Perhaps Turhan detested his mother as much as ever, but there was the slightest crack in the stern, unforgiving hatred he bore her.

"What do you feel about women, Turhan?"

"Huh?" The youth glanced up sharply from his evening meal. It had been a month since their first serious talk.

"I said, 'What do you feel about women?'"

"*Effendi?*"

"You seem nervous as a jittery cat every time I – ahem – bring a lady home for the evening."

"Well, uh, ummmm, that is..."

"Turhan, you can't have forgotten our talk about... 'feelings.'"

There has never been an easy way for the older generation to indoctrinate the younger into the mysteries of sexual discovery. The talk between Turhan and Jalal that night was no exception.

The worldly-wise butcher did the best he could to explain to the pubescent Turhan that desire did not stop when babies came, and that despite what he may have seen in his mother's hovel, a relationship between man and woman need not be limited to drunken grunting and ugly coupling. In fact, it could be a most pleasurable way of sharing everything from companionable friendship to deepest love.

"My wife and I were married more than twenty years when she died. We have two strong, wonderful sons to show for it. Throughout our lives together we bickered and talked and worked together. But we made a rule and stuck by it. We never ended the night angry at one another, and we invariably found a time and a place, even when the boys were growing up to..."

Jalal's talks with Turhan were by no means limited to the sexual aspects of the boy's education. There were many evenings when Jalal read to himself. When the butcher learned Turhan could read, he found great delight, not only in loaning the youth books, but in discussing them as well. "There's no reason why one need be a boor simply because he works in the marketplace."

It was because of Jalal that Turhan first started a journal. Turhan had been reading a tattered copy of a travel book and mentioned to Jalal how he'd like some day to see the world. He told Jalal about his talks with Shadran and of the magic cities of old that his grandfather had described.

"What a shame we Ottomans must read translations of the works of others to get a feel for what the rest of the world is like," Jalal said.

"What do you mean, effendi?"

"For the most part, travel books are nothing more than someone going to a foreign land and writing down his recollections."

"So?"

"Turhan, how many people in your village could read and write?"

The boy thought for a few moments. He remembered that Grandfather had had to find an Armenian tutor. Had that small act, in its own way, led to Shadran's death? To Turhan's exile?

"Very few."

"Very few or almost none?"

Turhan hesitated. Then, quietly, he said, "Almost none, Sir."

"You're proving my point, boy. Very few people in Diyarbakır – in fact very few people in Anatolia – can read as well as you. And as for letters...?"

"I know, effendi." Turhan brightened. "I've seen the lines in front of the scribes' stands every day. They seem even busier than you."

"Indeed. And what do they do all day? They write flowing, overdone love poetry, or ridiculous, overstated requests for our governor's assistance. They write the same words over and over until they can do it in their sleep. Each precious young girl thinks the poetry was written for her ears alone. And the scribes make a veritable fortune."

"So you'd have me be a *scribe*, Effendi?"

"No, but you could do worse than learn how to write."

"I *do* know how, Effendi. Shadran taught me."

"And when was the last time you put quill to paper?"

"Long ago. Too long, I'm afraid."

"I'll tell you what, Turhan. When is your birthday?"

"February, Sire."

"Alas, we've missed it by half a month. Ah, well, perhaps a belated gift..."

Next evening, when Turhan returned home, he found a quill pen, an ink bottle, and a pad of fine vellum paper waiting for him in his room. And the day after that, he started writing his journal.

Each night, before he fell into exhausted sleep, Turhan would write a few lines about his experiences that day. By month's end, he'd filled the first book.

By the end of the year, Turhan had saved enough money to rent a clean, bare room near the marketplace. Despite Jalal's protestations that the youth was no trouble at all, Turhan felt he was occupying too much of the older man's time, and that he was interfering with the butcher's social life. He continued to eat dinner twice a week with Jalal, and found that he was no longer uncomfortable when the man brought home a female companion. In fact, he noticed that quite often Jalal would invite him to dinner on evenings when a particular woman joined them. Turhan was not surprised when, several month's later, Jalal proudly announced that he'd squired enough women about since his wife's death, and that he'd be remarrying shortly. Turhan continued to write each night. More and more, though, he found himself possessed by those 'feelings' that Jalal had mentioned.

Time flew by, and before he knew it, Turhan had been working for Jalal for two years. Since Jalal was known for his cleanliness and the high quality of his meat, he catered to a much higher grade of clientele than most other butchers in the marketplace. Occasionally, he asked Turhan to deliver orders to the homes of Diyarbakır's wealthier residents, making sure that the boy washed himself thoroughly and changed into a fresh apron before he made such rounds.

One afternoon Jalal sent Turhan to deliver a small package of lamb cutlets to a home on Barbaros Caddesi. Turhan was surprised when the mistress of the house, Gönül, invited him to come inside. The interior of the two-story stone building was sumptuous, crowded with chairs, divans, pillows, carpets and burnished wood tables. Mirrors and paintings hung on the walls.

Gönül prepared tea and beckoned him sit on a nearby sofa. She told him that her husband, a wealthy merchant many years her senior, had gone to Syria on a gold trading mission, and that her children were spending the month with relatives at the seashore in Antalya. She'd let the servants have the week off since it was summer. Gönül revealed she was twenty-nine years old, bored, and had asked him in because she felt like talking with another human being.

Turhan told her of his early life in the village. He repeated his grandfather's early admonition about the value of learning, and became passionate when he spoke of his friend's murder, his own exile, and the lives of the downtrodden. "Your home is very beautiful, Madame," he said, "but what I envy most is all the books in this room. They offer so much. Some day, I will leave this city and see the world. Perhaps even a great lady such as you will hear about me."

Gönül looked directly at Turhan. He was nearly fifteen now, slender, athletic in build, quite handsome. She raised her skirt, ever so slightly. He stopped talking and stared at her slender legs, which she crossed and uncrossed every few moments. Although not particularly beautiful, Gönül, a product of Eurasian-Middle Eastern bloodlines, was a sensual woman. Her hair was jet black, of medium length. Her slightly thickening waistline gave promise that within a few years she would spread and become matronly. For now, she was voluptuous.

The house, so cool when he first arrived, seemed uncomfortably warm. He spoke faster and louder to cover his discomfort. He asked Gönül for another cup of tea. Her hands trembled as she lifted the teapot to refill his cup. He reached out to steady the pot. Their fingers touched. Both felt the shock at the same instant and quickly withdrew their hands.

As if guided by unseen wires, Gönül rose from the couch opposite the boy. She sat next to him and moved closer. He was dizzied by the fragrance of her light perfume. Very gently, Gönül pulled him to her and pressed her lips to his. Her tongue darted in and out of his mouth, creating a thrilling sensation as she kissed him hungrily. She arched and strained against him, her breath coming in short gasps. Turhan's hands reached into her bodice.

"Wait," she whispered. "Have you ever been with a woman?" He felt himself blush. "I thought not," she said, smiling. "You must follow my instruction until I can't speak any longer. Then do what your body tells you."

She led the youth into her bedroom. Moments later they resumed kissing and caressing in the comfort of a huge, soft bed. Gönül, now driven by passion and urgent need, removed her clothes, revealing a milky white, wonderfully rounded, soft body. Her large breasts were firm and high, flushed pink, their nipples rigid to his touch. She ground her body against his, tugging at his shirt and pants. Turhan rapidly shed his garments. He looked down, embarrassed.

"Don't worry, my little lion. That's exactly the way it's supposed to be." With a delighted gasp, she reached down. Turhan was stunned by the intense sensation her warm fingers brought.

She took Turhan's hand in hers, and pulled it gently down to the delicate black hairs that formed a delta patch over her womanhood. His fingers soon discovered a soft, slick moistness. She arched her back and moaned involuntarily. A sudden gush of wetness engulfed his fingers.

Turhan closed his eyes and felt the woman slide down his body. She grasped his organ in her hand and encircled it with her mouth, pressing her tongue in and out, emitting low animal moans as she did so. Just when he felt he would explode, she squeezed him tightly, bringing him up short. "Slowly, my lion," she gasped, hardly able to control her own squirming. "We must make this last. It's your first time. I want you to remember me for the rest of your life."

She teased the youth, stopping him time and again just before climax, until neither could wait any longer. He rolled on top of her and entered her tight, slippery cavity. Her body bucked. She shrieked in ecstasy as she climaxed with deep spasms. Seconds later, Turhan came, his own explosion ripping through him like fire.

Exhausted, they lay still for several minutes. Then, Turhan felt himself hardening again. Gönül's eyes widened in lustful delight as she looked at him. It had been a long time since she'd experienced such satisfaction. She smiled wantonly, pulled his mouth to her breasts, and reached down again.

Turhan spent that night and many afternoons thereafter with Gönül. During the next several months, whenever her husband was gone on his frequent journeys and her children were away at school, they continued their joyous adventures. Soon, their friendly intimacy allowed for delightful pillow talk after they'd made love. "Gönül

Hanım, I have to find a way to leave this city. I've been writing more than ever. Unless I see more of the world, I'll become old and stale in Diyarbakır, and my dreams will die."

"I hope when you write, you don't mention me by name. How would it appear if someone discovered such a book?"

"I would never reveal such things, My Lady. What we've done is burned in my mind, but your identity remains your own."

"I hope your memories of me are burned in other places as well."

9

"We must get you out of Diyarbakır immediately."

"What do you mean?"

"My husband, Ertuğrul, suspects I'm unfaithful. He's sixty years old. His pride's at stake, even though he's not interested in me sexually. That means only one thing if I'm discovered. And if he finds out it's you... Ertuğrul is a wealthy man, well connected. It would not be your hands he'd be interested in cutting off."

Turhan shuddered. "What should I do, Hanım?"

"Caravans pass through Diyarbakır at least once a week. I've met several caravan masters over the years. One of the best will be stopping in Diyarbakır within the month. Perhaps you could travel with him."

"What would I do for merchandise?"

"Ertuğrul keeps our storehouses filled with wares. He trusts me to keep the books. It's commonly accepted that twenty percent of any shipment vanishes between consignment and delivery. We'll prepare a camel-load of things to sell. Ertuğrul showers me with gold and jewels. He'd never notice if one or two baubles or trinkets disappeared. You'll send me half what you receive from selling the goods."

69

Within a week, Gönül had put aside one thousand kurush – a veritable fortune – worth of textiles, gold and jewelry. She warned Turhan that the *visible* goods he carried must appear modest. Any ostentation in one so young would arouse suspicion. He must seem to be dealing in common commodities, second rate bolts of cloth, worth perhaps two hundred *kurush*. He must hide the really valuable things on his person.

Gönül asked her cousin to intervene on behalf of her young lover so that Turhan might join a caravan headed north to the Black Sea coast. In those days, such arrangements were made through an intermediary. Not only were direct negotiations considered crude and barbarous, but Gönül could not risk anything that might hint she was somehow involved. Thus it was that one afternoon a week later, Gönül's cousin entered a certain coffee house prepared to meet a swarthy, fat little man with pencil-thin moustache and a wen on his nose, who'd been told to expect him. The caravan agent was already there when Gönül's cousin arrived. He immediately recognized the tall, middle-aged man with brown eyes, black eyebrows that arched upward, and thick, graying moustache.

Over the next three hours, the two men bargained hard, but in the end each knew exactly what amount would change hands to insure that Turhan would sign on with Ibrahim, one of the most respected caravan masters plying the region between Syria and the Black Sea – and the maximum commission each of them could secure for his efforts.

Ibrahim's caravan arrived at the end of August. The caravan master sent word he would meet Turhan during next afternoon's rest period, immediately after prayers. Shortly before noon the next day, Turhan, dressed in his neatest clothes, walked across town to the caravanserai on city's outer perimeters. He'd often viewed the hostel from afar. The closer he came, the less impressive it seemed, a hollow, square structure, two stories high. The top floor contained sparsely furnished rooms. The ground level housed animal stalls. The building surrounded a courtyard. Animals and men drank from a common pool in the center of the closed-in space. The place smelled of animal droppings, fodder and old sweat. Its leaky walls were thick with centuries' worth of clay and mud caulking.

The hosteler told Turhan that Ibrahim was in his summer tent, a kilometer distant. The youth thanked him and headed toward the three gray-white tents the innkeeper had pointed out. Although tufts of grass and even a few scruffy trees grew in some parts of the city, the land here was parched, nothing but stony sand. Turhan stopped at the largest of the tents. A deep voice boomed from inside, "Is that Turhan who goes about outside my tent?"

"Yes, sir," he replied.

"Would Turhan approach Ibrahim to speak?" The voice was warm and held a glint of humor.

"If Ibrahim Bey Effendi wishes and if it be Allah's will," Turhan uttered with exaggerated politeness.

"Ibrahim does so wish. And Allah will have to be ruled by that wish for the moment." Turhan heard hearty laughter. "Come inside, young man."

Turhan parted the curtained entry and hesitantly stepped into a large, light, airy space. A very tall, middle-aged man, whose dress was quite ordinary, greeted him. No flowing robes out of Arabian Nights tales. Solid blacks and grays accentuated the master's strong, weathered features. His great, fierce moustaches were caked with dust, flecked with gray. His brown eyes twinkled. "You need not be frightened, Turhan. I am a man, no more, no less. Let's speak with one another and decide whether we shall be friends and move on together, or whether Allah wills otherwise."

He clapped his hands. A servant brought two glasses of hot tea. "Now, boy, why do you wish to leave your beautiful city of Diyarbakır?" It was hard not to catch the cynical tone.

"It's not my city, and I no longer find it beautiful, Sire. Some years ago, I was banished from my village by the provincial governor for trying to save my friend's life when villagers burned the Armenian Church to the ground."

"You knew the Armenians were enemies of the Ottomans?"

"I knew they were human beings, Sir. Shadran, who taught me reading and writing, was my closest friend."

"Do you still read?"

"Whenever and whatever I can, Effendi."

"Oh? You read things other than the Koran?" The man's eyebrows lifted.

"One finds edicts in the Koran. But the world is larger than the Prophet foresaw."

"And you write?"

"Every day, Sir. That's how I remember what's important in my life. Effendi, how many men are there in the caravan?"

"It varies. As few as fifteen. As many as fifty. Women and children as well. You'll learn more about our group as you travel with us."

"Effendi," the boy said, barely concealing his excitement. "Does that mean...?"

"It does, Turhan. You're welcome to join us and share the perils and rewards of the road. My caravan leaves at dawn, day after tomorrow.

Our trip north will be rapid. We must be over the passes and on the coast before the winter winds make travel impossible. Your sponsor has paid for one camel load. You will work hard and see many things. You'll find the journey well worth your efforts."

"*Salaam aleikum,* Sire, and many thanks."

"*Aleikum salaam.*" When he heard those simple words, Turhan knew his fate was sealed. He would be departing from his old life forever.

But first, he would make a final visit to Jalal, who has been so instrumental in starting him on the road from the gutter to a future of such great promise. And, of course, his second visit would be to Gönül. Who knew when he would next enjoy the type of entertainment she provided?

10

Noise. Motion. The clang of copper against brass as pots were packed. The dust raised by hooves and feet. The swirl of loose fitting red, ochre, black and white clothing.

The sun had barely risen in the east. The still air heralded another torturously hot day. Brown hills to the north gave scant promise of pastureland. Ibrahim had told them the caravan would arrive at fertile valleys in the west by nightfall.

He rode his white Arabian stallion through the camp, urging everyone to hurry so they could be on their way. An old woman wearing loose traveling clothes, her white hair tied in a single long braid bobbed at the back of her neck, shrilly shouted back at him to mind his own business.

"Old woman, if your hands moved as fast as your tongue, you'd be worth ten men and ten camels to me!" the leader said.

"And you, young upstart," the old crone, whose name was Alkimi, cackled, "bring me your men and your camels. I'll chew them up and spit them out, and you besides!" Her weathered, brown face was both kindly and mischievous. Alkimi had traveled with caravans for more years than anyone cared to count. Cook, seamstress, physician, diviner of fortunes, she was as valuable to the caravan as Ibrahim. None dared dominate her. She was universally feared, universally adored.

When Ibrahim's mother had died, shortly after his birth, Alkimi had raised him. She'd been the one Ibrahim approached with every problem, knowing she'd speak her mind candidly and keep confidences. Her advice was invariably sound, unerringly accurate. They shared a bond of love, welded by years together, roads more distant, less traveled.

"*Tamam,* enough of you, old raisin." He laughed and moved smoothly off.

In another part of the camp, Turhan watched as shepherds rounded up the fat-tailed sheep, which carried most of their body fat in their huge tails. "They're funny looking, but wait 'til you taste their meat."

Turhan turned and found himself facing a slender young man, a head shorter than himself, with brown eyes, a hooked, hawk-like nose, and light brown skin. "Are you speaking to me, Effendi?"

"I'm hardly an effendi," the other laughed easily. "I doubt I'm much older than you. You must be Turhan. I'm Zeki." He reached out his hand. "It'll be nice having someone my own age on this trip."

"You've been on many trips?"

"I have. I can't even remember my parents. Ibrahim told me they died when I was three. I've been traveling with the caravan ever since. Fifteen years."

"Sounds exciting, always new places, new people."

"Not always."

"Where does the caravan go after it reaches Sinop?"

"We spend most of the winter moving east along the Black Sea coast. We sell most of our goods in Sinop, since it's cut off from the rest of Turkey during winter. Prices will be at their highest. Many leave the caravan there."

"How do our suppliers get their money?" he asked, thinking of his promise to send Gönül half his profits.

"The caravan leader is honor-bound to give the merchants and suppliers money entrusted to him for their benefit. Ibrahim makes a complete round trip of this circuit every year, from Mosul province in the south, to the Black Sea coast, and back. He passes through Diyarbakır twice a year. The merchants know the honest caravan masters from the scoundrels. If a caravan leader cheats a merchant, he's out of business. More likely, he suffers the usual fate of a thief."

Their conversation was interrupted as Ibrahim rode by and shouted, "All right, boys, time to move out!"

The group expected to cover seven miles the first day, spending the night within a few miles of Turhan's native village. The youth felt momentarily homesick at the thought of passing near the place that held so many memories. By mid-afternoon Turhan, who'd been charged with a small flock, had run twice the seven miles covered by the group, trying to keep his sheep tightly together to impress Ibrahim. The result was not successful. Each of the stubborn beasts chose to go its own way, stopping for a patch of thistle, taking off at a gallop for an imagined shrub, or simply wandering off.

After hours of useless running, Turhan watched Zeki, who seemed content to let his sheep drift all over the fields, straggle back, dart forward, zip out on a tangent. When Turhan asked about this, Zeki replied, "They never stray beyond a certain point. I've yet to lose one. The older sheep follow the caravan. The lambs stay near their mamas for food and warmth."

During the afternoon, the young men continued their conversation. "Caravans often provide inland cities and towns with their only goods from outside," Zeki said. "The routes have been established for hundreds of years. At the southern end, we purchase dates, figs, Persian carpets, jewels and spices. There's always some small war or skirmish going on near the border, so caravans use safe cities this side of the Turkish frontier as storehouses for their operations.

"On the way north, we take on Turks and buy pistachio nuts and wheat. Southbound, leaders seek out Arab companions and purchase tea, tobacco, rice and... other things. Smuggling's a way of life. All caravan masters do it to some degree."

Turhan paled. Zeki continued, matter-of-factly, "You might as well know it now. Ibrahim's a wonderful leader, but he's no less human than anyone else. The *aghas* and the governors take their cut of everything. If you get into trouble, you simply put enough money into the right hands and the trouble disappears. If you bring a lawsuit to one of our oh-so-honest judges for a decision, you pray your opponent didn't pay more *baksheesh* than you."

"But smuggling's against the law."

"How else do you expect the little man to gain anything in this system? The powerful have their ways. We have ours."

Turhan was silent for several moments. Years ago a gang of soldiers, acting under color of law, had abused and killed his closest friend. A petty official had destroyed his life, humiliated his grandfather, taken what little that poor man had, and ultimately robbed him of his life. All perfectly legal. Turhan had vowed to fight back. How much fighting had he done in the years since? What had he accomplished? How wrong was it to fight a system so rotten on the inside by *any* means at your disposal?

"What kind of goods?" Turhan asked when he was sure they had distanced themselves from the group.

"Gold. Arms. Occasionally opium or hashish."

"And Ibrahim allows that?"

"Don't look so shocked, Turhan. Ibrahim's a man, not a god. Sometimes he doesn't have much choice. There are those who exercise considerably more – power – than Ibrahim."

The youths walked awhile in silence.

"Don't get me wrong, Turhan," Zeki said. "Ibrahim's very special. He's the most respected and learned trader of all. He travels north to the Black Sea and arrives there in winter, when most caravans are in the milder southern areas. He sells his goods at a premium in whatever coastal city he chooses. Once there, he buys things that are very dear in the hot, dry areas of Turkey and Syria. At Sinop, he packs in dried, smoked mullet and tunny fish. When he unloads this shipment in Diyarbakır, buyers soak the fish in water overnight. Next morning it tastes like it came from the sea the day before.

"Farther east, we buy the finest tobacco and tea. In spring, when the weather's best, Ibrahim starts south. He usually arrives in Mosul by the beginning of the summer, when no one wants to be in that harsh desert. He's often told me the secret of his success is to be in places where he can buy and sell at a time when few other traders are around. In that way, he consistently commands the best price."

The sun set. Village lights flickered in the distance. A dull, lifeless town. A place to be *from*. Yet in the gathering twilight, there was something that called Turhan home.

Night was upon the land.

Turhan heard the *muezzin's* wail, summoning the faithful to prayer. The caller's cry could be heard clearly as it sinuously wound its way over hills, into the valleys. Turhan felt a chill. There was something lonely, awesome, and beautiful about the centuries-old call wafting over the desert from a high minaret. The desert sky was filled with stars, more and brighter points of light than he ever remembered seeing before. He heard soft echoes in the distance. He felt very close to Allah and to his departed grandfather.

The travelers pitched camp a few miles beyond the village. Men had gathered wood during the day. They used it and dried sheep dung, to start a small fire. The women prepared *ich pilav*, rice mixed with currants, lamb livers, pine nuts, chopped onions, and spices.

A wonderful aroma filled the air and Turhan saw a whole roast lamb turning on a spit. Drippings of lamb fat sizzled as they dropped onto the fire. Soon the carcass browned. Turhan's stomach groaned with hunger. Courtesy made him stay back and watch how the others ate their dinner.

Ibrahim went to the roasting meat, sliced off a small chunk near the loin, and tasted it. Satisfied, he sliced a generous portion and presented it to Alkimi with a flourish. Then he signaled the rest to begin the feast. Each man cut a large chunk of meat. Zeki was just ahead of Turhan. The newcomer watched carefully. Turhan's face fell when Zeki carefully took a very small portion from the rib. Turhan dutifully cut a similar portion. He noticed that even some of the women had taken larger cuts.

"So now we have not one but two little birds in our caravan, eh?" Ibrahim, juices clinging to the sides of his moustaches, grinned broadly and winked at Turhan. "You were wise to watch the others, let them go first, then take according to their portion. However, you erred grievously when you chose to take the same portion as our camp sparrow. If you don't do better than that, you'll starve or collapse."

"But..." stammered Turhan, "I... that is... I'm not really that hungry, and..."

"Nonsense. You think I don't know everything that goes on in this camp? I saw you running after sheep all day. Now, young fellow, eat like a man!" With that, Ibrahim sliced a large piece from the haunch and tossed it to Turhan. With a hearty guffaw, he left for another area of the cantonment.

Turhan greedily bit into the lamb. He could not remember ever tasting anything so delicious. The freshly roasted meat was chewy, salty-sweet. The very thin layer of crunchy burnt fat was the most delectable of all. This *ich pilav* tasted wilder, dryer than he'd been used to in the city. Soon his stomach was full.

After dinner, men broke out coffee, tea, and *rakı*, the fiery, anise-flavored Turkish liquor. Someone produced a *saz* – a Turkish mandolin. The night was filled with the sound of old Anatolian folk songs. Firelight created dancing shadows, ghostlike figures of light on dark. Turhan lay near the warm, smoky fire. The slightest sliver of a crescent moon hung suspended in the clear, black sky. It was not long before exhaustion caught up with him, and he fell into a deep, dreamless sleep.

The next morning was warm, clear, stark white. Turhan felt stiff and sore all over. He groaned as he looked at his feet. Blisters lined the soles. Alkimi approached so silently Turhan didn't know she was near him until she warned him, in a gruff, but kind voice, that he must not run about herding sheep this day, but should simply travel as slowly and steadily as he could. She looked at his feet, grunted, dipped into a large pouch and extracted a handful of foul-smelling, brown unguent, which she kneaded into his heels, the arch of his feet, and downward toward the toes. The medicine burned for an instant, then felt very cool. He smiled thankfully at the old woman.

"Sulfur, zinc, camel urine, other things," she mumbled. The soreness seemed to be going away. "You're not healed yet, little traveler. Your feet will feel all right for now. In a few hours, they won't feel so good. We'll stop and do this again."

"How long will we have to do this, Alkimi *hanım*?" he asked.

"Two or three days. Your bare feet will toughen on the desert sand and rocks. That's the least of your worries. How are your shoulders? Your back? Sore?"

"Very stiff."

The woman produced a large vial containing a gold-colored liquid of pungent but much different scent. "Menthol, camphor, leaves and herbs," she said. "You'll stink enough by midday that no one else will want to be near you, but you won't be so sore."

Alkimi administered ointments at least twice more during the day. Ibrahim seemed especially solicitous. At one point, he offered to let Turhan sit astride his own steed. Turhan declined politely. By day's end, his feet felt somewhat better.

The evening meal consisted of *güvetch*, a lamb stew with peppers, eggplant, tomatoes and rice. After the meal, Ibrahim invited Turhan to his tent.

"Do you feel better this evening?" Ibrahim asked.

"Yes, thank you, Effendi."

"Do you wonder why I called you to my tent?"

"I haven't had much time to think about it, Sire."

"I want to find out more about you, what's happened in your life to make you what you are." Ibrahim poured two glasses of tea and handed one to Turhan. "Do you want to talk for a while, Son?"

Turhan felt a warm kinship with this tall, kindly man. But the thought of what Zeki had told him yesterday stuck like a bone in his throat.

"Ibrahim Effendi, may I be honest?"

"I'd prefer that, Turhan."

"Very well, Sire. When you and I first spoke, you talked of adventures of the road, and I thought, 'How I wish I were like this man.' But yesterday, sire, Zeki and I spoke of... certain other things..."

The older man waited quietly for Turhan to go on, sensing his acute discomfort. Ibrahim displayed neither anger nor impatience, only resignation. "You mean the goods we pretend we don't have, Turhan?"

"Yes, Effendi."

"Turhan, every man starts his life believing he's on the side of good. When you're young, it's easy to know exactly what's right and what's wrong. But as you grow older, the borders of good and evil start to blur. That may be hard for you to comprehend. I only ask that you think back to what I say when you're twenty or thirty years older. When I was young, I was no different from you. I saw a political system rotten with corruption, and believed I was Allah's chosen, the hero who would single-handedly bring justice to Turkey and the world. I didn't.

"The real world is a place where you do what you must to survive as best you can. You learn to pass messages, deliver certain goods, and not ask questions. Otherwise you wake to find your camels poisoned, your merchandise destroyed.

"Then you start to ask different questions, the kind it never occurred to you to ask when you were young. Such as, who really gets hurt? A man so poor he could otherwise hardly feed himself sells a small amount of opium. From the money he makes on that single sale he cares for his wife and six children for a month. The man who buys it is ridden with cancer, or he's so old and feeble he longs for death to end his misery. For a few hours he smokes the opium pipe and, like magic, his pain is gone and he's a young man again, dreaming the dreams of his youth. Do you understand what I'm saying, boy?"

"That what our eyes show us is wrong is not. That if enough people tell you black is white you start to believe it."

"No, Turhan. On the contrary, you come to understand right and wrong more deeply. You understand your own shortcomings the better. Then, one day you realize your 'some days' are past."

"Must it always be that way, Effendi?"

"That's the most difficult question, my son. We must all grow older. Perhaps it will be granted to you to realize the dreams of youth. Only time will answer that. Now that you know I'm not a god, that I'm simply a man, perhaps we can talk as friends."

Something about Ibrahim's tone of voice, the clear, kind look in his eye, affected Turhan more deeply than he'd ever felt at any time since he'd spoken with Jalal. As the evening wore on, Ibrahim listened quietly as Turhan spilled out his heart.

Turhan's story stopped short of the adventure he'd had with Gönül and of the hidden treasure on his person. On these matters, Turhan knew enough to keep his own counsel.

As Turhan spoke, the caravan master's eyes misted with the thought of what might have been, had his own child lived.

"Have you ever heard of the university, Effendi?" Turhan asked. "My friend Shadran once mentioned it to me."

"I have, Turhan. There are many universities throughout the world. I, myself, attended the one at Alexandretta."

The boys' eyes widened. "Shadran told me such a place has more books than one could read in a whole lifetime."

"That's true, but if a man limits his learning to what he finds in those books, he becomes as stiff and brittle as the paper on which the words are printed. Real education begins when you use the entire world as your school. When you talk with people in different parts of the world you start to learn about the important things. Books and newspapers give you the insights to use that knowledge."

"News-papers, Effendi?"

"In many places men publish journals of events such as you keep, Turhan. These are not personal diaries. They speak of important events throughout the land and even beyond. They help men learn things that will affect them in their daily lives."

"I'd like to see a news-paper one day," the boy said, fascinated.

"In Kayseri, they publish one every day. I'll make it a point to buy one for you."

"Effendi, my grandfather once told me there was a place in Anatolia where people built an entire city under the ground. Have you heard of it?

"I have. There are many such wonders in our motherland, not all of them underground. Perhaps we may take a few extra days to see some of them."

Turhan's eyes widened. In his lifetime, he'd seen little more than a dusty village and a shabby city. Alkimi finally interrupted them, coughing and growling outside the tent, "The young fool listens to the older fool. You may learn the wisdom of the world, but you'll both be worthless tomorrow. It's time to stop now."

"Away, old gossip," snapped Ibrahim. "Where is it ordained that man's talk should be annoyed by the angry buzzing of worthless insects?"

"You two will be together many days. You can talk. You can learn. The smaller one still has sore feet and a sore body. He needs medicine and sleep. An old woman like me needs rest, too."

"Will you never stop torturing me?" Ibrahim asked in mock exasperation. "May I say one thing to the boy in private?"

"There's nothing you can't say without me here. It will be said much quicker if I stay." The woman stubbornly stood her ground.

"Very well," Ibrahim sighed. "Turhan, earlier tonight you asked if things must always be as they are. Your answer lies within you. I can only give advice which, like much I've said this evening, might be considered the ramblings of a tired old man. The merchant learns only about his world. The shepherd scarcely ever inquires of the universe beyond his sheep. In their limited worlds they become expert. There will always be men who know how to do things. But those who count in life are the ones who know *why*. Don't accept something for what it *seems to be*, but learn what it means in the larger circle of things. Most men are content to trust to Allah or the government. When they do that, they abandon responsibility for their own lives.

"When you were in your village, horrible things happened to you, things over which had no control. Too often, a man's destiny is governed by the whims of others. The vast majority of mankind is pushed about by the few.

"If you refuse to accept what seems wrong to you, if you dare challenge an injustice, you will suffer defeat, humiliation, even death. But your life will make a difference. Do you understand?"

Turhan nodded.

Ibrahim smiled warmly at the young man. "The old woman is right. It's off to sleep with you."

After the boy left, Alkimi and Ibrahim remained, speaking quietly with one another. "When I first saw him this morning, he reminded me very much of what you were like at that age," Alkimi said. "You were taller and skinnier, but he's as eager as you were to absorb the whole world. Allah, where did the years go? Did you tell him about...?"

"The drugs, the weapons?"

"No, my friend. The other?"

"How could I?" Bitterness and pain mingled in his look. "I told him you wake to find your camels poisoned."

How could he have told a lad so full of righteous fire that the strongest man can be broken? Or that what others might call "wrong" repaid, in part, a debt much stronger than principles.

Willow.

Even now the memory was too painful to bear.

"I couldn't tell him," he said softly to the old woman. "My child might have been very much like this one. He would have been about the same age."

"There was nothing any of us could do." She looked down at the ground, her voice strained.

The caravan master turned away momentarily, and blew his nose. "I walk with her every day of my life. Even now, each time I pass those graves near that village..." He coughed.

"Why do you feel such closeness for him?" Alkimi asked. "Why not Zeki, or others who've traveled with us over the years?"

"Who knows, my friend? Perhaps because my son would have been the same age. Or perhaps I see the proud, stubborn morality I had at his age. A reflection I would have wanted in my own child."

"That may be, Ibrahim," she replied. "But if you truly feel that way, you must tell him what happened. And that knowledge may help him become a man."

11

ISTANBUL

Abbas could never quite recall when Kerem came into his father's life. Soon afterwards, the beatings stopped. Ahmet seemed to have enough money for rakı *and* food – and plenty of it. Abbas had neither seen nor heard from his older brothers since they'd left. He often wished they'd been here to witness the remarkable transformation in their father.

At first, Kerem came to the house about twice a week. He was a small man, with an abnormally large, hooked nose, a thin moustache, and a pot belly. The routine was invariably the same. Kerem greeted Ahmet respectfully and the two men departed almost immediately. Ahmet was gone an hour, no more, no less. When he returned, he carried a bottle of the finest *rakı* and two loaves of fresh bread. Father's mood was always better after he'd been with Kerem. For that, Abbas was eternally grateful.

One morning, six months after he'd come into their lives, Kerem came to the house earlier than usual. Ahmet was about to leave for work – he carried much lighter loads lately – and Abbas had an hour before he had to be at school.

"*Salaam aleikum*, Gentlemen," Kerem greeted them courteously. Abbas was mildly surprised. Kerem's dealings had always been with his father, and the youth was flattered at being addressed as an adult.

"Kerem Effendi," the older man nodded.

"Ahmet, you and I have spoken of many things. I've never had a chance to speak with your son, who's fourteen, almost a man." The boy beamed with pleasure. "Do you suppose our state institution of learning might spare the lad for a day? I'd like to learn more about him and perhaps educate him in our view of the world as well."

Abbas' father seemed pleased. Despite the cessation of physical abuse, the two still had difficulty offering more than perfunctory greetings to one another. "I see no reason why not. What say you, boy?"

"As you wish, Father." Abbas could barely conceal his excitement. A full day away from the drudgery of classroom work. He'd far surpassed his schoolmates. The teacher had little initiative, certainly not enough to suggest that Abbas, one of thirty-five ragamuffins from the poorest part of Istanbul, do more advanced work. After all, what good would reading do a *hamal*?

"So be it." Kerem clapped his hands. "Come, Abbas. Let's have a *real* breakfast at *Kapali Charshi* – the Covered Bazaar."

Abbas could not remember a better day in his life. The older man listened patiently as the boy poured out his story. Kerem seemed to value what Abbas said, nodding at appropriate moments, clucking his tongue sympathetically at others.

"I never realized things had been so hard for you at home," he said at one point. "You've shown remarkable courage in the face of adversity." He put his arm around the boy's shoulder and squeezed affectionately. Abbas was struck by a sudden, warm feeling. It was the first physical contact, other than the beatings and holding his little brother at night, that Abbas had ever experienced. It felt good. Validation at last that he, Abbas, was worth something.

After they'd traversed Kapali Charshi – Kerem seemed impressed that his young charge recalled the location and owner's name of at least a quarter of the shops in the Grand Bazaar – they crossed the floating Galata Bridge into Pera, the European part of the city. This was a world apart from the rabbit warrens of Abbas' quarter.

"Your father's an angry man, Abbas. You understand that?"

"Yes, Sire."

"No need to be so formal. If we're to be friends, you may call me Kerem – when we're alone, of course."

"Thank you, S –, Kerem Effendi."

"Do you know why he's so bitter?"

"I believe so. He blames the foreigners."

"Indeed." They walked in comfortable silence for a while. "What do you feel about the 'foreign elements?'"

"I've never given it much thought. Probably the same. After all, this is the *Ottoman* empire."

"Is it the *Ottoman* empire, boy?" the man asked seriously.

They'd entered a decidedly better part of town. They passed a series of elegant stone-and-brick houses. "That one's owned by Georgiopoulos, a Greek shipping magnate. The one next to it by Latakian, one of the sleaziest drug dealers in the Empire." As the homes became more and more palatial, Kerem continued to name each householder. "LaFontaine, Frenchman. He and Latakian work together. They ship opium to Marseilles. HaLevy. Lends money to most of the Turkish banks. Foreclosed on two of them this year alone. Baruch, ten rug shops in the Bazaar. He's priced his merchandise so low five Ottoman merchants went out of business in the last six months. Brotzky. Smuggles people out and arms in to Russia." The list went on. Englishmen, Frenchmen, Germans. Not one Ottoman name in the neighborhood.

"What does this all have to do with me?"

"Abbas, one of the reasons we've lost control of our own destiny is that we've *given* it away to others. Our poor are so busy fighting among themselves for a single kurush that they let a hundred go to the foreigner who charges a little less. We cheat ourselves by drinking raki until we're drunk and falling into blissful opium dreams, not realizing that someone is making money – a lot of money – from our misery. Sometimes it's the Jews and Armenians. But the drug lords among our own kind, men like the Agha Nikrat, are worse, for they prey on their Muslim brethren. Somehow we must reclaim our souls if we are to salvage our own destiny."

The boy nodded. Kerem expressed his feelings in a far more meaningful, eloquent way than his father did, and he was obviously very wise.

It was early afternoon when they crossed back to Stamboul. "Are you hungry, Abbas?"

"Starved, Si –, Kerem," the boy grinned. "But the time's passed so fast I'd hardly noticed."

They stopped at a nearby *lokanta* where the youth filled himself on *dolma* and *döner kebab*, thin roasted lamb slices, cut from a vertical spit. The best meal Abbas could remember.

Afterward, Kerem invited the youth to his home. The older man apparently lived alone. His house overlooked the Bosphorous and was comfortable rather than flamboyant. "You must be tired from all that walking. Why not lie down for a while? I'll massage your sore muscles."

The boy did not argue. Kerem was expert in his ministrations. The boy relaxed, absorbing the pleasure of Kerem's touch.

"Does that feel better, Abbas?"

"Wonderful, sire."

"Do you like me, Abbas?"

"I praise Allah every night for your coming into our lives."

"Will you trust me if I tell you I'm about to do something which will make you feel *very* good?"

"Mmmm-hmmm." The youth started to doze off.

He felt himself being rolled over on his back. Suddenly, Kerem's hands started massaging a different place on his body. Abbas felt himself hardening, but lay there and said nothing. It *did* feel better than anything. When it was done, Kerem said, "Now you must do the same for me."

During the next year Abbas and Kerem shared their secret liaisons once a week. Kerem showed his young charge affection the boy had never received from his parents. They talked about a variety of things. It was tacitly agreed that they never discussed what Kerem did or the relationship between him and Abbas' father.

By the time Abbas was fifteen, he was a strapping, muscular youth. Kerem secured him a job on the docks, helping unload shipments from around the world. Often, Kerem pointed out that the Greeks controlled all the shipping while the Turks did the menial, low-paying labor.

Abbas soon found that by gambling with Turkish stevedores, beasts of burden with brains to match, he could easily best them at *tavla* – the backgammon game they played during their brief lunch break, and he usually increased his pay by nearly a quarter. After work, they drank away life's burdens at the *Altın Boğa*, the Golden Bull rakı bar. Most decent men wouldn't think of going to such a place, much preferring their coffee houses. But these men were not so 'civilized.' Their conversations were invariably the same. The Ottoman Empire was crumbling. It was the damned Greeks' and Jews' fault. They kept getting richer while the Muslims were worse off than ever.

The men easily accepted "clever Abbas," as they called him, into their circle. He gave eloquent voice to their feelings and urged them to be proud of their heritage. While work was hard and wages low, at least they engaged in honest labor and did not earn their living from the sweat of other men like the Greeks did.

One evening, shortly after work, Kerem approached him just as he was leaving work. "Abbas," he said, "your father's dead. He was stabbed in the marketplace."

Abbas considered the words in silence for a few moments. He and Ahmet had never quite made their peace. Rather, it had been an uneasy, wordless truce. After he and Kerem had cemented their relationship, Abbas' presence in the house had been minimal. He could not say he'd miss the old man. It was almost a relief to have him out of the way. But there were Mother and the girls to consider.

As if reading his thoughts, Kerem continued. "I've spoken with your mother. She's decided to go back to her village. She never liked Istanbul, and she's got family back home."

"Does she expect me to go with her?"

"No."

"Where would I live?"

"Why not move in with me?"

"Do you mean that, Kerem?" He brightened.

"I don't know why you shouldn't."

"Who stabbed him?" he asked.

"Probably an anti-government subversive gang in the Bazaar."

"Why?"

"Abbas, perhaps it's time I told you some things about our operation – your father's and mine – that you might not know." The two walked away from the port, and Abbas found himself in a newer part of town. "You've no doubt noticed that since your father and I became friends things have changed for you."

"Of course."

"My sources provided Ahmet with his extra income." Abbas said nothing, but kept walking. "He was a patriot in his own way, your father. He believed in Turkey for the Ottomans. Remember when you and I discussed that we must take back our land from the outsiders?"

"Yes, Effendi."

"Whatever you might think of your father, he believed in that goal and worked for it." The youth remained silent. "We can't afford to buy back with money what foreign elements have stolen from us. The only thing on our side is the law."

"What do you mean?"

Kerem reached into his jacket pocket and pulled out a small leather case. He opened it and displayed a card and badge. "Abbas, I've never told you this before. I'm an officer in the Internal Security Police. Our job is to protect the Ottoman government. You'd be surprised how many threats there are. A Jew who drives his Turkish neighbor out of business causes dissatisfaction which unfortunately erupts as anger at the Ottoman government. If the Jew is accused of a crime against state security, he may voluntarily choose to pay a substantial fine. If he doesn't, he risks conviction and confiscation of his business. Word soon gets out in the community. The Turkish businessman who has suffered so dreadfully feels vindicated, and the government secures additional revenue to carry on its good works. Eventually the property stolen from us is returned to its rightful owner – through our government, of course."

"What does all this have to do with my father, or with me?"

"Our government is responsible for the well-being of all its subjects. Unfortunately, our budget does not allow for a sufficient number of investigators. There is a special allowance for unofficial agents."

"You mean informers?"

"Now I understand why they call you 'clever Abbas.'"

"You want me to take my father's place?"

"With your father gone, we need an immediate replacement."

"You'd expect me to spy on my neighbors? Report them to you? Is that what my father did?" Abbas felt for the first time that his friend was betraying him.

"We'd like you to assist us in making sure there's full compliance with the law. We don't consider that spying. When we're dealing with criminals, we must use effective means. Naturally, we don't mean for you to work for nothing. Besides, I have other, better plans for you."

"Such as?"

"You're fifteen. In three years you'd be old enough to enter the Police Academy. You're certainly bright enough. With my strong recommendation and a proven record of honorable service to your country, getting you in would be easy. You'd never have to dirty your hands with manual labor again. And think of the power you'd eventually have."

Abbas was anything but stupid. It took him no time to read between the lines of what his mentor was saying. "But I've been away from the bazaar for over a year. It would look strange if I suddenly showed up back there."

"You don't have to. Crime is everywhere. The docks as well as the marketplace. Sometimes things are not as they seem. Greek shippers are very clever when they transport drugs or arms. It's often impossible to know where they hide the bulk of their contraband. Of course, if a dock worker leaves a small amount of such things in a place where they could be easily found..."

"You mean plant illegal goods...?"

"We don't speak in such terms. Criminal elements are very much aware of our vigilance. They do everything possible to foil us. It's only fair that the Ottoman Empire recover the smallest portion of what outsiders steal from us. Our ends are worthy, nothing less than preservation of the Empire. The means justify those ends."

Abbas considered what Kerem had said for a long time. Without his being aware of it, they'd traveled in a circle and returned to the area of the docks. The sun was setting behind Abbas' back, blocking him from the view of the Greek shipper and his manager who were speaking in jocular tones, unaware of their proximity.

"You're sure you were able to buy off the foreman? There'll be no trouble from the dock workers."

"It was easy, Mister Parios. They're nothing but stupid, greedy Muslims. A little extra money in the foreman's pocket, a few bottles of rakı. No difficulty at all. Dumb buggers they are. A wonder they were able to put together an empire at all."

"Christ be praised they need us to keep the machinery of commerce oiled, eh Vasilios?"

The two men laughed and headed down the quay to the harbormaster's office.

Abbas glared after them. "You're right, Kerem Effendi. It's time we purified our land and took control of our own destiny."

12

By the time the caravan reached the Euphrates River, five days west of Diyarbakır, Turhan no longer required Alkimi's ointments. Although it was not so oppressively hot, the land remained hard, barren, uninhabited except for a few small villages that dotted the horizon. Turhan thrived on the combination of hearty food, hard physical work and sufficient sleep.

Ten days out of Diyarbakır, the harsh desert grudgingly gave way to the foothills of the Taurus Mountains. Turhan marveled at his first sight of pine trees, green even in the dusty, late summer days. To Ibrahim, who was used to the mountains of Turkey, the Taurus woods were sparse, scraggly. It was hard to believe that three thousand years earlier, the entire land had been virgin forest, separating Europe from the Fertile Crescent. Goats and sheep had nibbled the forests to the ground. Then their small, sharp hooves dug up the seeds of any vegetation that tried vainly to take hold.

Shortly before noon, Ibrahim rode up to Turhan, leading a saddled mule and two fully-laden camels. "Turhan," he said, "I'm not going to pretend you're ignorant about certain things we carry." He pointed to a series of hills to the right of the caravan. "Ride with me along that trail. I believe it's time I told you the full story of *why*."

Although Turhan had never ridden a camel before, his confidence in the caravan master dispelled his fears. They left the rest of the group and rode up a narrow trail into the hills.

Turhan was the first to speak. "Effendi, you said you wanted to talk to me?"

"Yes, I do. The other evening, we spoke of drugs and weapons. Sometimes it's not easy to tell what is right or wrong, good or bad. Things happen in life that you can never foresee." Turhan noticed the man seemed to be lost in thought. They rode side by side in silence for a time.

"I am going to tell you a long story, Turhan. I ask that you listen and not judge until you've heard it all."

The boy nodded.

"Once upon a time – our folk tales often start that way, and I see no reason not to, in a small village in Mosul province, there was a girl named Willow..."

Her father was a small merchant who, to augment his meager income, sometimes dealt in opium and hashish. It was an accepted way of life. You paid *twice* to stay in business in that province: the requisite *baksheesh* to the authorities, and favors for the Agha Khorusun, who was the *real* power in the province.

Ibrahim had traveled through the village many times over the years. He watched the child Willow emerge from pig-tailed urchin, to coltish adolescent, and finally to young womanhood. At sixteen, she was the loveliest girl in the village. To Ibrahim, she was the most breathtakingly beautiful girl in the world. She had brown eyes. Her hair was dark as night and fell to her waist.

By then Ibrahim realized he'd fallen hopelessly in love with her, and he knew Willow shared that love. When he was absent from Mosul province for several months at a time, his heart ached, such was his longing. This had never happened to him before. He was strong, virile and led a life of excitement. Since he'd left university five years before, he'd never wanted for female companionship.

Ibrahim had done business with Willow's father for some years and the older man had become his friend. Occasionally, the merchant asked Ibrahim to carry small shipments of drugs to and from Anatolia. The caravan master saw no harm in this. He was not unaware that smuggling was done all over that part of the world. If Ibrahim didn't help the man, someone else would. And besides, there was Willow. The risks were small, the potential rewards great.

Soon Ibrahim found his eyes weren't the only ones that feasted on the young woman. Mosul's provincial police chief wanted her for himself. He was a large, ugly man, forty-five, with a pockmarked face, who sweated profusely and hardly ever bathed. But he was a force to be reckoned with and feared.

When the police chief became aware of how Willow and Ibrahim felt toward one another, he threatened her father. "Gothai, Effendi, as you know, I am aware of your dealings, not that they're better or worse than anyone else's. But certain things disturb me greatly. Your daughter disports herself in public, freely and immorally, with that camel driver Ibrahim."

"Ah, Police Chief Effendi, nowadays one cannot control women as we could in the past."

"A father must always exercise authority over his child, Merchant. If he cannot, he must make haste to marry her off to a man capable of doing so."

"Would this were so. But she's sixteen and very headstrong." He shrugged his shoulders helplessly.

"That may very well be, Effendi. I cannot waste time on argument. Gothai, for some years you have assisted me in helping the people of this province." The merchant was surprised and alarmed by the chief's lack of manners. One simply did not mention *baksheesh.* "I think, Merchant," he continued, "that the successful continuation of your business may no longer depend on *monetary* assistance."

"What do you mean, Chief?"

"I will have the girl Willow to wife thirty days hence."

The father paled. He neither liked nor trusted the police chief, but he had lived in his village all his life. To move away and start over again was unthinkable. The police chief exercised the power of life and death. All it would take would be an arrest.

"Well?"

"You shall have my answer in three days, Your Honor."

"I expect it is because you must talk with the girl, convince her what a fine match she's made."

"I must talk..."

"Very well, then. Three days. *Salaam aleikum.* "

That night, Willow's father and Ibrahim talked for a long time. At the end of the evening, when Willow was asleep, Ibrahim formally asked him for her hand in marriage.

"Ah, Ibrahim, I could wish for no greater joy than to welcome you to my home as son-in-law. But what can we do?"

"The Agha Khorusun?"

"Yes, that is a possibility." The merchant smiled for the first time in several hours. "That is most definitely a possibility."

There was only one man in the province more powerful than the police chief. The Agha Khorusun. If Ibrahim was to have Willow and his prospective father-in-law was to survive, the only way to handle this would be by seeking an audience with the Agha.

The Agha understood their problem perfectly, and said he'd personally deal with the police chief. A day later, he not only insisted they marry in his home, but further assured the delighted men that the chief of police himself would be in attendance and would propose a toast to the bride and groom.

The day Ibrahim married Willow was glorious. Even the police chief mouthed words honoring the happy occasion. Only Ibrahim saw the hateful glare in the other man's eyes. He knew he'd have to guard his flank thereafter.

The next year was the happiest of his life. Willow traveled with him. She was an eager, exciting lover, a wonder to be with on the trail. Each day Ibrahim discovered something more remarkable about his woman. It was not long before she announced she was carrying his child. His happiness knew no bounds.

But Ibrahim heard disquieting things from his father-in-law. Every caravan master who dealt with Gothai found his finest camels poisoned. Gothai's warehouse was ransacked. Bolts of his finest cloth were torn, grains were laced with rat droppings or worse. Bags full of opium and hashish, not all of them his, were slashed open, their contents scattered about the storage facility. One morning, the man discovered a severed pig's head on his front doorstep, its blood slathered over the entry to his home.

Ibrahim hurried south to help his father-in-law. There was no question the man had to get out of Mosul province, regardless of the difficulty. But now was not the time to travel. Willow was due to give birth within the month. Travel would be dangerous for her.

Two evenings after they had returned, Willow went missing from her father's home. Had her time come early? Then Ibrahim heard a keening wail coming from a shallow wadi at the far end of the village. It was Alkimi. When he approached Alkimi's tent, the horror in the woman's eyes answered the question Ibrahim was afraid to ask. Alkimi tried to stop the caravan master from going to the wadi.

"Not yet, Ibrahim Effendi. I beg you not yet. Let the women deal with this first."

But Ibrahim shoved her roughly out of the way and ran to the wadi. For the rest of his days, he'd wish he had not done so.

Willow's face was beautiful and at peace. From the neck up it appeared she was sleeping. But her body had been slit from breast to belly by a clean knife-line. The unborn child, a baby boy, lay dead in the dust. A kilogram of opium lay in the cavity which had housed the fetus the night before. Alkimi stood by Ibrahim as he vomited.

For days he neither ate nor slept. All he wanted was death. He was soul-dead, without the capacity for anger or revenge. Several days later, Alkimi came to him with broth and hot tea.

One day he came awake. "Why?" was all he could ask.

"There is no why. There is only 'who.'" Ibrahim looked at her, stunned. She continued, "The women say it was the police chief."

When he heard those words, Ibrahim was consumed with one thought: to destroy the unmentionable beast who'd murdered his wife and son. As days went by, he found that impossible. The police chief had redoubled his guard. He was surrounded by officers everywhere he went.

There was only one answer. Ibrahim went to the Agha Khorusun. He humbled himself and cried in the great man's presence. The Agha was very understanding. He had five sons and three daughters. Unlike most men in the Middle East, his daughters brought him as much joy as his sons, and he loved them equally. Ibrahim knew how the Agha had come to power. It didn't matter. He was the only man strong enough to deal with this terrible travesty of justice. The Agha listened and tears came to his eyes. Finally, he said, in a very soft voice, "Ibrahim, on my father's grave I swear you shall have your revenge."

Three days later, a stranger came to Ibrahim's tent and directed the grieving man to a small hovel on the outskirts of a remote village, just beyond the northern boundaries of the province. When Ibrahim reached the place, he heard a soft moaning. The messenger said, "Go and finish the work."

Not even Ibrahim's great anger and rage prepared him for what he saw, and he gagged. What remained of the police chief hung from a large meat hook. He was still alive. Barely.

"I hesitate to go into detail even now," Ibrahim said. "He had no power to implore me with the bloody stumps of arms he had left. His one eye fixed me with a stare that begged me to kill him. He couldn't speak. His tongue had been cut out. Nor could he hear. There were other things – Perhaps it was an undeserved kindness that I plunged my dagger into his heart right then. But I couldn't allow even so loathsome a creature to suffer any longer.

"After that, the Agha requested, from time to time, that I take certain of his friends on my journeys north. Invariably they brought several camels, all loaded down with carefully packed goods. I knew better than to ask what they transported. The Agha never demanded. It was simply understood that if he requested anything – anything at all – I would obey his will. He is a good man. Some debts can never be fully repaid."

Turhan said nothing. The tears running down his cheeks told Ibrahim he understood everything. And that Ibrahim had done right to tell him.

Shortly afterward, they came to a shallow depression between the hills, where they found a small wooden shed. At Ibrahim's direction, they tied the camels to a post in front of the building. Ibrahim pushed the door of the lean-to open and emerged with a large paper envelope. He opened the packet and counted out five thousand *kurush*. Turhan gasped, amazed. Ibrahim handed Turhan six hundred *kurush*. "Even the Agha never demanded we work for free."

After they left the shed, the trail continued climbing. Shortly, they came to a plateau a thousand feet above the surrounding countryside. The broad, flat basin stretched to the far horizon. The air was so clear that Turhan could see the purple outlines of hills in the distance. Except for the caravan, a group of slow-moving ants, the land was empty. The silence was awesome.

They were about to head down the trail to meet the caravan when Turhan heard the sound of running water. A few feet off the trail, there was a narrow defile with several shrub like trees. "Come," Ibrahim said.

They entered the gorge where a small cascade of water descended a nearby cliff into a sparkling pool. The men disrobed and dove into the cold, fresh water. Like children, they splashed and dunked one another as each tacitly acknowledged that the time of deep understanding had come and it was now time for the mood to lighten.

Three days later, they entered Malatya. Zeki and Turhan wandered about the wealthy, modern city, which boasted wide boulevards and elegant houses set amidst gardens and orchards. There were no old buildings, no ruins.

The caravanserai where they stayed was far different from the one in Diyarbakır. Stables were clean. Pallets for travelers did not stink of sweat and urine. That night, Ibrahim invited local merchants to a feast. The women made stuffed, pickled *dolma*, and *güvetch*. The men roasted two whole lambs. For dessert, there was baklava, a many-layered pastry interlaced with chopped pistachio nuts, and *tel kadayif,* shredded wheat covered with honeyed syrup.

After the women retired, the men talked of events beyond Malatya. Ibrahim listened with growing impatience for half an hour, then drew Turhan away from the group. "I don't have the patience to suffer these ostriches who bury their heads in the sand and deny that changes are coming."

"But Ibrahim Effendi," said Turhan, "I see no signs of unrest in Malatya. No troops. Shops are full. Everyone goes about life as they did in Diyarbakır."

"Appearances often fool a fool, Turhan. Many of these fat nobles and the sycophant merchants who prosper from them, believe that regardless of what happens in the west, things in this part of the empire will go on as they have in the past. Such pretense is idiotic. Did you notice how clean and modern this city appeared?"

"There was hardly an old building or a ruin anywhere."

"Yet a town has existed on this site for four thousand years. This place has had almost as many rulers as people. Hittites, Persians, Greeks, Romans, Christian Crusaders, they've all been here. The Ottomans who came west from the Central Asian steppes with Timurleng have been here less than five hundred years. Now it seems our days of glory are coming to an end. In the past few years alone, we've lost the Balkans, Greece and our last African lands. The Ottoman Empire shrinks every month. Once the jackals smell the blood of a decaying nation, they feast."

"What do you think will happen, Effendi?"

"Who knows? To stay alert to change is to stay alive. "But enough of such talk. If we live the years of the future before they arrive, we can't enjoy the days immediately ahead. I've arranged something very special for the next four days. You and Zeki will need your rest and your strength. It's time for me to ask our guests to depart. Off to bed with you."

13

Dawn. A slight breeze rustled the dying fire in the caravanserai's courtyard. Turhan felt himself gently shaken awake. He stirred through half-sleep. "Come," Ibrahim whispered. "Zeki's gotten the horses ready. We'll stop for breakfast an hour after sunrise. Wear your warmest clothing."

Turhan dressed and followed Ibrahim to the stables. Zeki was holding Ibrahim's white Arabian, Lightning, and two other horses, a grey gelding and a chestnut mare, which were saddled and ready. "Yours is the smaller one, *Yildiz*, named after the star on her forehead. She's gentle, but she'll have no trouble keeping up with us," Zeki said, handing Turhan the reins of the compactly-built chestnut.

Ibrahim approached with a pack mule. "We'll be gone four days. If we're not back by sunup the fifth day, the caravan will start northwest toward Kayseri. We'll catch up to them enroute."

"Where are we going, Ibrahim Effendi?" Turhan asked.

"A mountain two days' journey from here, Nemrut Dağ."

"Four days' time to see a mountain?" Zeki asked. "There are several mountains on the way to the Black Sea, Ibrahim Effendi. Why stop at this one?"

"I'll let Nemrut Dağ speak for itself," replied Ibrahim. "We must get moving before sunlight."

Although it was only Turhan's second time on horseback, he got used to the horse's easy lope within the hour. Later that morning, their mounts grazed in an abundant pastureland, while Ibrahim, Zeki and Turhan ate *ekmek*, the broad-grained Turkish peasant bread, olives, feta cheese and rose petal jam, which Ibrahim had packed the previous night, and drank strong black tea which he'd brought in a burlap-wrapped container.

After breakfast, they remounted and continued their steady pace through the hills and valleys. As they climbed into the highlands, travel became slower. By noon, hot and tired, they arrived at a flat, grassy knoll near a mountain spring, where they stopped for lunch. Afterward, Turhan slept for two hours. When he awoke, he was not at all certain this adventure was as wonderful as Ibrahim had promised. His backside was painful with saddle sores.

"All you can do is keep riding.," Ibrahim said. "Tomorrow, it'll be better."

By sundown, they came to a sheltered area halfway to their destination. The travelers pitched their tents and gathered enough wood for a fire. After a simple meal and tea, sleep came easily that night. Another day of traveling and Turhan was not quite so sore.

Ibrahim led them to a protected, flattened shelf of land, two thousand feet above the valley floor. The well-hidden aerie jutted out from the peaks behind. Its leading edge dropped off a sheer cliff face. The two sides were hemmed in by higher mountains. The explorers entered from a narrow, ascending trail, with dry brush all about. The shelf, invisible from the valley floor, commanded a broad sweep of land far below. Turhan picked out the dim lights of a village and, farther away, the more substantial lights of a small town.

Shortly before sunset, the travelers tethered their animals in an area several yards down the path and lit a campfire. After surrounding the fire with stones, to reflect and hold the heat all night, the three of them bedded down early.

Shortly after midnight, Ibrahim woke to a rustling below their campsite. He edged his way along the rock face leading from their small fire to the trail. He was so quiet that not even the crickets stopped their busy chirping. When got to the trailhead, he heard the animals nervously shuffling about. After searching in vain for the cause of their agitation, he retraced his steps back up the trail. When he reached the entry to the mesa, his attention was caught by the reflection of moonlight off a piece of metal. His eyes widened.

Four men were edging their way across the mesa from a cave he had not hitherto noticed. Twenty feet separated the men from the two sleeping youths. Suddenly, one of the men reached out and grabbed the sleeping Turhan from behind. A second man seized Zeki and stuffed a gag in his mouth. Ibrahim heard the loud whisper of the man who was holding Turhan. "One sound, my young friend, and you are dead. Do you understand?" The boy nodded. Within moments, the two boys were trussed and gagged.

"I could have sworn there were three of them," one of the men muttered.

"There were," one of his companions replied.

"Where's the third one?"

"I've no idea. These two are just boys."

"The other was an older man. He could be close by. Bashak, check the trailhead. Make sure no one's there."

Ibrahim hid in a narrow crevice, off the trail. His dark clothing blended into the rocks, making him invisible in the shadows. The robber reached the trail and looked about. He called out softly, "Nothing here. The horses are down below. Should I check there?"

"No, stay where you are and guard the trail. We'll go over to the cave for a couple of hours, then one of us will take your place. No sense searching at night. Those two won't go anywhere. We'll search for their friend later. Besides, we can always use fresh horses and theirs looked fit."

The sentinel sat down to crack and eat some nuts. Forty minutes later, he stood and walked over to the trailhead. All was still. He turned to make sure the two boys were still bound. That was all the time Ibrahim needed. He emerged from the shadows holding a rock slightly larger than his hand, which he used with speed and precision. The man collapsed with a soft exhalation.

Ibrahim crept forward until he reached the boys. He motioned them to remain silent, then released them. Turhan and Zeki were dazed, but not injured. Ibrahim took the rope and gag that had been used to bind Zeki and bound the unconscious sentinel. They quickly gathered their gear and noiselessly moved down the trail.

Turhan started to whisper something, but Ibrahim's raised hand stopped him before any words came out. Once they'd descended to the valley floor, he asked, "Ibrahim, who...?"

"Bandits. This area's full of them. It's in the center of a triangle formed by three important trading cities, Diyarbakır to the east, Malatya to the north, and Urfa to the south. Under normal circumstances, it's at least a week's hard journey between those cities, with hardly a small village in between. There are no protected land routes, very few policemen or soldiers, and limitless mountains to hide in. It's a perfect place for such men to ply their trade."

"What if they follow us?" Zeki asked, not a little nervous.

"That's hardly likely," Ibrahim replied. "Even though they outnumbered us, they weren't in any hurry to attack while we were awake. Jackals!" He spat derisively to the side of the trail.

"Cowards always hunt in packs and strike the weaklings. I'm sure they've had more than their fill of us. Besides, there'll undoubtedly be travelers coming down the main road today with much more to steal than we've got." He pulled out his pocket watch and nodded. "Two hours past midnight. Good. We'll be able to start the final ascent before daybreak."

By this time, the youths had recovered from their shock and were eager to get started. A gibbous moon suffused the area with bright, silvery light. Turhan felt he could reach out and touch the mountains. The land rose steadily. The small party cast infinitesimal shadows against the vast landscape. After some time, Ibrahim reined in his horse and directed the others to stop. "From here, it's on foot all the way. We'll turn the animals out to pasture."

"How far is it from here, Effendi?" asked Zeki.

"An hour at most, but it's a steep climb."

They reached a large, flat mesa just as the sun was coming over the crest of the mountain, three hundred feet above them. Turhan was stunned. If he lived a hundred years and ultimately went blind in his old age, he'd never forget the sight.

Nemrut Dağ was the highest peak in the region. The panorama in all directions was astounding, but this paled when Turhan confronted what he saw *on* the flattened escarpment. A long, broad mound was flanked by twin terraces, the closest of which faced into the rising Sun. The embankment was lined with massive statues, several times the height of a man. The tallest, a young woman thirty-five feet high, was the only one with a head on its body. On the ground immediately beneath the colossal structures, were four huge male heads. Off to one side were an eagle and a lion. Each head was taller than Turhan's entire body.

In the early morning light, the stone heads glowed reddish pink. As the sun rose higher, they turned yellow, then blazing white. The statues were not carved from single stones, but were constructed of several large blocks of alternating black and white marble.

Ibrahim approached Turhan quietly. "Beyond words?"

"Would Allah sanction the creation of such powerful images, Effendi?"

"Probably not," Ibrahim said. "But this is not the work of Allah. It is the eternity of Turkey. I brought you here to show you that Anatolia is more than poor villages and drab cities. For you to grasp the magnificence of our motherland, you must know what came before us. Man has always believed in a superior power. What you see was not created by any god, but by a man who believed he was more than mortal. Two thousand years ago, this place was part of Commagene, a very small kingdom surrounded by the Parthian and Roman empires. Its ruler, Antiochus, claimed he could trace his royal line back a thousand years. He signed treaties with his neighbors, so he didn't have to worry about war. This land was very fertile then. The king grew fat and rich.

"Antiochus's explanation for everything going so well was that he was a god. Since gods deserved proper monuments, he ordered the construction of Nemrut Dag. An army of slaves dragged blocks of cut stone from thousands of feet below to this summit. No one knows how they placed one atop the other."

"But, Ibrahim Effendi," interrupted Turhan, "if mankind worshipped these stones from that day forward, wouldn't they have made certain the heads were kept on the bodies?"

"That's one of history's ironic jokes. Work started fifty years before the prophet Jesus was born. It took twenty years to erect the monument. Shortly after he completed these structures, Antiochus forgot how the world really works. The 'great god' insulted Rome, and soon he was replaced by a more complacent puppet. Antiochus's golden empire lasted barely twenty-five years.

"These magnificent statues sat forgotten until they were accidentally discovered by a German civil engineer, thirty-five years ago. The next year, a young German archeologist, Otto Puchstein, came to investigate. I've met Otto a few times during my travels. He's still busy uncovering ruins in Anatolia. He must be sixty by now."

"How old were you when you first saw Nemrut Dağ, Effendi?"

"About your age."

"Who are these stone people, sir?"

"Antiochus's favorite Greek gods. The lady who managed to keep her head is Tyche, the goddess of fortune. On this side you can see Heracles, Apollo, and Zeus, King of the Gods. The fellow without the beard is Antiochus himself. The eagle and the lion symbolized strength."

The tall man lost himself in thought for a moment, then murmured quietly, "Our motherland. What a tortured history it's had. How many civilizations it has nursed. Ripped by earthquakes, plundered by conqueror after conqueror, tramped underfoot to brown nothingness. It's been shorn of its bounty, but never its dignity. *Inshallah*, may it be better for you."

Their reverie was shattered as shots rang out.

"Get down!" Ibrahim shouted. The three of them instantly dropped behind the terrace.

"You may as well pray to Allah, for all the good it will do you," a voice snarled from above. Turhan looked up. A hundred feet above him, in a rock crevice, he saw the man who'd tied him up the night before. His three accomplices surrounded the scraggly-bearded, unkempt assailant.

Ibrahim whispered to Turhan and Zeki, "We've got to keep him talking. It's our only chance." He called out to the spokesman. "How did you catch up with us so fast?"

"Where else would three well-heeled travelers with fine horses be headed in these parts, my friend?" The brigand cut loose with a string of caustic invectives.

Ibrahim quietly told the boys, "We've got only one rifle. I'll try to draw his fire. See if you can make it to that ledge. It will give you some protection." He gestured to a large rock about twenty feet away, which was covered by an overhang.

"If you knew where we were going," Ibrahim called back, "why didn't you just cut us off before we got here?"

"No sense making ourselves obvious. You're our guests in this territory. We thought we'd ride ahead and welcome you."

"Very gracious of you," Ibrahim replied, trying to gain time, so he could concoct a plan. Out of the corner of his eye, he caught the slightest movement as the boys ran for cover.

A storm of gunfire erupted. Two bullets hit Zeki, almost simultaneously. The boy spun and his body seemed to leap in mid-air before he collapsed in a heap. Turhan kept running until he was under the ledge. Ibrahim saw the boy's dazed expression. The outlaws blasted away at Turhan's cover. The youth looked as if he would run out from under cover in sheer panic unless Ibrahim took immediate action. He unleashed his own barrage of rifle fire. One attacker fell into the scree at the base of the slope. A second followed. Ibrahim scurried toward that part of the mountain farthest away from Turhan's rock fortress.

"All right, Hero!" Ibrahim yelled out. "You've murdered a young boy. See if the two of you can take on a man!" He deliberately aimed for a small pile of rocks above the gunmen and pulled the trigger. He noted with grim satisfaction that a small cascade of rocks starting to fall from that precipice. But now his rifle was empty. He wouldn't have time to reload before the two survivors located him.

The rivulet of rocks became a torrent. Suddenly there was a great rumbling, as if unseen forces were beating a huge drum in the bowels of the earth. The roar grew in magnitude. It was louder than any thunderstorm Turhan had ever heard. The ground started wobbling, rolling and shaking under him. Turhan could not keep his balance and fell. Above the commotion, he heard Ibrahim shout, "Avalanche! Get under the ledge!" and the agonized screams of their two assailants on the higher ground as they were buried alive by a hundred boulders. Rocks continued rumbling down the mountain, burying Zeki's remains. As quickly as it had started, the noise stopped. There was an eerie silence. The sun, shining through dust, had turned blood red.

Turhan heard nothing. No moans. No shouts. No life. "Zeki!" He cried his friend's name over and over.

The rocks remained silent.

The dust started to settle.

The place where Zeki had fallen moments before was still, as though the stones that buried him had occupied this space for hundreds of years.

Ibrahim ran quickly to the boy.

"Zeki," the lad mumbled in a daze, his face streaked with muddy tears.

"Let us pray for Zeki's soul, Turhan. When death arrives, we cannot bar the door," Ibrahim said gently.

As the next hours passed, the two friends, bound in the immutability of death, talked about Zeki. Man and boy slowly descended from the mountain where horses, food and warmth awaited. Exhausted, Turhan collapsed in deep sleep as the moon rose once again.

Ibrahim had difficulty resting that night. Although he'd had little to eat that day, he felt a stab of indigestion earlier in the evening. Later there was a strange tightness in his chest. He dismissed it as a reaction to the day's terrible events.

14

The caravan was about to depart northwest toward Kayseri, when Ibrahim rode up to Turhan and asked, "Could you come to the back of the caravanserai for a moment?"

Turhan followed dutifully. The small chestnut mare, *Yildiz*, was tethered to a post. "She's yours, boy. She can't bring Zeki back, but she'll make the trip far more pleasant than walking. Ride alongside me for the rest of the journey. I need someone to listen to an old man tell his stories."

Kayseri was one-hundred-fifty miles distant. Four days after they left Malatya, the Taurus Mountains gave way to a treeless steppe. Each night, the caravan stopped in a different forgettable, shapeless, and boring small town. "Why do we stop at these places, Ibrahim Effendi?" Turhan asked. "There must be several routes that go through larger cities and towns."

"That's so, Turhan. However, when you're the only source of goods coming through, you not only realize higher prices, but you're always appreciated."

At each stop along the way, their arrival was heralded as a major event. The *muhtar*, the headman, inevitably ordered a feast. Villagers found bed space for their guests, and placed comfortable matting on the floor. There was always talk, for the caravan brought news from the outside world, a letter or message from a loved one in a distant place, a source of fresh life. The villagers wanted to hear gossip, not the political messages spread by the government in far off Istanbul.

Often people asked Turhan whether he knew so-and-so's relative in this village or that. Was he going to Kanesh? Would he mind carrying a letter to this woman's cousin or that man's great uncle? Turhan learned how lonely and tedious life on the steppe could be, and how great were distances that separated those who had left their loved ones when they departed their native communities.

On the first day of autumn, Turhan called out to Ibrahim and pointed south in amazement. Rising in the far distance was the highest, most perfect mountain the boy had ever seen. "Mount Argaeus," Ibrahim said. "As we get closer, you'll see snow at the top. It's there year 'round. Legend says if you climb to the summit, you can see from the Black Sea to the Mediterranean. At one time, it was a volcano. It's been quiet for as long as anyone can remember."

The mountain dominated the horizon as they approached their destination. They reached Kayseri late that afternoon. Turhan immediately felt the bustle and drive of this large plains city, a caravan crossroads since ancient times.

"We do a great deal of trading here," Ibrahim said. "We'll find some of the finest Anatolian carpets at the lowest prices in Turkey. There are several excellent goldsmiths in the city. We'll purchase jewelry we can sell at profit in the north." In a quieter voice, he said, "It's also the closest we come to Afyon, the town that gave its name to opium. The Agha Khorusun has many friends in this city."

Turhan was hot, dusty, and tired from so many days of travel. He was in no mood to do business today. The older man saw this and smiled knowingly. "However," Ibrahim continued, "this afternoon I've got something in store for you that will get you ready for the days ahead. As soon as we've put down at the caravanserai, join me."

"Would you mind if I didn't? I'm tired. I feel sticky and greasy. I just want to collapse and go to sleep."

"Yes, I would mind," the man answered with a gleam in his eye. "You will come with me this afternoon and you may consider that a command."

"Very well, Sire," the boy sighed.

Within the hour, Ibrahim and Turhan departed the Vizier Caravanserai and walked southeast along Talat Road. Everywhere Turhan looked, there was a bustle and hum to the city. The wheels of commerce spun noisily. Less than fifty yards beyond their hostel, they felt the tug of insistent hands. "Carpets, *messieurs,* the finest *Bünyan* designs. *Herekes, meine herren*, from the Sultan's own looms." Ibrahim clucked his tongue at the two middle-aged hawkers and raised his eyebrows, the Turkish symbol for "Begone!"

It was hard to see the buildings, for merchants had set up booths on both sides of the street, barely leaving room for carriages to pass. There was a riot of colorful clothing, reds, yellows, greens and blues, suspended from makeshift lines strung along the tops of the booths, which contrasted with the somber grays, browns and blacks of shawls and *shalvar* worn by women and young girls, who resembled nothing so much as plain, round little hens, pecking about a yard filled with a cornucopia of needs and luxuries. Most of them had money sufficient only for a bolt of the coarsest cloth, or for the lowest priced fruits and vegetables.

"Mosque mice," Ibrahim remarked, good naturedly. "The *real* trade in this city is left to the professionals."

A mile down Talat road, the stalls thinned out. Turhan saw sturdy two and three-story stone buildings, mostly brown and dun, but occasionally bright, garish blue, red, or brown-yellow. Some were residences, but most of the buildings had signs suspended from metal bracings attached to their second stories, *Dish tabibi,* dentist, *avukat,* lawyer, *noter,* notary public, and the like.

Just beyond the citadel, the road turned right. A few yards farther along, Turhan saw a massive, faded brick building with a huge, silver-colored dome. Ibrahim said, "Here we are. When you see what's in store, you'll quickly wipe that sullen look off your face."

They entered the *Hand Hamam,* Kayseri's largest Turkish bath. Many years ago, Grandfather had taken Turhan to the hamam in the village, a small, wooden shed with cracking beams and a sour smell. This place was much different. As he entered, the stolid brick on the outside gave way to cheerful blue tiles. There was a fountain in the entry hall, which continually sprayed water into a round, tile-covered fish pond. Fat, orange carp swam lazily about, oblivious to men who lounged about the pond, nursing a glass of tea or, perhaps, stronger stuff. Turhan had learned early that in the land of Sunni Muslims, the Prophet's injunction against wine was taken literally. Had Mohammed wished to enjoin the use of *rakı,* the anise-flavored lion's milk of Turkey, he would have done so. He hadn't, and that was the Ottomans' blessing.

During the next hour, Turhan and Ibrahim moved from the washroom to a series of ever hotter steam rooms. Turhan experienced his first Turkish massage. The kneading, thumping, pummeling, and rubbing caused every one of his muscles to slacken. He was so relaxed that by the time the masseur was finished, he could hardly move. But there was more pleasure to come. After they'd returned to the washroom, they entered a large heated pool, where they paddled about with nothing more to do than luxuriate.

Half an hour later, they entered a small room, where more attendants poured buckets of warm water over them, then rubbed and scraped Ibrahim's and Turhan's bodies with a coarse sponge, flaking off the outer layers of skin. When the attendants were done, they doused Turhan and Ibrahim with more hot water, then soaped their bodies with a horsehair brush, working it up to a rich lather before pouring buckets of cooler water over the two travelers.

"*Tamam*. Finished," the chief attendant said handing Turhan a thick white robe, a Turkish towel, in which to wrap himself. When Turhan returned to his cubicle, two hours after he had entered the *hamam*, he found his clothes washed, dried, and softened. As he alighted from the dressing room, he found Ibrahim waiting at a nearby table with two small cups of steaming Turkish coffee. That night, Turhan slept refreshed and at peace.

The next day, while Ibrahim tended to business, Turhan spent the day wandering around the city, deeply feeling the loss of Zeki. That evening Ibrahim noticed that Turhan was restless at supper. After the meal, he handed the youth what looked like a large, unbound book printed on both sides of thin paper. The masthead at the top read "*Günlük Gazete*."

"*Daily News*, Effendi?"

"I told you when we got to Kayseri, I'd find you a newspaper. There's still plenty of light to read by."

"Thank you, Ibrahim Bey." There was not much excitement in the boy's tone.

"Not a good day?"

"I'd rather not talk about it."

"Very well. Many times I've found that when I read about the problems other folks have, mine don't seem so large."

Turhan went to his room. Within a few minutes, he became so engrossed in the newspaper he almost forgot Zeki's death. He read that in faraway places whose names were totally unfamiliar to him, men were discussing something called "the dismemberment of the Ottoman empire." He linked the words to what Ibrahim had told him in Malatya about troubles ahead for the Turkish people. The newspaper was written in Arabic script. Here and there throughout the paper were advertisements printed in a different kind of lettering.

Long after he would normally have gone to sleep, he read the newspaper a second time. What an incredible, wonderful device. Turhan thought back to the dreadful injustices he'd seen and his desire to avenge Shadran's and Grandfather's deaths. He recalled Ibrahim's words about questioning what seemed wrong to him, challenging others to think. A newspaper did this every day.

Here was a way he could tell the truth to the world. Within the pages of the newspaper, he could fight injustice, give a voice to people who had no voices of their own. *Could this be a way of accomplishing things he had thought impossible? Things he knew were more important than anything else?*

Next morning, Turhan sought out Ibrahim, even before breakfast. "Effendi, thank you for the newspaper last night. With Zeki's death on my mind, I was not properly appreciative. I apologize."

"Think nothing of it. Everyone has moods. Like storm clouds, they pass, like seasons they change."

"Effendi, remember when you told me about speaking against injustice to the world?"

"Yes."

"After I read *Günlük Gazete*, I thought, 'This may be a way for me to speak to the world.'"

"Indeed." The caravan master suppressed a smile. "It's not a job for everyone. A writer's work in such a journal should be like a clear mirror. It's not always flattering. The journalist makes many enemies."

"But at least the world might listen."

"Turhan," the man said, laughing. "I very much doubt if *Günlük Gazete* speaks to the *world*. However, you're right, that paper does speak to *Kayseri*."

"Meanwhile, my young friend, you've been little more than a porter and a shepherd until now. It's time you learned the art of trade. "

15

After a delicious breakfast, Ibrahim took Turhan to the center of the bazaar. Ibrahim was as shrewd a bargainer as any merchant there. "Real gold does not have a brassy color, and it's soft," he said, at one jeweler's stall. At another, he remarked, "Pearls are extraordinarily rare in these parts. Although this ring is beautifully set and looks rich and exceptional, the pearl's counterfeit. Rub your teeth over it."

The boy did, and noticed its creamy smoothness. He commented on it to Ibrahim.

"Very observant, Turhan. A real pearl will feel gritty to the teeth, like hard-packed sand. Smoothness fools the unwary."

Somewhat further along the alley, Turhan watched a pair of merchants vigorously exchanging hand signals with one another. "A means of trade as old as mankind," Ibrahim remarked. "By their dress, the shopkeeper is a Jew. When the Hebrews were thrown out of Spain four hundred years ago, Sultan Mehmet invited them to come to Turkey with the comment, 'They say the King of Spain is wise. If he threw out the Jews, he must be a fool.' Spain's loss has been the Ottoman Empire's gain. For centuries, Jews have fueled Turkey's commerce. The other fellow's Persian. Neither understands the other's language, but hand signals have worked for as long as the market has been in business."

"Ibrahim Effendi, I'd like to purchase some rings to trade in the north."

"Very well. A few words of advice before you go off on your own. Don't buy the first thing you see. Don't buy from the first merchant, even if he has exactly what you want. Appear disinterested. Leave, return a few times. Never betray your eagerness. Merchants know in a moment if you're anxious to purchase. Let them treat you to *chay*. Tea lubricates the wheels of business in the *bedestan*. If I'm not within the distance where you can see me, don't go into any shop. You're young, alone and easy prey."

For the first hour, Turhan obeyed Ibrahim's admonition to the letter. He bought nothing, but went from stall to stall, examining merchandise. He drank numerous glasses of tea and voided his bladder behind the stalls several times that morning. Just before mid-day, Turhan noticed that many places were closing their doors. He remembered a shop in the next block that had looked particularly attractive. As Turhan approached, he saw it had remained open. He looked around for Ibrahim. The caravan master was nowhere to be found. "Oh, well," Turhan thought. "No doubt Ibrahim meant I should remain where we could see each other during the busiest part of the day. Surely there's no harm in going into an open shop when there are so few people on the street."

Turhan entered the shop. The man behind the counter was different from the one he'd seen there in the morning, but he was an engaging chap. Within minutes, Turhan was actively bargaining. After thirstily downing a glass of tea which the clerk provided, talk became serious.

"Donal Effendi, the rings you've shown me are of minimal quality. What would you take for these five?"

"A brilliant choice for so young a trader. You've no doubt had training and are most discerning. These rings are genuine gold, twenty-four carat. You can tell by the markings on the side. Two have clusters of pearls, sapphires, and topaz. Run your teeth over the pearls if you doubt my word. The others have single stones. You deprive me of my five choicest pieces, but it is my honor to serve you. Even if I lose money, I gain a friend who'll no doubt trade with me for many years. I want to help you get started, young man, so I'll part with these for half their true value, two hundred fifty *kurush*."

"Effendi, I said I might consider five rings as a group, to relieve you of your burden. I saw rings like this for fifteen *kurush* apiece a block away."

"Hüssein's stall, no doubt. He'll ply you with ten karat gold plate. His stones are manufactured in Russia. He'll only cheat you. Pay him the fifteen if you want. On the other hand, should you wish to pay two hundred twenty *kurush* for the lot, I might be persuaded to forego any profit I'd make."

"*Chohk pahala*, too expensive, the youth said, rising to leave. He replaced the tea on a table, surprised that he felt dizzy.

"Wait, Effendi. How much do you wish to spend?"

"Perhaps one hundred *kurush* for them all."

"Ah, I see I'm dealing with a true professional. Is something wrong, Sir? Your face seems a bit pale."

"No, I'm all right."

"Why not lie down in the back of my shop for a while? Perhaps it's the heat of the day?"

"No, I'm fine," Turhan remarked, not feeling well at all. Should he call for Ibrahim? No, it would pass in a moment. "I think a breath of fresh air would help."

"Nonsense. Have some more *chay*."

"If I may, thank you." Turhan sat down heavily. The tea tasted very sweet. He heard Donal's voice through a fog.

"Come, boy, let me escort you to the back. Lie here for a few moments 'til you feel better."

Turhan's legs felt like blocks of wood. He felt himself guided into an area in the back where he lay down on a pile of carpets and pillows. "Perhaps I'll relax for just a little while." Within moments he was in a deep sleep.

"Wake up! Wake up, I say! What are you doing in the back of my stall? Answer now or I'll call the market police!"

"Hnnnh?"

"Awake this instant! Allah's shame upon you, a young boy, a drunkard in the middle of the day! Up and out right now! What's this? You've two of my finest rings in your pocket! A thief to boot! Allah! Police! Police!" The man ran to the front of his stall. "There's a thief and a drunkard in my shop! Help! Help!" The market was instantly abuzz. One market policeman and two city constables entered the shop. Bozkurt the jeweler was livid. Ibrahim, who'd heard the commotion, immediately went to Bozkurt's stall.

By the time he got there, the police had grabbed the drowsy Turhan and were pummeling him with their clubs. The boy seemed oblivious to what was going on. The moment Ibrahim saw them he shouted, "Stop! For Allah's sake, stop! He's neither a drunkard nor a thief. He's my young companion, Turhan. Stop it this instant!"

They froze and stared at Ibrahim. This caravan master was well known in Kayseri.

"But Ibrahim Effendi," Bozkurt replied. "I caught the boy *suchustu yakalanmak*, red handed, with the rings on his person."

"Was he trying to run from your store?"

"Of course not, he was too drunk to do so."

"Bozkurt, the boy was in my charge the entire morning. I swear he had nothing but tea."

"See for yourself, Effendi, the boy is clearly intoxicated."

"*Donal Bey, no more than one hundred twenty-five kurush,*" Turhan mumbled incoherently.

"What?" one of the policemen said, startled. "Did you say 'Donal Bey?'"

Turhan did not respond. The policemen said, "Did any of you hear what the boy said? Did he mention the name Donal?"

"I think I heard him say that, officer," Ibrahim replied. "Why? Does that name have any significance?"

"It may," the other said. "Allow me to smell the boy's breath." He did so, then said, "The youngster's not drunk, but drugged."

The officer looked about the stall and found two half-empty glasses of tea on a tray. Nothing significant. A sign of business throughout the marketplace. Still, it wouldn't hurt to inspect. He sniffed both glasses, then spilled a small amount from one of them onto his fingers. "Drugged all right. Hashish. The boy must have ingested a lot of it. The sugar in the drink undoubtedly covered the taste. Get him some strong mint tea and let him sit for a couple of hours. Perhaps then he'll be able to help us."

"The last thing I remember, he quoted me two-hundred-twenty *kurush* for the five rings."

"Was he here when you first passed the shop?"

"No, Officer. The other man, the one who shouted at me, was here the first time."

"I remember the boy," Bozkurt said. "He kept wandering from stall to stall. I didn't pay attention to him. He seemed too young to take seriously as a customer. Just looking."

"When I came back, a man who introduced himself as Donal was standing behind the counter," Turhan continued. "He told me he owned the shop and he'd just sent his assistant – you, sir – on an errand."

"I had an early lunch engagement," the merchant said to the police officer. "I trusted my fellow jewelers to keep their eyes on my stall, as I do on theirs from time to time."

"What did this Donal look like?" the constable asked.

"Slightly taller than me, swarthy, dark moustache."

"Wonderful," said Ibrahim. "That describes three quarters of the men in the bazaar."

"Not necessarily," the officer said. "Were there any unusual marks on his face?"

"He had a scar over his left eye."

"*Bohk!*" the officer said, involuntarily using the word for dung. "It's him all right."

"Who?" Ibrahim asked.

"A known thief. He strikes regularly every two or three months. We haven't been able to catch him so far. He invariably seeks out shops with small, very expensive goods, goldsmiths, jewelers, dealers in

Hereke carpets. He tells the merchant he's a trader from out of town. He's very generous and insists upon buying tea instead of accepting it from the merchant. He offers a price somewhat higher than the going rate, then excuses himself for a few moments, leaving a small deposit with the seller. The shopkeeper is found some hours later in back of his stall, drugged, with his most valuable merchandise gone."

"I didn't notice anything missing except the two items that I found on the boy."

"You probably came back early and frightened him off. When he heard the commotion, he must have run out the back of your shop."

"Allah be praised, there's no harm done," Bozkurt said. "I apologize, boy. I'd offer you some *chay*, but you've undoubtedly had enough. By the way, were you interested in purchasing those rings?"

"I was, Effendi."

"And you offered?"

"Twenty *kurush* apiece, sir."

"A little low, but we can bargain."

"I was offering a hundred *kurush* to buy five pieces, and I was prepared to go to a hundred fifty if they were of good quality."

Turhan walked over to the nearby jewelry case. "I was interested in these other three as well."

"The five rings together would be one hundred sixty *kurush*, my best price. You're aware these are fourteen karat gold?"

"Fourteen?" Turhan asked. "Donal said twenty-four."

"Turhan," Ibrahim said. Twenty-four karat is the purest gold, but it's much too soft to make a ring that will stand up under constant wear. Most rings in this bazaar are ten, fourteen, occasionally eighteen karat, certainly no more." Then Ibrahim became the seasoned trader. "Bozkurt, these five rings are worth a hundred twenty-five at best."

"Ibrahim, you know these are my finest. A hundred fifty?"

"Thirty."

"Done."

Turhan reached into his tunic to withdraw his money purse. He paled. "It's gone! My money is gone! Two hundred *kurush*! Allah, Allah!"

The boy looked as though he would weep. Ibrahim saw the shock and said, gently, "According to the accounting your agent gave me back in Diyarbakır, you have five *lira* – five hundred *kurush* – left. Did you want to spend it on these rings?"

"I don't feel much like buying right now," Turhan said miserably, "I promised I'd send half to my partner."

"A partner? You never said you had a partner."

"Perhaps not really a partner. The person who supplied me with goods to sell."

"Oh, Ertuğrul," Ibrahim said, brightening. "That old man has been around long enough to know these things happen. It's a grave misfortune for you, Turhan. I'm sure they won't catch the thief before we leave Kayseri. Be glad it was your purse, not your head."

16

Two days later, Ibrahim awakened Turhan earlier than usual. "For the next days, you and I leave the trading to others. There's a special place, not too far from here I'd like you to see: the Valley of Göreme. It's different from any place else on earth. If you didn't see it, you'd always be sorry."

Turhan was wary. "The last time you said that about a place..."

"Allah controls what happens, not you or I, boy," the older man said sharply. "If you'd rather not see it, that's your loss."

"No, Effendi, I want to go with you."

So it was that two hours later Ibrahim and Turhan rode west over the old Roman-Byzantine road toward Göreme. Although there were no trees to shade them, a slight breeze off the foothills to the south made travel pleasant. When the sun reached its zenith, they stopped for lunch on a rise by the side of the road. Three superb peaks rose from the steppe, Argaeus, nearly thirteen thousand feet high, and the two Hasandağs, twelve and ten thousand feet. Even in early autumn they were snow-capped.

West of Ürgüp, Turhan noticed hundreds of small blisters in the earth on either side of their trail. "Small volcanoes, extinct geysers," Ibrahim remarked.

"How far are we going, Ibrahim Bey?"

"Once we're over the next rise, we'll be there."

As they crested the rock highland, Turhan gasped. Thousands of years before, the three giant volcanoes spewed rocky eruptions into valleys of soft tufa stone. Over the millennia, the Kizilirmak River, the hot sun, floods, rain, the winds of the Asian steppes, and the hand of God sawed away at the lava, creating a bizarre landscape. As far as Turhan could see there were fairy chimneys, slender rock cones, many with mushroom shaped stones covering the top. Some of these structures climbed the sides of their neighbors. Others were separated by as much as a thousand feet. Some rose higher than the tallest buildings Turhan had ever seen. Others were only a hundred-fifty feet in height.

"These stones were so soft even the earliest men could bore into them with the most primitive tools," Ibrahim said. "People dug out houses of every kind. Each tower was large enough to house several people. Early Christians carved more than three thousand churches in this valley. Their frescoes look as fresh now as when they were created. Let's ride down into the valley and get a closer view."

They chose one of the cones at random. Inside, they climbed a circular staircase neatly carved in the rock. At each landing, spacious rooms led off a small central hall. Windows cut through the rock flooded the rooms with light. As he looked out from one of them, Turhan realized they were fifty feet above ground. There was not so much as the twitter of a bird. The entire valley was silent.

"Well?" Ibrahim asked.

"It's everything I was told. More."

As they rode through the valley, they were surrounded by high tufa cliffs. They were the only souls in the vast expanse. The few trees in the area had shed their leaves. It was a place of ghosts. "Ah, here's the cave I was looking for," Ibrahim said.

They entered a teardrop-shaped opening, twice Turhan's height. Immediately inside the cave, the youth saw several large stones, placed where they could be moved to make the entrance look like a shallow, dead end. Twenty paces beyond the entryway, a path turned right and descended into a large hall, from which half a dozen passageways branched out.

"Choose any one you wish," said the caravan leader. "But make sure you have some way to find your way back."

"What do you mean?" Turhan asked.

"This is one of the underground cities your grandfather told you about. It has nine different levels. A few miles from here, there's one that goes down fifteen stories and has air shafts coming up four hundred feet to the outside. Each city is connected to others by an underground tunnel. When marauders came through the Göreme Valley in ancient times, scouts alerted the inhabitants, who immediately fled to these caves. It's cool in here. They stored food and water easily. When they needed to cook, they burned fires. To a stranger who'd heard of volcanoes and seen geysers in this land, smoke rising from shafts hundreds of feet from any visible cliff or cave would simply appear to be another of nature's mysteries."

"How large were the cities?"

"The largest was a mile wide and nearly two long."

"Where are all the people today?"

"Gone. No one knows where. Why don't you go down a couple of stories? I brought some rope and two candles with me. I'll stay here and hold one end. Don't go too far."

The boy disappeared down one of the passages, the candle casting a faint glow along the walls. Several minutes later he shouted, "Ibrahim! Come quick! See what I've found!" The caravan master anchored the thick cord to a solid stanchion and descended toward the voice. As Turhan beckoned, Ibrahim followed him through a small hole, which led to a large cavern. There was more than enough room for them both to stand to full height. At the far end of the hall, a pathway led still deeper into the cave. When they reached the end of the room, the path led to a huge grotto, penetrated from above by a natural shaft of light. Spiky, stone formations hung from the ceiling. Similar shapes rose from the floor.

Beyond the damp grotto, they reached a small, dry room about the size of a large tent. Turhan glanced up. His eyes went wide in wonder. Brilliant frescoes in shades of red, gold, silver, bronze, yellow, green, and blue covered the walls and ceiling. There were vivid depictions of men on horseback, men in white robes bearing gold crosses, and demure, gray-garbed women.

"As miraculous as Nemrut Dağ?" Ibrahim asked.

"Oh, yes. Was this the work of man?"

"It was the work of men who believed in a God and wanted to share that belief with others. They had to hide to do it. Early Christians were no more popular with Rome's rulers than Greeks and Armenians are in Anatolia today. When they were persecuted, Christians hid in these caves. They created places of worship and painted symbols of their beliefs everywhere in these valleys." Suddenly, Ibrahim clutched at his chest.

"Is something wrong, Sire?"

"I don't know. I felt a tightness. Perhaps if I rest for a moment..." The man slithered down into a sitting position. "Is it very warm in here, Turhan?"

"No, Effendi. Perhaps we should go back now," he said, worried by Ibrahim's inexplicable condition.

"I'd like to rest for a little while." The man was pale and perspiring. "Maybe we should get to the cooler part. Can you lift me, boy?"

Turhan did as he was asked. They left the dry chapel. It was cooler when they entered the grotto and Ibrahim seemed better. The ledge gleamed with moisture. They'd gone several yards when suddenly Ibrahim lost his balance. Instinctively he reached out and grabbed a rock at the side of the path. Then he clutched at his chest again and fell to his knees. Turhan reached for his friend, but it was too late. The older man slipped onto a secondary ledge below the pathway. Beyond him, the floor dropped fifty feet to the base of the cavern. Stiletto-sharp formations jutted upwards, crowding each other. A fall would be fatal.

Ibrahim dripped with sweat, despite the coolness of the cave. His face was bone white. Turhan stood transfixed. Eventually, Ibrahim's breathing evened out. He tried to grasp the ledge from which he'd slipped, but failed. Turhan could not reach far enough to pull the man up. There was a large, bleeding gash on Ibrahim's left leg.

"Turhan, listen to me," Ibrahim said in a calm tone. "I don't know what's happened to me, but I feel dizzy. Get the rope from Lightning's saddle pack. Go as quickly as you can, but be careful. We can't risk your falling, too."

When he returned, Turhan was alarmed at Ibrahim's worsening pallor. "It's all right, boy," Ibrahim said, breathing laboriously. "It comes and goes. Now is not the time to lose your courage. Find the most solid rock outcropping you can." Turhan found a thick rock ledge at the height of his waist, where dripping water had bored a large hole over the years. He described it to Ibrahim.

"Good," the older man said. "Tie one end of the rope, as securely as you can, through that hole." The boy did.

"Now, throw the other end down to me."

Slowly, inch by inch, Ibrahim and Turhan worked to pull the caravan master up the rope. Turhan looked back at the ledge. The hole was becoming larger as the pressure of his friend's weight sawed the rope through the soft stone. With a last pull, the caravan master made it to the ledge and held on. Turhan followed the rope to its anchor. A little more strain and it would have cut through the soft rock, sending both of them to their deaths. The two cautiously made their way back to the entrance. Once outside, Ibrahim saw that his leg wound was superficial. He bathed it and doused his face in a nearby spring. His color returned. His breathing became regular.

After they bedded down outside the cave that night, Turhan fell asleep immediately. Ibrahim stayed up much later. He was worried about what had happened inside the cave. If he didn't feel better, he'd see a doctor when they returned to Kayseri. This was the second time in the last few weeks he'd had chest pains. Probably nothing serious. Better not to alarm the boy.

The next day, Turhan learned that the "Valley of Göreme" was really several valleys, each distinct from the others. "Why doesn't the world know of this place?" he asked.

"The same reason lots of things are ignored in Turkey. Anatolia is vast. Those few wealthy Europeans who travel aren't interested in anything east of Istanbul. Perhaps that's just as well. Those who've come to Anatolia have done so, for the most part, to plunder our antiquities."

"What about our own people?"

"How many do you think travel for pleasure? But for an accident of fate, you'd have remained where you were born, ignorant of the world around you."

The following morning, Ibrahim suggested they return to Kayseri along the south fork of the Kızılırmak River. Time passed quickly when the older man spoke of ancient days in Asia Minor. "Twenty-five hundred years ago, the Lydians lived in a city called Sardis, a few hundred miles to the west. The city was capital of a wealthy empire. Cereal grains, grapes, currants, olives, and figs supported a rich life. Cattle and sheep provided meat, wool, and leather to feed and clothe everyone. The Lydians took fortunes in gold from the nearby Paktolos River, using nothing more than sheepskins as their filters.

"They built travelers' inns and invented dice games, using marked, box-shaped sheep and cattle bones, to entertain visitors. The Lydian king was so wealthy that even today people speak of someone who is 'as rich as Croesus.' Yet all that wealth didn't save his kingdom.

"Cyrus the Great, Shah of Persia, dreamt of an Empire that stretched from India to the Aegean Sea. Lydia was the only major kingdom that stood in his way. The Persians were in no hurry to conquer the kingdom. They knew that if they outran their supply lines without pacifying the local populace, they'd be cut off from home without much chance of returning alive.

"Their approach worked very well. Most of the time, they simply surrounded a town or an area, moved an armed force in and set up a *satrap*, a provincial governor. Soon, Croesus realized he was losing a lot of territory and a lot of tax revenue as a result of the Persian campaign. He became concerned."

Ibrahim and Turhan came to a small, sluggish river, slightly wider than a stream. They turned right and proceeded east toward Kayseri. "The Lydians called this river the Halys. Croesus went to Delphi to consult the Oracle, who advised him, 'If you cross the Halys, you will destroy a great empire.' Croesus relied on this advice, massed a huge army, outfitted it with the best equipment money could buy, and sent the forces east. The Lydian soldiers managed to cross the Halys – barely – before they were destroyed. They were no match for Persian cavalry, which cut the charioteers off from one another and proceeded to slice the Lydian army to shreds. The oracle at Delphi had been correct. Croesus had destroyed a great empire. Unfortunately his own." Ibrahim and Turhan rode wordlessly for awhile.

"After they'd captured the capital, the Persians completed the royal road from Susa to Sardis. They built over a hundred post stops along the way, where soldiers could get a fresh horse or stay overnight in cleaner places than we've stayed on our own journey. Soldiers traveled from the Aegean to the Persian Gulf in a week – a quarter of the time it takes to make the same trip today."

"What happened after that?" Turhan asked.

"The Persians and the Greeks mauled one another for the next few hundred years, using Anatolia as a battleground. Eventually a Macedonian boy, barely five years older than you, blazed a trail of glory and destruction that led from Greece to India. Thirteen years after he'd started, Alexander the Great had conquered the widest-ranging empire the world had ever known. The Persians couldn't stop him. Fever did. He was thirty-three when he died."

The caravan remained in Kayseri an additional day. The physician Ibrahim hoped to see had taken a brief holiday and was not expected back for a week. Ibrahim decided an examination could wait until Sinop. He'd had no recurrences of pain.

From Kayseri north, the steppe turned progressively browner and colder. One town resembled every other on the route: a mosque, a *bedestan*, a few nondescript ruins. Ibrahim seemed to know the history of every place they stopped. This plain old wall was the remnant of a citadel that had staved off Ottoman invaders. That chipped, raised area of old stones had once echoed with the tragedies of Aeschylus and Sophocles. Cold, barren fields stretched to the farthest horizon, where once great cities of antiquity had stood. On the ninth day out of Kayseri, they reached Yozgat. Ibrahim told Turhan, "This is a huge country. You'll see more and more each day as we get closer to the Black Sea."

The sun, which had blasted them like a furnace in the south, disappeared, replaced by a cold, northeasterly wind. The day dawned drab, gray. Ibrahim and Turhan wore many layers of clothing and blanketed the horses for the trip. It seemed an ordinary day, like most of the others. Late that evening, Alkimi approached Turhan. "I must speak with you privately, boy."

"What is it, Alkimi Hanım?" he asked, surprised at the urgency of her tone.

"Ibrahim cares about you like you were his own son. You know that." He nodded. "The man looks vigorous and strong, but for the past few nights, I've had strange, distressing dreams. Everything is not right with Ibrahim. He does not say anything, but I think he suspects it. Stay close by him. Make sure he's safe."

Turhan shuddered and thought back to Göreme. As if divining his thoughts, she said, "I know all about what happened in the cave. He was fortunate you were there to help him. He may need you again, sooner than you think."

Her words were ominous. Ibrahim had told him this woman was rarely, if ever, wrong. She saw the look on his face and softened. "Turhan," she said, "will you listen as a silly old woman, schooled only by life, prattles on for awhile?"

"Of course, Hanım."

"Very will then. You may choose to ignore or forget what I say, but since Ibrahim loves you like a son, I want to say it. Every young man dreams of the great things he will do. Some hold on to their dreams, waiting for the right time and place to make them come true. A precious few hold on to their dreams for as long as they live. The vast majority of men put their dreams away for another lifetime. Days pass into weeks, weeks into years. Then comes a wife and, *Inshallah*, children. The dream shrinks and fades. Most men die and ten years after their deaths, hardly anyone remembers them at all.

"Some people live beyond their death. They observe the world and write about it or paint it. They are remembered. Turhan, don't let your dream be buried. It is only if you dare the absurd that you may accomplish the impossible. This is a strange time. Things are not right with Turkey and things are not right with the world."

"Alkimi Hanım, what can I do?"

"Be ready. The torch is being passed to you."

"Allah, Allah," he murmured.

"Yes, little one," she said gently. "You must go with God."

17

Next morning, the telegraph wires crackled. Within hours, word spread through Yozgat like wildfire. War! Montenegro, Greece, and Bulgaria had declared war on the Ottoman Empire. Veiled women scurried silently through the streets, laying in stocks of every available comestible. Ibrahim quickly grasped the significance of what had happened, and bought everything he could.

"This afternoon, prices will be double. Tomorrow they'll double again. It's urgent we make it to the coast by December first. We'll buy more at Sungurlu and Chankırı. Prices won't rise as fast in Anatolia as in Thrace. By the time we get to Sinop, there'll be severe shortages in the capital. Every available ship will be running supplies to Istanbul. There are fortunes to be made."

"What should we buy, Effendi?" asked Turhan. "Gold, diamonds?"

"Food and clothing. You can't eat diamonds. Jewels won't keep out the winter wind." Ibrahim handed Turhan a sack containing a great deal of money. "Here is all your accumulated money. I've given you some of mine as well. You shouldn't miss this opportunity simply because you lack funds. Pay me back when you dispose of your goods at Sinop. With luck, you'll sell enough to pay for your entire education."

During the next four days, Ibrahim worked eighteen hours a day. He seemed more tired than usual, but Turhan attributed this to excitement and the long hours the caravan master spent scouring the countryside for all kinds of goods, and for beasts of burden to carry them. By the time they left Yozgat, the caravan had swelled to three times what it had been a few days before.

"Turhan," he said, "with our caravan increased so greatly, travel will be difficult, but we must cover twice our normal distance each day until we reach the coast. We can't afford to miss this opportunity. Lately, I've been more tired than usual. Ride by my side, be my eyes, ears, and voice if necessary."

"Effendi, I'm sorry I've been the cause of your discomfort."

"Nothing of the kind, boy. I wouldn't have missed these side trips for anything. Neither of us could foresee this war." Turhan felt a sharp sense of foreboding as he recalled Alkimi's words.

The bloated caravan moved north. Ibrahim continued to buy goods of every kind, and animals to haul them. Each place they stopped, news from the front was more appalling. Greek forces had annexed the island of Crete, then smashed their way up the Greek peninsula and captured Salonika. The Turkish star and crescent was trampled underfoot. The blue and white Greek flag flew from the windows of the city.

At Sungurlu, the news was worse. The Serbs had demolished the Turkish army at Kumanovo and Monastir, taking ten thousand prisoners. By the time the caravan reached Chankırı, Bulgarian troops were less than twenty-five miles from the Turkish capital. Except Istanbul, Edirne, Ishkodra, and Ioanina, all of which were under siege, the Ottoman Empire had lost its remaining territories in Europe.

Ibrahim expanded the caravan to five times its normal size. "Regardless how large the caravan is, we must increase our speed to the coast," he said. "They say that in Istanbul the defeats and food shortages have led to violent demonstrations. Thousands of refugees are streaming into the capital from the north. They'll need everything they can get. Price is no object."

Just before they departed Chankırı, Ibrahim told Turhan, "The war is lost. Within two months, the siege will be lifted and goods will flow into the capital from everywhere, driving prices down. Unless we make Sinop by December first, we'll lose not only a good share of the profits to be made, but many of our animals as well."

After the caravan put down each night, Ibrahim ranged the countryside looking for food and supplies. The caravan was now a moving force of thirty men, one-hundred-fifty draft animals, and two hundred sheep. Most women and children had left the caravan at their various destinations. At Tashköprü, they picked up the last of their supplies before heading into the mountains.

The interminable steppe finally gave way to foothills. It did not seem as cold as before. As the caravan climbed higher, the land turned from sere gray-brown to forest green. There were vigorous stands of pine and fir, more and larger trees than Turhan had ever seen. When Turhan remarked about this, Ibrahim smiled. "Looks like we'll make Sinop by tonight, *Inshallah*. We'll arrive at port in time to sell our goods at peak price. Turhan you've truly been my lucky charm on this journey."

The caravan master looked exhausted. "Tell me about Sinop, Effendi," Turhan asked, to keep the mood light.

"According to legend, the city was founded by a race of huge, warlike women, Amazons. Sinop was well-known in ancient Greece. A philosopher named Diogenes was born there. He is said to have gone around Athens with a lamp, searching for the face of an honest man. Sixty years ago, a Russian squadron destroyed the Ottoman fleet off the coast, setting the stage for the Crimean War.

"Tonight we'll spend the night with one of my closest friends, Professor Isaac Ben David, a Jew." Ibrahim brightened noticeably. "He and I go back a long time. He was a professor of history in Istanbul, one of the most brilliant in the Empire. Fifteen years ago, he ran into political problems with the sultan's education minister and left the capital to teach in the small local college. That's when I first met him. It was one of those happy coincidences where you find a kindred spirit in the most unlikely place. Whenever I'm on the northern coast, I spend as much time as possible with him."

They climbed higher. Snow covered the ground in deep, soft patches, totally unlike the thin, sleety ice Turhan had seen in the bitter winters of eastern Turkey.

"Come, Turhan," Ibrahim said. "I'll show you something much different from ruins and old tales." They dismounted and walked to a wide, bare, hilly area, covered top to bottom with snow. There was a small shed at the top of the rise. "Several years ago, I found a most important provision in that shack." They approached the place together. The door was unlocked. Ibrahim entered alone, then emerged with two long wooden sleds with iron runners, old, but sturdy and serviceable. "Turhan, today you're going to fly."

"Fly, Ibrahim Bey?"

"It will only seem that way. Grab one of these and follow me."

They carried their sleds to the top of the hill. "Lie flat on your stomach. Steer by using the handles in front. No matter how dangerous you think it is, stay with the sled. Remember how I told you not to fear the horse."

"Yes, sir." Turhan lay obediently on the sled. Ibrahim positioned him.

"Hold on tight!" He gently shoved the board forward. Slowly, then with gathering speed, the sled took off down the hill. Faster, faster! Not even the horse had gone so swiftly. It was exhilarating, breathtaking. Turhan heard the smooth whoosh of crunching snow under the runners. Moments later, the sled slowed and came to a halt where the hill flattened out.

"Look out!" Turhan heard a shout behind him. Ibrahim whizzed by to his left, steering his own sled carefully to avoid the young man. The caravan master laughed, an excited, elated sound, the sound of a young boy.

"Again!" Ibrahim shouted, as he ground to a stop a hundred feet ahead of Turhan.

For the next two hours, time lost meaning. Teacher and student played together. Ibrahim hauled Turhan about like a horse pulling a cart. They cavorted in the powdery snow until the older man was puffing heavily for breath. Too soon they realized they must return to the caravan.

"Turhan," Ibrahim smiled. "This has been one of the finest times I can remember. Not since Willow..." The man was shaking. Intuitively, Turhan went over to him, put his arms around him, held him. Ibrahim stood still for a few moments, then took a handkerchief from his coat and blew his nose. The moment passed in silence. Suddenly, he clutched his chest. "*Willow!*" he gasped, and fell onto the snow.

"Ibrahim!"

"My heart," the older man rasped, his breath coming in shallow gulps.

"Ibrahim, you'll be all right! Allah, will protect you!" Turhan said, desperate to comfort his companion, but overwhelmed by the certainty that the caravan master would not be all right.

Ibrahim shook his head slowly and smiled very gently, with infinite sadness. "What a shame. What a terrible shame I won't live to share more of your life. In the past three months, you've become a son to me. Perhaps it was our shared need, or the loneliness we could never talk about with anyone else."

He was gasping harder now. Turhan felt the bitter tears start to come. He couldn't stop them, didn't want to.

"I know, Ibrahim. I never had a father. I wanted one so badly. I wanted him to be you. I need you, Ibrahim. Please, please be all right."

"Too late." The man's breathing took on a rattling quality. "I love you, boy. Carry on for me. Make my spirit as proud as if you were the son of my loins. For you are the son of my heart. Don't be afraid to show emotion. Cry out against injustice. Fight for what you believe is right. Most of all, don't be afraid to love. This is my testament to you. Be strong, my son."

Ibrahim ceased breathing and lay still. A look of peace settled on his face. Turhan sobbed uncontrollably. He gently closed the dead man's eyes. "I love you, Ibrahim. I love you, father of my heart. You've handed me the torch. I promise I won't let it go out."

Three men returned with Turhan to where their leader lay dead in the snow. They carried Ibrahim's body back to the caravan and lifted it onto his white horse. Turhan mounted *Yildiz* and held Lightning's rein as well. The caravan started down the trail to Sinop.

The mountains gave way to grassy knolls. The green took on a lighter hue. The wind was gentle and warm, despite the fact it was December. Turhan saw a bright shaft of sunlight reflected in the distance. As he looked toward the source of the light, he gasped. From one side of the horizon to the other, he saw water. Ibrahim had told him that somewhere across the vast body of water lay Russia, and to the West this sea ran into another and then another, connecting Turkey to the world. He looked at Alkimi, who nodded. "We will bury Ibrahim here," Turhan said quietly.

And so it was that, obedient to Ottoman custom, Turhan buried the father of his heart in a grave overlooking the Black Sea. Ibrahim's remains would guard Turkey's northern border, just as Willow's stood sentry over its southern frontier. Afterward, Turhan stood silently, his head bowed, for a long time.

"It's time, Effendi," Alkimi said, addressing him in the honorific reserved for a man.

"Yes, it is," he replied. "*Allaha ismarladik, Baba.* Go with God, my father."

18

"Will you be leaving the caravan here?" Alkimi asked.

"Yes. Ibrahim wanted me to go to school. Before I do, I'll help sell our goods. What will happen now?"

"The caravan will carry on as it did before there was Ibrahim. Tashkin has been with us for many years. He'll assume command. He's a good man. He's not Ibrahim, but he's honest and diligent, and," she said, with the slightest trace of a smile, "I can train him. Where will you go from here?"

"Istanbul. I'd like to go to school there. Will you be all right, Alkimi?"

"Of course. The caravan's heart must continue to beat, even though half of it is gone," she said gruffly.

"Alkimi," he blushed. "I've a favor to ask."

"Will I take the lady her money? Of course. By the way, Ibrahim said that if anything happened to him, I was to give this to you." She reached into her many layers of clothing and drew out a goatskin bag, which she handed him. Turhan opened the purse. His eyes widened. It was more money than he'd ever seen in his life.

"Ibrahim wanted you to go to Istanbul and complete your education. He thought this would help. When you're in Istanbul, you must present yourself immediately to the Agha Nikrat, the Agha Khorusun's brother. He controls the trafficking of illegal goods there, just as Khorusun does in Mosul province. Ibrahim wrote Nikrat about you. The man promised he'd protect you and see you through your schooling. Now, enough. Go to the university and find his friend, Professor Ben David. It's time you told him what has happened."

Turhan walked toward the college. He was impressed by the dramatic layout of the city. To his right, was a protected bay with waters so quiet that small children waded in them. Beyond and to his left, where the land hooked around, the sea was so violent that no one dared venture near. Straight ahead, a huge, high promontory jutted out to land's end.

Shortly, he arrived at the school, only to learn that Professor Ben David had gone home for the evening. The young man who greeted him said he'd guide Turhan to the professor's house.

Turhan had expected Ben David to be frail and elderly. The picture could not have been less accurate. Isaac ben David was a hearty, solidly built fellow, fifty years old, with thick black hair, a full beard, only starting to go iron gray, and warm, green eyes.

"Professor Ben David?"

"That's me," the man responded.

"My name is Turhan. I am a friend of Ibrahim..."

"Indeed, come in, come in!" the professor said expansively, holding the door wide open. "Where is that rascal?"

"I'm sorry. He died this morning, Sir."

"No," the man said, shocked. Then, seeing the look on Turhan's face, he said, "You loved him very much?"

"As a father."

"Where is he?"

"We buried him on the heights overlooking the city."

"Have you erected the stones?"

"No, Professor."

"We'll do that together in the next days. With the headstone facing toward Mecca as the Prophet decreed."

"Will there be a turban?" Turhan asked. In the Ottoman Empire, a turban at the top of the gravestone signified rank.

"Yes," the professor replied. "If I had my way, it would be that of a sultan. How are you feeling?"

"Shaky, Sir."

"And Alkimi?"

"She is stronger than I."

"Stay with us a while. Ibrahim would have wanted that."

The professor was delightful, courtly, charming and hospitable. At dinner, he reminisced about the times he'd shared with Ibrahim. It had been several hours since Turhan had eaten and he partook ravenously of the huge dinner. There was lamb, beef, fish, fresh garden vegetables and new potatoes, mint tea, pastries and sweet Russian liqueur.

Professor Ben David's wife, Leah, was a dark, attractive woman of thirty-five. Their son, Avi, was a strapping youth, who gave promise of his father's brawn. Most of all, Turhan was struck by the professor's thirteen-year-old daughter, a girl who barely came up to his chin, who had long-flowing, dark hair and sparkling brown eyes. She had a fawn complexion and the softest looking skin he'd ever seen. Beneath her modest dress, he made out the faint outlines of a beautifully curved young figure. During the dinner, Zehavah Rebecca Ben David – Zari – favored Turhan with well-timed smiles and nods. Turhan found it hard to speak.

That night, he slept at the Ben David's home. When he awoke the following morning, Professor Ben David said, "We have one more task. How far is it to Ibrahim's grave?"

"An hour's ride, Professor."

"We must bury him properly, Turhan. And it is time."

"Yes, it is," Turhan responded quietly.

So they rode into the hills and piled stones on Ibrahim's grave, and afterward Professor Ben David handed Turhan a turban to place at the head of the stone. And thus Turhan truly and finally buried the father of his heart.

When they returned home, the professor took Turhan to his study. "Now we have made our peace with the departed. Many years ago, when I first met Ibrahim, he showed me words he'd composed after his first journey in Turkey with his father. I'm certain he'd have wanted you to have it." The professor moved a heavy chair and peeled back a luxuriant carpet, exposing a small safe in the floor. He opened it, reached in, and extracted a piece of paper, yellowed with age, which he handed to the youth. Turhan read the words which Ibrahim had written in a strong, clear hand:

> "Since the dawn of mankind, our land has been a bridge.
> East and West meet within its frontiers.
> Warrior and vanquished have spilled, shared, merged blood.
> The footsteps of forever have crossed our motherland.
> They have never diminished our spirit, but have added to it.
> Come, visitor. You are but the latest.
> Enter, and look into the mirror of man's soul."

Professor Ben David squeezed Turhan's hand.

"He is one with the past. You are his future. Tomorrow we will start to carry Ibrahim's soul forward into the ages."

Two days later, Turhan received the first letter ever addressed to him. He opened it eagerly. The note, in beautifully written Arabic script, said simply, "Dear Turhan: My brother and I regret as deeply as you the passing of Ibrahim. He was a great man and a good one, who knew injustice must be fought, whatever the cost. It will be my honor to carry out his wishes that you finish your education in Istanbul. My home will be yours as long as you desire. I am enclosing a small amount to help you come swiftly to me. Yours most sincerely, Nikrat, Agha of Istanbul-Sultanahmet."

Turhan's eyes widened when he saw the Agha had sent three hundred lira. What kind of land was this where bad was good, and authorities so corrupt? Perhaps the Agha Nikrat would finish the answers Ibrahim had started.

ISTANBUL

"Three hundred lira, Abbas," Kerem said, counting the money out. "That's your part of the bounty. Who'd have dreamed a young lad could have gotten inside the place and secreted so much? The month you spent as his servant was certainly well worth it. When the police invaded the house, they found drugs every place you told them. You should be proud. You helped bring about the downfall of the mighty

Agha Nikrat himself! Soon everything will be gone. His home, the fleet of boats he used for his smuggling operations, the accounts he had in Turkey, all confiscated by the state. Best of all, after his conviction that criminal will languish in prison for the next fifteen years. You were brilliant, boy! You'll make a superb law enforcement officer, a protector of the public good. Bravo to you!" He hugged the young man warmly.

Abbas relished his success in bringing down the Arab, an enemy of the Ottoman Empire, more than he appreciated the money. He smiled broadly at Kerem. "Let's go to a nearby raki bar and drink to our success, Kerem Effendi. This time, *I'll* pay for it."

PART TWO:

HALIDE 1897–1917

1

Halide came bouncing into the room wearing a particularly lovely dress. She looked at her reflection in papa's bedroom mirror. Yujel Orhan had never hidden mirrors from the child. After preening a while, she looked at her father and said, "Papa, I'd be much prettier if I didn't have this big thing on my back."

"Halide, you're a lovely child." His daughter was nearly five years old. Because of Yujel's patient teaching, she could already read as well as many children twice her age.

"But I don't look like other children. They think I'm funny. They think my big hump is ugly."

The professor cleared his throat. "Halide, I think you and I need to have a long, serious talk."

"All right, Papa." She sat on the bed, hands folded.

"Darling, this is very hard for me to say. Do you know what the word 'brave' means?"

"Yes, Papa. It means you don't run away, even if you're scared."

"Good, Halide. Some people have a very easy life. Others have to be much braver all their lives, because of things they can't help. You were born with the hump on your back. There's nothing anyone can do about it. Not doctors. Not even me. I wish more than anything I had the hump instead of you. Because of it, you will have to be very, very brave."

"Why, Papa?"

"You'll be starting school in a few weeks. Grownups hide what they feel when they see something they think is ugly. Children are more honest and more cruel. They'll tease you. Or they'll make up what, to them, seem clever or funny remarks about you. They may think if they come near you they'll catch the hump on your back. Some children won't want to play with you at all."

The girl turned pale. Yujel felt a tightening in his stomach. "Even grownups can be cruel, my darling. Some of them will try to touch your back, because some very stupid people think it is a sign of good luck. Others will be overly sweet to you because they don't know what to say. People will say and do awful things that will make you very sad. I want so badly to be there with you, to protect you from harm, my sweet baby child. But I can't always be there. If I throw a protective cloak around you, there will still be holes in it. You must be very brave."

Halide listened thoughtfully. At the end, she said, "Maybe there will be some people who'll see that I'm pretty inside. Besides, Papa, you'll always love me."

Yujel's mind flashed back to those vivid scenes that had taken place a few years before – memories that would always be with him. His mind reeled back to the morning he'd sat nervously in the waiting room, pretending to read Rostand's *Cyrano de Bergerac*, which he'd brought with him to the hospital. On the table by his side lay yesterday's *Le*

Monde. Its headline blared news of the Dreyfus trial. Mathieu Dreyfus claimed the document that convicted his brother Alfred was actually written by Major Esterhazy.

Yujel had risen as the obstetrician approached him. The doctor had been very pale. "Professor," he said quietly, "might I see you in my office a few moments?"

"Is the baby...?"

"May I be brutally frank, M'sieu?"

"I would prefer you to be, Docteur."

"It is a very rare, pronounced form of congenital kyphosis, an unnatural reverse curve to the upper back and spine. She will appear quite deformed. Her back will have a hump. Depending on the degree of curvature, it may be greater or less, but it will be noticeable. The problem is inoperable."

"Will she be able to walk?"

"Yes. Her appearance will not affect her body's ability to function, nor will it cause her physical discomfort."

"Praise Allah!" Yujel sighed. "At least she won't be in pain."

"Not physically," the obstetrician remarked sadly.

"Does her mother know yet?"

"I'm not sure. They were getting ready to take the child in."

A horrified scream answered their question.

Yujel had to retain a full time nursemaid. His wife, Colette, refused to acknowledge the child's existence, let alone nurse her. Colette soon disappeared from their lives.

Yujel Orhan had lived in Paris for fifteen years before, at age fifty, he'd finally been promoted to full professor, ten years behind his colleagues. They never *said* it was because he was Turkish, or because he did not attend chapel each week. The excuses had always been sincere, delivered in a most sympathetic manner. When Yujel reminded them that teachers ten years younger than he, carrying half his class load in English Literature and drama were regularly made full professors, his superiors simply changed the subject. Ultimately, in 1897, the university ran out of excuses. Yujel's learned treatise, *The Role of the Ottoman Empire as a Twentieth Century Pivot*, created a stir at Oxford and Heidelberg, and enjoyed modest popular appeal. His dream of a full professorship was finally realized.

His domestic life, however, was anything but triumphant. Four years before, when he was a vigorous, virile forty-six, he'd met Colette. Since his first wife's untimely death from cancer a decade before, he'd enjoyed the companionship of one or two women, but there'd been no serious attachments. Colette, twenty years his junior, thought it quite daring to take a course in Ottoman history. She told her friends she'd always been fascinated by the sinister, mildly frightening Muslim world. Besides, the tall, urbane, mustachioed professor with graying temples and strange accent was "exotic," his reserve a challenge to her womanhood.

Ultimately, he had proposed to Colette and they'd married in a civil ceremony. From there, things had gone rapidly downhill. Yujel tried to appease and satisfy his young wife in every way. Nothing worked. Colette found him dull, drab, *old*. She had nothing in common with his stuffy friends. And, of course, he was beneath her station. She went dancing with her old girlfriends. Soon, she found that rumors about Impressionist painters looking for slender, small-breasted models were true. She sat for them, first modestly clothed, later *deshabille*. Within a year, when she was not spending her nights elsewhere, Madame Orhan and her husband slept in separate bedrooms. The more wretchedly she treated him, the more inflamed with desire he became for her. On the rare occasions they slept together, she treated him with such undisguised contempt, he damned himself afterward for his weakness.

"What do you mean you're pregnant?"

"You heard me, you stupid bastard. You've knocked me up."

"Me?" he shouted. "What about your numerous 'friends?' Half of Paris, for all I know."

"Very funny," she sneered. "You kept me such a prisoner during the winter holidays I had no opportunity to be with anyone else. I'd certainly much rather have been, old man. Besides, I am lawfully married to you. You are conclusively presumed the father of the child I am carrying. Of course, I could be persuaded to abort the child."

"What are you inferring?"

"Perhaps if I were settled in a small villa, south of Paris..."

"How can you, a Catholic, speak of such an idea?"

"Oh, so now it's 'You're a Catholic' is it? Listen, don't forget I turned my back on Mother Church when I entered into an 'unholy' union with you. I'm almost thirty years old. If I can't get a good settlement now, when am I ever going to find it? Besides, you're a full professor. You can afford it."

"I won't hear of it. We'll simply try to adjust to one another as best we can."

"You believe that?" she screamed. "Listen, you miserable excuse for a man. I will wait until this child is born. Then I will find the most bloodthirsty shark in the Paris legal system and tell him exactly how a dirty old man, a *Turk* to boot, seduced an innocent, young French girl, forced her to marry him and submit to his filthy, unnatural demands. I will crucify you in court! See how *that* word offends your *Muslim* sensitivities!" She laughed bitterly at her pun. "And I will never allow you to see my child! Never, never, never!" She slammed the door of her bedroom. He heard the lock click into place.

2

The other children taunted Halide mercilessly. They told her she was a monster. They jeered that no mother came to pick her up because no one wanted to claim her. Then some children started a rumor that she was neither French nor Christian, and that she worshiped the devil. The child could not comprehend such cruelty.

"Papa, why do they hate me so much?" she asked, tearfully.

"Darling, it is horrible and it makes no sense, but often children blame their own failures on others. It's easier for them to pick on someone who looks different or doesn't have a mother or who may have a different belief than it is for them to look inside themselves for any faults."

"All I want is to be left alone. Is that asking too much?"

"Oh, my baby girl," he said, holding her and rocking her small, trembling body. "It's not too much. It should never be too much to ask. I want to tell you a story that may not seem like it will help, but please think about it, all right?"

"Yes, Papa."

Yujel told his daughter the Hans Christian Andersen tale of the ugly duckling, a cygnet who looked so much different from other baby ducks that he was an outcast. Even the mother duck shunned him. He finally learned he was a swan, far more beautiful than any duck, and found peace within himself. When Yujel completed the story, he played her the recording of Saint-Saens' "*Le Cygne*," which had become her favorite melody. She fell asleep in his arms, her tear-stained face at peace.

As time passed, Halide tried to escape her unhappiness. The usual distractions of childhood did not tempt her. She directed her energies elsewhere. By the time she finished her first year at *École des Étudiants*, she was so far ahead of the other students that no one attempted comparisons. The teasing increased, for now the children resented her talents. They called her, "Hunch Brain." Yujel's heart broke each afternoon when he saw Halide walking home slowly, sadly, always alone. Other children avoided her. Often he wanted to scream out in anguish as he saw them mimicking his child behind her back.

One day, a little girl who'd been one of Halide's most constant tormentors, fell and broke her arm. Infection set in, and the girl was homebound. Yujel suggested Halide visit the child.

"I'm afraid, Papa. She always calls me terrible names. She tells the other children I'm a dirty, smelly hunchback and not to play with me. She even tries to imitate the way I look."

"It never pays to return pain with pain, darling. Remember when you and I talked about being brave? I think it would be an act of courage for you to visit this child."

Halide went to the girl's home. She brought flowers and a book. When she came to the door, the child's parents inquired who she was. She felt a stab of pain as she heard a child's voice from the other room. "I don't want to see *her*."

"Hush, Jeannette," a man's voice said sharply. "None of your other friends have come to visit. You will see her and you will behave."

Halide wanted to turn and run from the house, but she stood rooted to the ground, remembering her father's words.

"Come in, dear," Jeannette's mother said. "Our daughter is delighted that a friend from school has come to visit." Halide hid the cringing she felt, and went inside. When she brought the flowers to Jeannette, the child reached out and took them stiffly. Her mother said, "I'll leave you two alone to talk."

No sooner had the door closed than Jeannette pulled the covers completely over her head, leaving Halide sitting there embarrassed. After a while, the girl had to come out for air. She glared at her visitor. Halide continued to sit quietly. The other girl finally broke the silence. "All right. You've brought flowers and come to visit. Now go away."

"You don't like me, do you, Jeannette?"

"No, and nobody else in school does either. Why don't you just go away?"

"I can't. My papa sent me to this school. If you mean why don't I go away from my body, I can't. I'm stuck inside."

For the first time in Halide's memory, the shadow of a smile crossed Jeannette's lips. "Why don't you look like everyone else?"

"I don't know. I didn't ask to look the way I do, and I can't always see what I look like, because I'm on the inside. Are you afraid that if you talk to me or act nice, you'll start to look like me?"

The sick child looked down at an imaginary spot on the blanket. Then, very quietly, she said, "Yes."

"You'll never look like me, Jeannette. It's what's inside that's important. Papa told me a story about an ugly duckling once."

"I know that story. My mama read it to me. Does your papa tell you fairy tales?"

"Sometimes. Mostly I read a lot of books myself."

Jeannette cast her eyes down again. "I don't read very much at all. I'm not very clever."

"Is that what teacher says, Jeannette? I don't think she gives you a chance. Do you like to read?"

"No."

"Why not?"

"It's boring. And very hard."

"Would you like me to read the book I brought you?"

"All right."

Halide opened the book of mythology tales and began to read. Time passed more quickly than either girl imagined. While Halide was reading about the mighty Hercules and his feats of strength, Jeannette's mother came in. "Jeannette, I hate to interrupt, but your friend has been here over three hours. You need your rest."

Jeannette pouted. "Halide, could you come back tomorrow and read some more?"

Halide never flaunted her academic excellence. In time, she discovered that modesty and thoughtfulness consistently gained her new friends. Eventually, she no longer walked home alone. She was invited to a few parties. Although some children continued to harass her, the teasing gradually became manageable, then simply tiresome. As Halide became more popular, her resultant happiness spurred her to become even more gracious, poised, and generous.

She and Papa went to museums, concerts and exhibitions together. Halide was always curious and Papa always made their outings so much fun. Invariably, he asked if she wanted to bring a friend. Sometimes she did, but mostly it was glorious just to be with him. When Halide asked about her mother, Yujel did not evade her questions, but he refused to speak ill of Colette.

"Why would she leave us, Papa?"

"Sometimes people become very upset. Things happen in their lives that make them so unhappy they cannot live with other people."

"But wouldn't she want to visit me?"

"The last I heard, she had moved far away, south of the equator."

"Perhaps some day, when I'm a professor like you, I shall find her and surprise her."

"Perhaps," he murmured.

"Papa," she said, changing the subject. "How come we never go to any of the large, beautiful churches other children go to each Sunday? We go to a mosque in a poor *arondissement* on Saturday. When you pray, you call God 'Allah.' Once Jeannette said she didn't think I was really French. I asked her what she meant, and she said I should ask you."

"Darling, have you heard of the Ottoman Empire?"

"Of course. The capital is Constantinople." She started to recite facts she'd read in a book. Father held up his hand to stop her.

"My precious child, your mama was – is – French. I'm not. I was born in Istanbul. The French still call it Constantinople. Even though we live in France, my adopted country considers me a subject of the sultan. Since you're my daughter, you're also considered Turkish."

"Did your parents come from there?"

"Yes, darling."

"Then I want to go and visit Istanbul as soon as I am able."

The principal of the école élémentaire had observed Halide over the years, and when Halide was in her fifth year, the principal asked Yujel to come to a private conference. When Yujel arrived, the principal introduced him to Maître Paul Weygand, a distinguished-looking man his own age, who was headmaster of a very prestigious lycée – the high school that Halide was to attend the following year.

"Professeur," the headmistress began, "You have an exceptional young daughter. Most exceptional."

"Yes, Madame Dassault. Is something amiss?"

"Amiss?" she repeated, then shook her head. "Not at all, M'sieu. What I should like to suggest is that perhaps you might be of a mind to retain a *précepteur*."

"A tutor, Madame? I had no idea she was behind in her studies."

"Behind in her studies? *Behind*, M'sieu? Mon Dieu, Professeur, I have been principal of this school for a dozen years. Before that I taught for fifteen. I've never seen the likes of Halide, Professeur Orhan! The child soaks up knowledge like a sponge. She is ten years old. A year ago, she completed the entire curriculum we offer in our *école élémentaire*. I consulted Maître Weygand, the principal of the *lycée*, who suggested certain advanced studies as a means of maintaining Halide's interest. The girl completed those projects with an ease that left us dumbfounded. She is extraordinary. She adjusts to her, ahem, disfigurement. She's modest and courteous. She is so far above the rest of her classmates it is impossible to use the same measure for her as for them. She is now doing work equivalent to a second year lycée student. At the rate she is going, Maître Weygand's school will run out of things to teach her in a year, two years at the very most."

Maître Weygand nodded, emphasizing Madame Dassault's words.

"Then why a précepteur?"

"Professeur, perhaps I can best answer that question," Maître Weygand said. "It would be sinful to waste this child's mind. Your daughter's promise must be developed to its full potential."

"To what end?"

"I believe she would qualify for an early – very early – admission to the Sorbonne, the premier college of the University of Paris."

"A child prodigy with a – unique – physical condition. You'd make her a double oddity? Her deformity has caused her enough problems even here."

"Sir!" Madame Dassault said sternly. "You dwell on Halide's appearance. The hump, which is not nearly as pronounced as you appear to believe, is something she cannot help. She deals well with her handicap. She has won the loyalty of teachers and classmates with her open and caring ways. It's true some children never cease their taunting, but surely you can see that by moving her up with more mature students, the tormenting will diminish rather than increase?"

"But the Sorbonne?"

"What's wrong with the Sorbonne? You're a professor there, are you not?"

"That has nothing to do with it."

"Come, come, Professor," the woman said, smiling. "Are you concerned your daughter will eclipse you as a scholar?"

"Have you a précepteur in mind?"

The principal indicated that the headmaster of the lycée should answer the question. "At first a university student would be appropriate. But in two years or so, I recommend no less than Hélène Durein. She is most influential with the university admissions department. She is quite expensive, Professeur."

"I'm not concerned about expense."

"Very well. I will notify you when it would be appropriate to seek out Mlle. Durein."

In December, 1910, Maître Weygand asked Halide to take a series of written tests. He told her, "Our lycée is part of an educational experiment. We've been asked to see how these examinations can be employed by other schools."

Halide answered the questions easily. Afterward, Maître Weygand thanked her and introduced her to a tall, stiff woman with close-cropped red hair. Halide did not give the tests a second thought. She was looking forward to the winter break. After she'd left the room, Weygand said, "What did I tell you?"

"You're correct, Paul," the woman replied. "Her papers are astounding." She stroked her chin, reflectively. "I believe I could prepare her for admission quite easily."

The following month, Maître Weygand summoned Halide to his study. "Halide, Mademoiselle Durein, whom you met last December, has asked that you visit her in her office. It is situated in the *Rue Metz* near *Place Lafayette.*"

"Who is she, M'sieu?"

"She's one of the best known educational specialists in France. Your father, Madame Dassault, and I discussed the possibility of Mlle. Durein as a special instructor. She is most selective and takes on only a very few private students each year. Last month, when you took those tests, she evaluated your abilities. I'm delighted to say she has decided to accept you."

⤫

Mlle. Durein worked Halide harder than any of her teachers had in the past. There wasn't a subject in which the woman lacked knowledge. She directed Halide to closed stacks at the university library and guided her through the conflicting authorities in many fields. The *précepteur's* breadth of knowledge challenged Papa's. Occasionally, Halide daydreamed that Mlle. Durein was her real mama. What a shame Mlle. Durein and Papa had not met years ago. The instructor seemed oblivious to her student's hero worship. Sometimes Halide brought flowers, pastries, or other small gifts to the Rue Metz. Mlle. Durein was cordial in her thanks, but was more interested in the quality of Halide's preparation.

In 1913, Raymond Poincaré, was elected President of France. Aristide Briand became Premier. Impressionist painters gave way to Cubists. The foxtrot was the year's dance sensation. Stravinsky's "Rite of Spring" debuted on the Paris stage. Parisians, enamored with motion pictures imported from America, giggled at the antics of a hilarious little man with a square moustache, who wore ragged, ill-fitting clothes and waddled like a duck. Since Henry Ford had pioneered new assembly-line techniques in his car factory, some of his automobiles had made their way across the Atlantic. Doctor Albert Schweitzer opened his hospital in Lambarene, French Congo.

And, in September, a small, slight, young woman, barely sixteen, with a noticeable humpback, took her seat in her first year classes at the Sorbonne.

3

Most university students concentrated on their studies, not the physical appearance of classmates. For the first time in her life, Halide was no longer an ugly duckling. She took part in several study and discussion groups. Talk spilled over into day trips with friends to the opera, films, the sidewalk cafes. It was a delightful time for Halide.

Although Mlle. Durein had given Halide a firm grounding, particularly in history, literature, the arts, and mathematics, for the first time in her life Halide found that not all classes at the university were easy. Chemistry in particular was daunting, and although her test scores showed she was doing remarkably well, she knew in her own mind that she was slowly falling behind.

Halide redoubled her efforts, dramatically cutting back on her social activities. In order to try to understand the subject that was slipping from her grasp, Halide asked one of her girlfriends who was doing reasonably well in chemistry whether the girl knew of a study group she might join.

"You've picked a perfect time to ask," the girl said. "We limit our group to six, and one of the girls just transferred to the University at

Dijon. Why don't you come with me tomorrow evening and you can see how you like it."

The group consisted of three boys and two other girls. She recognized faces from her class, but not names. During the first session, she sat and listened quietly as the members explored what they had learned earlier in the day. One slender, dark-haired young man in particular, without being pushy or overbearing, seemed able to explain the most difficult concepts in simple language, using examples that were familiar to them all. He greeted Halide politely, and even though he was quite reserved, he made her feel very welcome in the group.

The meeting lasted three hours, and by the time the meeting concluded, she was exhausted. Still, she acknowledged to her friend, the evening had been worthwhile and the day's lesson now seemed clearer to her. After that, Halide started coming to the twice-weekly study group meetings. She found herself more firmly in control of the subject matter and also found it easier to participate actively in the discussions.

From time to time, she noticed that while she was talking, the dark-haired young man who'd so impressed her the first evening seemed inordinately interested in what she had to say. He made a point of emphasizing the value of what she said without patronizing her. There were times when he looked candidly at her. For the first time in her life she felt delighted little shivers when he did. The young man was somewhat taller than average and not at all bad looking.

At the conclusion of the third group meeting, Halide got up the nerve to actually approach him to introduce herself. "Please don't think me forward," she began, "but I've heard others call you Metin and you've no doubt heard those in our group call me by name. I'm Halide Orhan."

"Metin Ermenek," he said, bowing ever so slightly and smiling. "Not to be rude, but I'm aware you're Halide Orhan, the youngest and, from what I've seen one of the brightest students in our class. I was absolutely delighted when I heard you were thinking about joining our study group. I had wanted to approach you myself, but I didn't know how you'd react. I hope my dominating the group didn't put you off."

"Hardly," she said, smiling back at him. "You explained things so clearly. It was as though I were sitting and listening to my father. Oh, did I say something to offend you?"

"Not at all," he said. "But I hardly pictured myself as old enough to be anyone's father. I'm only eighteen, and I've never so much as dated a girl."

"I didn't mean it that way, Metin. I meant that you somehow seem so mature. Anyone would feel very comfortable around you. You seem so confident. Are you a native Parisian?"

"No, I'm from Istanbul, Turkey. Why, Halide, you seem to be blushing. Now I fear *I've* said something wrong."

"Not at all. Are you aware that I'm half-Turkish? Come to think of it, I'm almost *all* Turkish. My father and I live alone. He's a Professor here." Her words came out in a rush. "And all my life I've wanted to see Istanbul." The janitor interrupted their conversation by indicating that all the other students had left the room and he wanted to lock up the place so he could go home for the night.

"Are you too tired to join me for a cup of coffee or tea at the cafeteria? It's open 'til midnight."

Months passed. Slowly, almost imperceptibly Halide and Metin came to look more and more forward to the time they spent together. After-group coffees expanded to light snacks together. Each was scrupulously polite to the other. Each felt a growing closeness with the other, yet convention held them back from speaking about what they felt.

At the end of the term, Metin finished first in the class, which was not unexpected. What was a total surprise to her was that Halide finished a close second in a subject that, scarcely three months earlier, she had thought she might fail.

"Metin," she said, uncharacteristically taking his arm, "I owe this success all to you. Every bit of it. I think we should celebrate. Would you feel me too gauche if I asked if I could treat you to dinner for your efforts?" she asked.

"I won't say no," Metin said. "I agree this calls for a celebration, but don't give me the credit. You're the one that never stopped trying, even when you must have believed it was impossibly hard. But I'd really prefer if you'd let me treat."

"We can argue over that all night, but the evening is so lovely, let's not waste it. I'm hungry as a bear. Could you suggest a place nearby?"

"As a matter of fact, I can," he said. Metin chose a small Turkish restaurant where he'd been many times before, inexpensive, but with excellent food. It was crowded, but he spotted a small table for two in the back. As they threaded their way through the crowd, both realized that Halide had not let go of his arm since they'd left the university.

"Good evening Metin," a big, burly bear of a man in his early twenties said. "Lovely young lady with you tonight. Will it be the usual?"

"Not tonight. Tarkhan, I'd like you to meet Halide Orhan, a friend of mine and a fellow student from my chemistry class. We've just finished first and second in the class and we're celebrating. The waiter nodded politely. "Halide and I have been walking the better part of a kilometer. We deserve something better than falafel. I'd like your roast chicken dinner, chips, salad and Coca Cola to drink. How about you, Halide?"

"The same, please." The waiter departed. "Now, Metin," she said, "The semester's done and I still know virtually nothing about you except that you're a third year student, that you're one of the kindest people other than my father that I've ever met, and that in the time I've known you I've seen you smile only once – a very handsome smile I might add."

Metin blushed. "I've always had trouble talking about myself with anyone," he said. "I read somewhere that women get very bored when all a man wants to do is talk about himself. I thought if I listened more, learned more, it might somehow make me a more interesting person."

"I don't know about other girls you've talked to, but I'd like to hear about your life."

She was about to say more, but at that moment the burly Tarkhan reappeared, bearing two huge plates filled with food. The chicken was done to perfection, with a healthy brown color and crispy skin. The chips were not greasy, and the salad, a concoction made of chopped onions, tomatoes, green peppers, cucumber and parsley, sweetened with lemon and sugar, smelled fresh and delicious. After the meal, over American-style coffee, they discussed their childhood memories of different places they'd been to and seen.

"Have you ever thought of what you want to do when you finish school?" she asked.

"Yes. My father's a physician in Istanbul. I'd like to go to medical school, but I'd like to do more than simply set up a clinic in the big city. If I can, I'd like to set up public health clinics throughout Turkey."

"That's … that's fascinating. I mean, being a doctor and all. You seem so sure of yourself at such a young age."

"I've wanted to be a doctor as long as I can remember," he said. "What about you, Halide?"

"Would I sound like a silly child if I said I had no idea what I want to do?" she said.

"Not at all. I'd be more surprised if you did know what you wanted during your first year in university. Besides, a beautiful, intelligent young lady like you has so many options."

Halide suddenly rose. "I think I'd like to go home now."

"Did I say something wrong? Please tell me if I did."

"You called me beautiful."

"And I meant it."

"Are you trying to humiliate me?" She tossed enough money on the table to pay the bill for both of them, then angrily stomped out.

Metin followed her into the street. The summer evening was dry and mild. "Listen, please, Halide, what did I say to offend you?"

"How dare you call be beautiful or even attractive? You have eyes, the same as anyone else."

"Wait a minute," he said, grabbing her by both shoulders. "You're saying because you have a kyphosis no one could find you beautiful? How shallow do you think I am?"

"A *kyphosis*? Is that what you call it? A polite way of saying a humpback?" She tried unsuccessfully to pull away.

"You can call it whatever you want. You didn't ask to be born with it, and if you think I care less for you because of it, why … why …?" He didn't say more because the girl was weeping copiously. He held her very gently until her sobs subsided. "Halide," he finally said. "Halide. There's so much beauty in you. Beauty that's inside, beauty that surrounds you when you speak, when your brilliant mind is at work, when I look at you in a crowded room. Maybe you don't see the beauty and maybe others who are fools don't see the beauty, but I tell you the beauty is there, and it's enough for me."

"Are you … are you serious, Metin?" she said between sniffles.

"I swear to you I am. I didn't mean to say it so soon. I thought maybe if we let our – our friendship grow into something more precious … But you're the one that raised the issue when you said you were a silly girl, and what I said just gushed out of me. Why do you think I never protested when you linked your arm through mine? Because it felt so good and because I was so proud to be seen with you."

"But the ky – the *kyphosis*?"

"What about it? Does it make you less of a woman, less of a human being? Does it somehow make you less worthy? In the time we're together, perhaps they'll find a way to perform surgery if it bothers you that much. I can tell you it's absolutely meaningless to me," he said hotly. "What is meaningful to me is *you*."

"Can you forgive me for the way I acted in the restaurant?" she said, her eyes brimming with tears once again.

"What's to forgive?" he said, gently chucking her under the chin. "They make lousy dessert anyway."

The months seemed to speed by. Metin and Halide went everywhere together – the theater, the opera, museums, exhibitions. Fortunately, since neither of them was particularly well-heeled, Paris had always retained a special place in its heart for its youth, and prices were well within reason. They talked about everything and nothing, and although kissing and cuddling were very much a part of the picture, both of them observed an unwritten, unspoken promise to one another that it was not right for them to go farther than that.

More and more, Metin spoke about his dreams for Turkey, and more and more often he almost unconsciously peppered his talks with, "When we go here," and "When we start to work together," and "When we can bring about changes that will help our people." Halide never dissuaded him and never rebuked him, for she felt closer to him than any man, perhaps even Papa.

Still, it wasn't until January, when he was into the final half of his third year, that things came to a head. They'd just come out of a performance of Franz Lehar's *Merry Widow* and Halide asked, "Metin, could we stop for tea and a sweet? I'm nowhere near ready to go home."

"Certainly," he said. She held his arm and nuzzled closer to him.

He was unusually quiet as they walked down the 'Boul' Miche' to a café frequented by most of their friends from the university. No sooner had they sat down in a far corner of the room, more to escape the bitter Parisian cold than anything else, than she said, "Darling, you seem awfully withdrawn tonight. Is something bothering you?"

He took her hands in his and looked steadily into her eyes. "Yes, there is. I'm in love with you, you know …"

Halide blushed furiously. The words had never been spoken, but now they were out in the open and she responded automatically, "Well, Mister Ermenek, it's about time you told me. I'm so much in love with you I could almost faint. I've been in love with you since last summer."

"That's the problem," he said. "You're barely seventeen and … and …"

"Yes?"

"Are you prepared to wait until I start medical school? That's two years away?"

"Wait for what?" For the first time in her life, Halide, always the most direct of young women, was being coy.

Metin sipped nervously at his tea. "You want me to come right out and say it?"

"Well, darling, it seems to me that's always been our way, hasn't it?" She smiled demurely, but her eyes were brilliant with happiness.

"All right." In front of everyone in the tea room, he got down on his knees. "Halide Orhan, will you ... will you ... allow me to ask your father for your hand in marriage?"

As if on cue, a quartet consisting of the members of the chemistry study group entered the tea room. Before Halide could say a word, before Metin could get up off his knees, they sang an original song, the lyrics exhorting Halide to say yes. Halide glared at Metin, who shrugged his shoulders helplessly. The quartet was not to be put off. They grabbed every student in the café and a raucous chant of, "Say yes! Say yes! Say yes!" erupted.

Halide, savoring the moment, stood and said to the assembly, "I'll need some time to think about it." She waited all of five seconds before she said, "Yes, my darling, you may ask my Papa for my hand. And if he loves me the way I think he does, I know what his answer will be."

4

In 1914, two events jarred Yujel's world. On June 28, in the small Serbian city of Sarajevo, Archduke Franz Ferdinand, heir to the Austrian throne, was murdered, with the end result that numerous European nations declared war on one another. Three days later, Yujel felt even greater turmoil when Halide came home holding the hand of a slender, shy young man and said, "Papa, I'd like you to meet Metin Ermenek. He comes from Istanbul and he's studying at the Sorbonne."

Yujel's heart skipped a beat.

"Darling, wonderful Papa, we wanted you to be the first to know. Metin and I are in love. As soon as he graduates and starts medical school, two years from now..."

"Professor Orhan," the lad said, clearly nervous, but in respectful, measured tones, "I'm most honored to meet you."

Allah, why did it have to happen so soon?

"Metin," Orhan said, not unkindly. "How old are you?"

"Nineteen, sir."

"My Halide is just a child."

"Seventeen, Papa."

Yujel glanced at her sharply, then melted. He'd never seen her so radiant. The girl was, dare he think it, beautiful. He felt a lump in his throat. Was it jealousy? Envy that time had passed him by? Or the very real thought that although she would always be his little girl, she was not *his* little girl any more. How on earth had he overlooked the obvious during the past several months? Praise Allah, how, in the whirlwind that was Paris, had she found an Ottoman?

"Metin," Yujel said, "You must forgive an old man." He winced at the thought of being just that. "Would you care to tell me how this all came about?"

"Of course, Professor. Halide and I met last spring during chemistry class. We worked together in study groups. I marveled at how Halide kept pressing on, even though chemistry did not come naturally to her. We finished in first and second place respectively in the class."

"Not bad for a couple of Turks," Halide interjected, smiling and squeezing the young man's hand.

"I invited Halide to dinner to celebrate our grades," Metin continued. "We talked about many things. Then we started going to the theater, museums. One thing led to another. It felt so much like being back home just talking with her."

"What would your parents say about this? Aren't marriages still arranged in the Empire?"

"That's true in the villages, Professor Orhan. But unlike most of Turkish families, where women are treated as little more than chattels, whose only talents lie in working the land and bearing sons so men can boast of their manhood, mine has always been liberal. We've had roots in Istanbul for a hundred years. Father's a surgeon and a professor at the *müderrise*. Mama's one of the very few women practicing as an *avukat* in the courts. I believe they'd want my happiness more than anything else, just as Halide's your greatest happiness. I've no doubt when they meet Halide, they'll share my love for her."

"Do you have brothers, sisters?"

"Yes, Sir. I'm the eldest of three. I have a younger brother fifteen and a sister twelve."

Yujel was pleased by Metin's answer. In the Turkey he'd known, girls and women were deemed so inferior that when a man was asked how many children he had, he would number only his sons.

"What are you studying, Metin?"

"I want to follow in my father's footsteps, Sir. My teachers at the French *lycée* in Istanbul suggested I test for admission to the Sorbonne. If my present grades continue, I hope to be admitted to medical school."

"Do you intend to practice with your father?"

"No, Professor Orhan. After I complete medical school, I plan to return to Turkey and set up public health clinics around the country. Ninety-eight out of every hundred people who live east of the capital exist much as they have for the past thousand years."

"What about Halide? She's known nothing but an upper middle class Parisian existence. Anatolia's a far cry from Istanbul, let alone Paris. Even though she's heard me speak Ottoman Turkish at home, I doubt either of you would fit comfortably into an Anatolian village."

The boy looked thoughtful for a few moments. Then he said, "I see what you mean, Professor. Neither Halide nor I have discussed how we're going to go about doing what we want to do. But surely, Effendi, there must be a way to help our countrymen."

"What about your military service, Metin?"

"I can only hope Turkey will stay out of Europe's latest conflict. The motherland has already shed too much blood. It's time for other nations to deal with their own problems, without our participation."

"Unfortunately, Metin, there are war clouds on the horizon. I don't think Turkey can help but become embroiled in the conflict. We can only hope she'll choose her allies wisely."

"With whom should the Turks align themselves, Papa?" Halide asked.

"The Argentines." The remark, made only half jokingly, broke the tension.

"If Turkey enters the war," the young man said, "I'll no doubt be called to duty, perhaps near Istanbul."

"*Inshallah*, Metin," Orhan said.

Metin left shortly after dinner. Yujel spoke seriously with his daughter. "I believe you've chosen wisely. Promise me only that you won't forget the old fellow back in Paris."

"Oh, Papa," Halide said, hugging him tightly, "that could never happen in a hundred years, a thousand years. Besides, it'll still be a very long time before we marry. What one wishes and what one can do aren't always the same. I'll still be under your roof so long you may well wish to get rid of me at last."

"That," Orhan said gravely, "will never happen during my lifetime."

Turkey stumbled into the war. By accident. On the wrong side.

The Turks ordered two ships from Britain. England canceled the deliveries when war broke out. The Germans, who had two warships trapped in Istanbul at the time, turned the situation to their advantage and gave the Turks the two ships. The Turkish government renamed the ships *Yavuz Sultan Selim* and *Midilli*, gave the Germans command of the vessels, fezzes and Turkish uniforms, and 'enlisted' them in the Turkish navy. The German admiral in charge took his two 'Turkish' ships into the Black Sea, bombarded the Russian coast and sank several of the Czar's vessels. The Ottoman chamber of deputies was furious and demanded that Enver Pasha, the most pro-German of the ruling triumvirate, apologize to Russia, Britain, and France. But it was too late, and Enver's "apology" claimed Russia had provoked the attack. Within days, the "sick man of Europe" was formally at war with Russia, France and Britain.

Late in the afternoon of November 17, 1914, Professor Orhan paced the room anxiously, then walked over to the living room window. He looked down and saw the last of the leaves blown by a cold gust of wind. The leaden sky promised an early winter this year. He shivered and turned the radiator up to its highest setting.

He heard Metin and Halide coming up the stairs. They were laughing. He was in no mood for gaiety. He was an "enemy alien." It would be difficult for him to retain his responsible position in Paris this winter. He greeted the young people warmly. They went into the kitchen to prepare the evening meal and he returned to his notes.

During dinner, the mood was tense. "What do you think will happen, Professor?" Metin asked.

"I hope you'll be able to sit out the war in Paris. I read in the papers that the Ottoman chamber of deputies passed a military conscription order. Let's hope they ignore those young people who've gone overseas to study."

"But what if they call me back?"

Halide looked at her young man with alarm. "Don't say such things, Metin," she said quickly. "You're going to be a doctor. Surely they need surgeons more than soldiers."

"You seem to forget, Halide," her father remarked, "that Metin's still two years away from medical school. There'll be a shortage of officers. Unquestionably, Metin would be commissioned."

"Papa! I'll not hear of such things!" she said, suddenly pale.

Metin glanced at Professor Orhan questioningly. "You don't think they'll really recall me?"

"One never knows. Let's pray Turkey can somehow extricate itself, before it's too late."

The war did not end quickly. The Ottomans marshaled eight hundred thousand troops. Within a few months, Turkey was fighting a war on not one, but four fronts. Enver Pasha mounted a catastrophic winter offensive against the Russians in the Caucasus. As 1914 gave way to 1915, the Russians inflicted staggering losses and drove the Turks all the way back to Lake Van.

Parisians escaped the ongoing war by forced gaiety. They went to the cinema and after the motion pictures, the students went to night clubs where they were entranced by the wonderful new American import, jazz.

The Orhans' worst fears soon came to pass. Metin was called back to Istanbul and entered military training. He wrote Halide every day, without fail. Because Professor Orhan had an influential friend in Geneva to act as go-between, their letters to one another arrived within a month of being posted. On January 17, Halide received the first of Metin's numerous letters. It was dated December 22 of the previous year:

Darling Halide:

I'm sorry to be so late in writing you. I think of you always. I got back to Istanbul on the fifteenth and was allowed two days with my family before I had to report to the military academy.

I told my parents all about us. They're anxious to meet you, but now would not be the time to visit. The city's in a state of near panic. There are all kinds of rumors in the streets. Only yesterday, Vatan *reported that British and French forces were steaming up the Dardanelles to lay siege to the capital and that the Russians were about to attack from the north. Fortunately, the "news" was false. Each day, hundreds of people take ferries over to the Anatolian side. Very few passengers return to the European side.*

Cousin Rauf, who works in the interior ministry, came over for dinner the night after I arrived. He says the government has two special trains on the Anatolian side of the Bosphorous, ready to depart on an hour's notice. One is for the Sultan, the other for the legislators. Supposedly the government has already shipped the archives and the treasury's gold to Eskishehir.

Another rumor making the rounds is that the police have stored oil cans all over town, ready to set fire to the city should the enemy break through. They say plans have been made to dynamite Aya Sophia and some of the other important buildings. I'm told that when the American ambassador protested, Talat Pasha, one of the ruling triumvirate, said there weren't half a dozen deputies who cared anything for the old; they looked forward, not back. If there's any truth to that tale, Allah help us all!

Food is in short supply. The prices are very high. Fortunately, father's practice continues to be very busy; there'll always be a need for doctors.

Papa used his influence to get me assigned to officer candidate school. I'll take a four week course, after which I'll be commissioned and assigned to duty. Career officers graduate from the Ottoman Military Academy, but there's such a shortage that anyone with a year of college behind him ends up a sub-lieutenant. I start next week. If all goes well, I'll get my commission in mid-February.

I miss you so much, darling. I wish you were here right now so we could hold one another, or even just talk. Give my love to your papa. I kiss your heart.

Your loving Metin

On February 13, the day of his graduation from officer's school, Metin sent a long, news-filled letter to Professor Orhan, which Yujel promptly read to his daughter:

Dear Papa Orhan:

Your future son-in-law, Sub-lieutenant Metin Ermenek, sends fondest greetings. You'd hardly recognize the fellow who left Paris a scant two months ago. I'm lean and trim, as you can see from the accompanying photograph, and you'll notice I've grown a most stylish moustache.

"Oh, Papa, let me see." Halide interrupted. She sighed as she looked at the photo, caressing it for a full minute. "How handsome he looks!" she said proudly.

"Hush!" Professor Orhan replied. "Let me go on, child." He continued.

*It's still hard to know truth from fiction in this city. Paris is a city **at** war. Istanbul is a city **in** war. You'd be surprised how many people are hoping the English and French hurry and capture the city. At least then Turkey will be out of the war.*

I was so worried about where I'd be posted. As you probably read in the papers, Enver's expedition in the Caucasus was a complete disaster. Most of our class has been assigned to Anatolia to try and stop the Czar's forces. I was really afraid I'd be sent there.

Again, Father intervened. I'm to be posted close to Istanbul. I might even be able to return home to visit occasionally. I'm assigned to the 57th Regiment, 19th Division of the Third Army. My classmates who're headed east are envious. Two weeks from now I arrive at what will undoubtedly be one of the easiest assignments possible, Gelibolu. Please send my fondest love to Halide and, of course, my respects and love to you as well.

Yours, Metin

"Papa, isn't that wonderful? Thank God he won't be going to the horrible eastern steppes and fighting Russians!"

"I suppose we can rest a little easier, child, to the extent anyone can feel less nervous about a nearby war. At least he'll be close to Istanbul."

"Where exactly is Gelibolu, Papa?" Halide asked. "I don't know much when it comes to small Turkish towns."

"It's not a town, my dear," the Professor said, reaching toward the bookcase for an atlas. He leafed through the volume, finally coming to a map of the Ottoman lands. If we start at Istanbul and move south," – his finger pointed to the map – "we go from the Bosphorous to the Sea of Marmara. From there, you follow that Sea south and west. You come to another narrow strait, the Dardanelles. That waterway is surrounded by two narrow land masses. We call the peninsula 'Gelibolu.'"

"Papa," Halide said. "What do you mean 'we' call the place Gelibolu?"

"I spoke as an Ottoman. Turks call a place one thing, Western Europeans always change the name to suit their language. Hundreds of years later they still insist on calling our capital Constantinople.

Edirne is Adrianople to them, although Hadrian, for whom the place was named, hasn't ruled there for more than fifteen hundred years."

"And Gelibolu?" she asked.

"Oh, the English and the French have a different name for that, too. They call it '*Gallipoli*.'"

5

When Turhan first arrived in Istanbul at the beginning of 1913, the Agha Nikrat's eldest son, Mattyo, an elegant man of thirty, met the boat as it docked at Galata Harbor. He immediately informed Turhan of the Agha's situation. "It's all part of the Internal Security Police's blackmail scheme. As long as Father paid them 'protection' he was left alone. First, it was five percent. We could live with that. After all, if it didn't go into one government pocket it would go into another. Governments exist to line the pockets of those in power. But as time went on, the monster's appetite got bigger and bigger. The Security Police wanted ten percent, then twenty. Eighteen months ago the Chief of Sultanahmet section came to Father's home in broad daylight and demanded a third of all receipts.

"That was more than Father could take. He met privately with the Interior Minister. Shortly afterward, the man who'd approached Father was send to Hakkarı, near the Iraqi border, and it was business as usual once again.

"The Interior Minister died a year ago. We harbored no illusions that the Security Police wouldn't try to seek revenge. We were quite surprised that they never even approached Father. But in guarding our outer flank, we ignored the devil that dwelt within. The police hire informers, people who are paid to infiltrate a household and quietly hide illegal caches of goods where the police are certain to find them. In our case, the plant was a boy about your age, who served Father for a month before the police broke into the house. The police confiscated whatever they could find, the house, a few boats, money. They prevailed on the Minister of Justice to bring the case to court. Father's being held in pretrial confinement because the Security Police fear his escape. The Public Prosecutor has asked the court to sentence the Agha to fifteen years."

"What about the informer?"

"He left our employ a week before the police invaded our home. We've never seen him since."

Mattyo insisted that Turhan stay with him in his comfortable home in the heart of Pera. Turhan enrolled in a local *lycée*, where he mastered English and German. He read everything he could get his hands on. He honed his writing skills to such a degree that when he submitted an anonymous article to *Vatan,* one of Istanbul's major newspapers, it was actually printed.

He also received education in how the world really works. Early on, he'd learned that what passed for justice in the Ottoman Empire was a charade propelled by power and greed. He was not ignorant of how the Agha's family had acquired its wealth. He knew enough not to intrude when a small cadre of men met with Mattyo behind closed doors at the Pera residence several evenings each week. Large amounts of money changed hands during these meetings. From time to time he caught snatches of German, English and what he recognized as French.

Just before the Agha's final court hearing, Mattyo invited Turhan to visit his benefactor. "Are you sure that's permissible?" Turhan asked.

"Wouldn't it be an affront to his dignity for me to see him in such a humbled state?"

"I think not, Turhan. You'll find the Agha a great and very wise man, regardless of how he's chosen to run his life. I doubt he'd feel embarrassed to meet you. Besides, my mother, my brothers and I have spoken highly of you."

The "prison" was a huge, well-appointed apartment. The Agha was attended by his private secretary and a chef who cooked all his meals. During the hours Turhan spent with the man, they were interrupted half a dozen times by well-dressed men who sought the Agha's advice and counsel. The Agha, a man in his late fifties, of some girth but only moderate height, wore a silk caftan and slippers and seemed in good humor from the moment Turhan arrived until it was time to leave. He was utterly charming. Turhan could not help but like him. The Agha spoke candidly about his world view, and answered Turhan's questions directly.

"My associates and I make no apology for what we do. If it wasn't us, it would be someone else, perhaps more greedy, and there would be chaos. At least we maintain order throughout our strongholds. There is always honor among us."

"But Nikrat, Agha Effendi, don't you worry about addiction to drugs or theft by the people with whom you deal?"

"Not at all. We exercise very strict controls. We may deal in hashish, opium or arms on behalf of others, but my associates are wise enough never to dirty their own hands by direct contact with such contraband. If they steal, they'd better not be caught. If they're even suspected of using illicit drugs, they quickly disappear, never to be heard from again."

"But Agha Effendi, something obviously happened to destroy the order you speak about."

"One can't always control what happens from the outside, my young friend."

"I've heard the Public Prosecutor is asking for fifteen years at hard labor. Surely, Sire, you must be worried."

The man smiled conspiratorially. "I don't say I'm not concerned, Turhan. But powerful men always play their games on a grander scale than most. One never knows what will happen. I have confidence that justice will be served."

Within two months of the visit, the Agha was found innocent of all charges. The judge ruled that there had been insufficient evidence to convict Nikrat. Although the money that had been seized was not restored to him, the family moved back into the Agha's palatial mansion far up the Bosphorous and Turhan moved in with them. He heard later that the judge had moved to an elegant new residence less than a mile from the Agha's home.

During the next year, Turhan resided with the Agha's family. He was treated as a favored younger son and introduced to many of the Agha's business associates from outside the country. The Agha waxed richer than before. Certain industries are affected most favorably during wartime. No one heard from the Security Police. But the Agha had made enemies within that force. Powerful enemies who thirsted for revenge.

In January of 1915, shortly before the beginning of Turhan's nineteenth year, the Agha Nikrat invited the German Ambassador to his home for dinner. Three hours before the dignitary was expected, the Agha asked Turhan to go down into a special hidden wine cellar to retrieve some pre-war vintage French wines for the diplomat.

Turhan had scarcely shut the basement door when he heard a loud crash above him, followed by screams and the sound of gunfire. For the next hour he remained absolutely still, listening in fear as the crunch of several loud boots and the voices of a number of men as they searched throughout the house. Finally there was silence. When he emerged, it was twilight. He climbed the stairs noiselessly, lest a guard be stationed in the house. When he'd reached the top landing, he remained still for five minutes, listening for any sign of life. There was none. Still cautious, he entered the kitchen. No sound. "Agha Effendi?" he called quietly. Nothing.

He pushed the kitchen door open and walked into the living room. "Agha…?" He stopped in his tracks and retched uncontrollably. Everywhere he looked there were bloody remains of what had been bodies scattered throughout the room. The Agha's wife and four younger sons were recognizable. Mattyo's head and that of his father had been blown off by shots from large caliber weapons.

Turhan forced himself to remain still, calm. He edged his way toward a small window near the front entryway of the house. Peering through it, he saw two Security Police guards stationed twenty feet away from where he stood, just outside the house. Silently, he made his way back down the basement stairs. The Agha had shown him the location of the secret tunnel some time before. An hour later, Turhan emerged two blocks from the residence.

He was certain the Security Police had seen him in the Agha's company. For all he knew, descriptions of him were now circulating within every precinct in the city. Fortunately, it was dark. There were not many people on the streets. He made his way to a nearby dock and caught one of several ferries bound across the strait to Üsküdar on the Asiatic side of the Bosphorous.

The next day, he enlisted in the medical corps. After a week of training, Turhan was posted to a place close to the capital. Gelibolu.

6

February 23, 1915   *Maidos*

My Darling:

There's an air of unreality here. Everyone seems to be waiting for everyone else to make the first move. After the British navy attacked the southern tip of the peninsula, the German General, von Sanders, came down from Istanbul to command a separate army to defend the Dardanelles. Our Division, under Colonel Mustafa Kemal, has been assigned to that Fifth Army. We're headquartered at Maidos.

No one knows where or when the British and French navies will attack. I've been supervising the stringing of barbed wire along the beach. The 'intelligence' thinks that will stop the assault. How idiotic! The English navy is out there shelling the shore. It won't take long for their ground troops to cut right through the wire.

Mustafa Kemal believes we've got to keep control of the high ridges if the attack comes. He and von Sanders disagree on where the Allies will land. The German general thinks they'll come ashore at Troy on the Asiatic side and Bulair on the European shore. Kemal says it'll be at Cape Helles on the southern tip of the peninsula and Gaba Tepe on the west coast.

196

I hear from my family frequently. Everyone is well. They appreciated the photographs you sent and thank you for your last letter. Allah, how I long to be with you! I can only console myself that our time will come, sooner than we think.

Father wrote that he's very tired. He said that with so many doctors in the field, everyone with a medical degree is seeing patients. He thinks most of the 'illnesses' are hysterical reactions to what's going on in the capital. Istanbul's residents are convinced that the British and French will break through by summer, and then Turkey will be out of the war.

Mama says maybe I should have gone east after all. No, thank you. I hear strange, disquieting rumors about the relocation of Armenians. It's all very secret. No one ever talks about it, but there have been stories of atrocities. The news is very confused. At least here I'm relatively safe and quite close to home. And the "enemy" are the civilized British and French.

The professional officers who've known Mustafa Kemal before say they'd rather be lieutenants under him than colonels under any general they could name. I'm told he's quite the ladies' man when he's not at war.

Who knows where all this will lead? So many young men thrown into war just so the politicians can justify their strutting and the industrialists can become wealthy. What a waste!

Well, Angel, I seem to be raging at the world. Mostly from boredom I'm sure. Let's both pray that by this time next year I'll be back in Paris, or that Istanbul will be safer and you'll be closer to me. Give my fondest to Papa. I love you, darling.

Ever your Metin.

In Paris, an early spring thaw and unseasonably warm, bright sunlight, caused the trees to sprout new leaves almost overnight. Flowers blanketed the areas adjacent to paths. Mothers and nannies pushed large-wheeled prams on tar-covered walkways, noisily berating older children and ordering them to play elsewhere, lest they awaken the babies.

Halide was miserable. "Papa, it's been two weeks since I've heard from Metin. Could there be something wrong with the postal service?"

"Possibly, child," her father replied. "Perhaps it's because of the action in the Dardanelles. Communications seem to have been cut off."

"Something's desperately wrong. Perhaps he decided we weren't right for each other."

"I rather doubt that, darling. I think he's caught up in a bout of mankind's most vicious disease. War."

Another week went by. Still no word from Metin. Halide was in a state of panic. She could not keep her mind on her studies. She cut classes and cried at odd times, often for no apparent reason. It was worse when she read stories in *Le Monde* about the Allied landings on both sides of the Dardanelles. If one could believe the French press, the annihilation of the Turkish forces was not more than a few days away. Papa purchased a week-old copy of *Vatan*, a Turkish newspaper. Since Papa had insisted from the time she was seven that she learn his native tongue, Halide had no trouble reading the Arabic-script Ottoman writing. Her eye immediately seized on a small item that read.

PERSONAL REPORT FROM THE FRONT.
OTTOMAN FORCES RETAIN KEY RIDGE IN BLOODY BATTLE!

"April 25. 1915. Soon after dawn, English, Australian and New Zealander troops landed just north of Gaba Tepe. French soldiers landed on the Asiatic Coast. Colonel Mustafa Kemal told us earlier he believed the Sari Bair ridge was critical to our defense of the Dardanelles, that if the enemy captured that high place they would dominate the peninsula.

"*This morning, he led that advance up the ridge to its summit. Our medical unit followed immediately behind. When we came to the top of the hill, we ran into a company of Turkish soldiers. They said they'd been the only force opposing the enemy for the past three hours. They were completely out of ammunition.*

"*The enemy was two-thirds of the way up the hill, three hundred feet below us at most, and the troops were firing. Colonel Kemal ordered the company to fix their bayonets and lie down on the ground in place. They did. Incredible as it may seem, when the enemy saw our troops cease their retreat, their forces lay down as well. For thirty minutes everyone held their fire. That half hour decided the fate of the battle.*

"*Kemal sent an officer down to bring the regiment up the hill on a dead run. When they arrived at the crest, I heard an order which will stay with me as long as I live.*

"*'I don't order you to attack. I order you to DIE! In the time it takes us to die, other troops and commanders can come and take our places! In the time it takes us to die, this hill will be saved. If this hill is saved, the capital will be saved. And if the capital is saved, the nation will be saved. If any of you turns and runs, I order that man be shot as a deserter. And should I do anything but LEAD you in this battle, I direct you to shoot me as well!'*

"*By the end of the afternoon, almost the whole of the 57th Regiment had died, faced continuously with a curtain of enemy rifle fire. Only two of my friends, Corporal Firat and Sub-Lieutenant Metin Ermenek survived.*"

Halide turned white. She re-read the part about her fiancé over and over. Finally, she forced herself to continue reading.

"*They are good fellows, both of them, typical of what Mustafa spoke of as the 'new breed' of Turk. Firat's a country fellow from Angora, eighteen, who graduated lycée just before he was inducted into the Army. Lieutenant*

Ermenek studied at the university in Paris. The enemy soldiers are no different from us. They, too, have wives, mothers, and sweethearts.

"The battle continued all afternoon. Mustafa Kemal rode away for a little while. When he returned, he brought reinforcements. During this day, I carried at least two hundred men to our field infirmary, less than a hundred yards from the battle lines. When the sun set, the Allies had been driven back to the lower ground they'd occupied early that morning. We'd kept them off the Sari Bair!"

That night, Halide made up her mind what she must do.

7

Halide was already dressed when Papa came down to breakfast the following morning. Yujel found the table set with the finest service they had. There was orange juice, a pitcher of coffee, and several warm, crisp croissants, which Halide had purchased that morning. He inclined his head toward her suspiciously. "What's all this about, daughter?"

"Papa, I'm going to Istanbul."

"*What*???"

"I'm going to Metin."

"Are you insane, girl? This is the middle of war. You're barely eighteen years old. Thousands are trying to get *out* of Turkey!"

"I'm not crazy, Papa. I must be near my man."

"In the middle of a battlefield? You talk like a fool. Halide, I forbid this rash act."

"Papa! Would you truly hurt me like that? In all my life, have I ever disobeyed you or done anything to shame you?"

"No, but..."

"Papa, please understand. I *must* go to him. I can't think of anything else! I've got to find out if he's safe, if he's even alive!"

201

"There are channels, Halide."

"Damn the 'channels!'" she said, slamming her orange juice glass on the table. "It could be weeks before I hear anything. By then I could be in Turkey."

"But, Halide, you're a child."

"I'm not a child, Papa. I've finished two years at the Sorbonne with honors, though God knows how I managed to study these last two months. The world won't need another teacher so quickly. And Metin means more than my life to me."

Yujel saw his daughter was determined to make the journey. He softened. There was no way he could ever deny her what she asked.

"Mind, I'm not agreeing to this folly. I suppose you've planned exactly how you're going to do this?"

For the first time in over a month, Halide smiled. Her eyes took on a lively twinkle that had been missing. She rose from her chair and hugged him affectionately. "As a matter of fact, Papa, I made no plans at all. A girl relies on her father to take care of such details."

Yujel buried his face in his hands for a few moments. When he looked up, his eyes were shiny with unshed tears. "Halide," he said. "A child is only lent to you for a very short time. You try to bring that child up to be the best human being possible. And you try, Allah, how you try to hold back the clock, make that child stay small a little longer. All too soon, the time comes to let the bird fly free.

"I'll help you get to Istanbul. What's so very hard for me to accept is that you might not return. Each child brings his or her own blessing to the world. May yours be special, my darling. Fly to the arms of your love with my deepest blessing."

Two nights later, over a simple meal of onion soup and sourdough bread, Yujel said, "This is wartime, Halide. The French consider you a hostile alien, even though you've lived here all your life. With their penchant for petty bureaucracy, they'll check everything out most carefully before they let you leave their sacred soil. Once you've left, don't expect to return for the duration of the war."

"I know, Papa. Once I get out of France, how do I get into Turkey? Won't the Ottomans suspect me as well, since I was born and raised in France?"

""Halide, you recall how smoothly you've been able to correspond with Metin during these difficult times?"

"Yes, you told me you've a friend in Geneva."

"Karl Feldkirche was a student of mine some years ago. Today he's Deputy Minister of Transport. He and I have stayed in touch over the years. We both saw the war coming. It was Feldkirche who suggested since no one knew who would end up on which side, one could always benefit by possessing a passport from the only European country everyone knew would not participate."

"What you're telling me, you sly fox," – she grinned – "is that..."

"*Fraülein* Halide Orhan, born 1897, the ward of Doktor Karl Feldkirche of Geneva, Switzerland, was issued a passport from the Swiss Confederation in March, 1914. The passport was forwarded to me in Paris for 'safekeeping.' I'll take you as far as the frontier. Geneva's a short boat ride from there. Karl's agreed to meet us on this side of the border. After that, we must leave the planning to him and to your escort."

"My escort, Papa?"

"I could not allow you to make such a journey unaccompanied, Halide. Despite the tragedy of war, we're truly fortunate. Feldkirche told me a junior brigadier general, Omer Akdemir, is in Geneva, involved in peace negotiations, and he'd be honored to escort you to Istanbul."

"Will you be all right, Papa?"

"Only when I know you're safe. I wish I could make the trip with you, but Doktor Feldkirche says that's impossible. Don't forget to write."

"Papa, I'll do more than write. I'll return."

"*Inshallah*, may it be during my lifetime."

"The war can't go on forever."

"But neither can life, my angel."

"Papa, years ago I told you I'd follow in your footsteps as an educator. I've not yet graduated. I have unfinished business here. I'll be back. You'll be proud of me, Papa. Don't you dare get ill or die! You say you're brave? So am I, Papa. We two must be there to help one another. And we will be!"

8

"I've never seen anything so breathtaking!" the girl gasped. They'd arrived near the border at Chamonix the night before. Professor Orhan had insisted they be up by sunrise. Halide, who'd never traveled more than fifty kilometers from Paris, awoke in an alpine town four thousand feet higher than the French capital. Though it was early June, the air was nippy. Yujel made certain his daughter wore her warmest coat, muffler, and gloves before they left their pension.

As she emerged into clear air and bright sunshine, Halide was awed by her first view of the ice-covered glaciers of the Mont Blanc massif, nearly sixteen thousand feet high. Bright green meadows ascended to darker forest green and ultimately to rocks and the eternal whiteness of the craggy summits. The girl hugged her father tightly. "Oh, Papa, Papa! Thank you so much for everything."

"I felt the nicest send-off for my only daughter would be a sight she'd remember until she returned to me."

They walked through the center of town until they reached Le Brevent funicular station, then boarded a tram, which took them up five thousand feet to the crest of Mont Blanc's smaller sister. What had been an enthralling view from the valley floor below was overwhelming.

205

As they alighted, they were met by a short, sprightly man of fifty, with thinning hair, rimless spectacles, and a slight paunch, wearing a smile almost as wide as his face. "*Grüss Gott, Bienvenue, Hosh Geldiniz,* my dear professor," the man said effusively, kissing Yujel on both cheeks. He bowed to the girl and continued, "This must be Halide. Welcome my child. I apologize for ignoring you, my dear, but I'm so delighted to see your father. Yujel, Mademoiselle, may I present General Omer Akdemir." He nodded in the direction of a tall, distinguished- looking man of forty-five, with neatly clipped moustaches and iron gray hair. The man nodded politely, then stepped back as the two old comrades jovially embraced again.

"How long has it been, Karl?"

"Twenty-four years, Yujel. June of 1891 to be precise."

"I wish you wouldn't have reminded me. That means I was a young man of forty-four."

"Ja, und I was a sprout of twenty-six. Your Halide is as old as I was when I first met you."

Despite the length of time since they'd seen one another, they slipped into conversation as easily as if they'd been together the night before. Years dropped from Papa's face. As the two men talked, Halide gazed in rapture at fifty peaks, each of which stood out in grand, snow-capped seclusion. Her reverie was interrupted by the general, who spoke for the first time, his deep, commanding voice, resonant with mildly accented French. "Excuse me, Miss Orhan, but it must bore you to hear old comrades reliving memories that took place before you were born."

"Not at all, General. I don't know when I've ever seen my father look so happy."

"I am indeed pleased to meet you," the general continued smoothly. "I'm overwhelmed that one so young has the courage and determination to go to our motherland when the rest of the world is fleeing from it." The man seemed very kind. Dignified. Strong, yet gentle, a younger version of her father. Halide felt protected in his presence.

"Would you care to take coffee with me? I'm afraid your father and Doktor Feldkirche will be in their own world for hours."

"It would be my pleasure, General," she smiled.

There was a small coffee house nearby. As they entered, Akdemir said, "This is the way to see the massif! All the comforts of home."

"Have you a home during this war, General?"

"As much as any soldier can. I was stationed on the Armenian border when war broke out. Last November the High Command ordered me back to Istanbul and promoted me to Brigadier. I was assigned as junior attaché to the Turkish General Staff. My wife and three of our four children accompanied me back to the capital. The last few months have been very – costly – for both sides. At the beginning of May, the General Staff requested I accompany Minister Eshref to Geneva. I'm afraid the talks have not gone well."

"What a shame, General."

"Indeed it is. The blood of all those young men." He stopped, and looked stiffly ahead.

"Is something the matter, General?"

"No. Yes, it is, damn it! Please pardon me, Miss Orhan. I've not been able to speak openly before, but meeting you, seeing your courage, makes me want to talk. My eldest son, Seljuk, was nineteen." He stopped, coughed roughly, pulled out a handkerchief and blew his nose.

"I'm so sorry," Halide said softly. "Where?"

"On the eastern front. Enver Pasha sent an ill-armed, suicidal mission into Russian Armenia. The aftermath was appalling beyond belief."

Neither Brigadier Akdemir, nor, for that matter, the world ever fully understood the enormity of what he referred to as "the aftermath." In November, 1914, Russian forces crossed the Turkish frontier, supported by Armenian nationalists who for years had borne the brunt of the sultan's repressive tactics. As the shattered Ottoman army retreated toward Lake Van, the government in Istanbul ordered the entire Armenian population be evacuated from Eastern Turkey and moved from all areas where they might undermine Ottoman campaigns.

The army was specifically directed to resettle the Armenians in Mosul province, to protect the Armenians against attack, and to provide them with sufficient food and supplies during the march. No one in Istanbul ever accepted responsibility for the holocaust that ensued. Turks and Kurds, their years of frustration heightened by agonizing defeats, turned the evacuation into a massacre. They descended on Armenian villages and slaughtered refugees along the road. How this occurred remained shrouded in mystery. The exact numbers were never known. The Turkish government claimed no more than three hundred thousand perished, through a series of "unexplained, illegal misfortunes in which the government played no part." The Armenians, shocked beyond anything in their history, insisted that more than two million of their countrymen were savagely annihilated by a genocide unparalleled in history.

The end result was that a large proportion of a population which the Ottoman Empire had considered a thorn in its side for hundreds of years, disappeared off the face of the earth. The western allies condemned both the atrocity and the Turkish government under whose authority it had happened. Fear and loathing of the "barbarian Turks" created a furor throughout Europe that was to have disastrous repercussions.

Under those circumstances, even one death would have been too many.

9

Although Halide was impressed by Geneva's spectacular mountain backdrop, and especially by the *Jet d'eau*, the 145-meter high water fountain in the midst of Lake Geneva, she was anxious to leave for Turkey.

"The Eastern Mediterranean's quiet. Most naval activity is centered in the Atlantic," General Akdemir said. "With the Battle for Gallipoli bottling up the Dardanelles, no one can get in or out. Trieste is a free port. We'll take the express train to Trieste, board a steamer to Smyrna, which we Turks call Izmir, then traverse the Turkish coast as far as the Sea of Marmara. From there, we'll take the ferry to Istanbul."

"When do you propose to leave?" Feldkirche asked.

"Today's June fifth. Two days from now."

In contrast to Geneva, Trieste was a filthy, open, sailor's town. Its buildings were grimy with the accumulated grease of centuries. The port smelled of fish, mildew, cordite, and stale beer. Its oily waters and tired, broken topography added to the sleaziness of the place. Ships flew their own national flags, disregarding the old rule of the sea that required them to fly the port's ensign. Trieste's ties with its nominal ruler, Austria-Hungary, were virtually nonexistent. Brigadier Akdemir and his charge walked as swiftly as possible through the crumbling streets. Halide kept her pride and stared grimly ahead as numerous hands touched the hump on her back, a peasant omen of good luck. Akdemir took pains to block the rude interlopers.

After dinner the brigadier, strikingly handsome in civilian clothes, suggested Halide might like to stroll on the quay. "It gets rugged as the night wears on, but you'll be safe enough if we go early. You'll be somewhat shocked at the low life you'll see. I'll understand if you'd rather not go."

"General, I felt stifled by the antiseptic starchiness of Switzerland. I grew up in one of the 'better' arondissements of Paris. Every girl needs to feel daring once in a while. As long as I have you to protect me, I'd *love* to go. And since I'm going to be in the Ottoman Empire for some time, would you mind very much if we spoke Turkish? I don't want my native nationality to be too obvious when I get there."

"*Chok güzel,* Halide Hanım," Akdemir replied, switching smoothly to his native tongue. "Your wish is my command."

As they descended toward the docks, the city became progressively seamier. Halide, who'd been warned what to expect, occasionally giggled. "General Akdemir," she said as they ambled down a side street. "There must have been at least twenty ladies near that hotel. They had everything but 'For Rent' signs hanging from their bosoms."

"Ummm, yes," the officer replied briskly, clearly embarrassed. "Not the type of woman one wants to associate with." He moved quickly to a larger street.

Soon they came to the harbor. The streets were lined with bars, tattoo parlors, shops filled with cheap, tasteless trinkets, sailors' hotels. By day these streets looked tawdry and run down, the buildings grimy and dark. At night, the district came alive with thousands of lights and the din of raucous music, off-key singing, and drunken violence.

Heavy trucks rumbled along the streets, delivering whatever could be sold at a profit to waiting cargo ships. At one point, Halide remarked, "General, it seems there are an inordinate number of trucks going by with huge crates marked 'water tanks.' Do they need so much water in wartime?"

"Our intelligence sources tell us those so-called 'tanks' are a secret new weapon the British have invented for desert warfare. We haven't actually seen any of them yet."

"Do I hear Turkish?" a man's voice spoke up behind them.

Halide turned and saw a man of thirty-five, considerably shorter than General Akdemir, who had a luxuriant, bushy moustache and clear, brown eyes. He wore a nondescript coat and fisherman's hat, and held hands with a plump, smiling dark-haired woman.

"I am Erdoğan Balıkjioğlu. This is my wife, Demet."

"Good evening. I'm Omer Akdemir and this young lady is Halide Orhan."

"I'm honored, General, Halide Hanım. May I invite you to be my guests for coffee?"

"It would be our pleasure, Balıkjioğlu Effendi," Halide said. "Where do you suggest?"

"Why don't we stroll along Front Street and pick the least disreputable looking place?"

As they walked, it became apparent this would be no easy task. Each bar competed with the last, with ever noisier, more obscene promises of delights. After a mile, they reached a quieter section of town. The view from the café's window was worth the walk. From this distance, the boisterous saloons cast bright, flickering lights over the oily water. The sound was just far enough away to be both exciting and harmless.

"What are you doing in Trieste, Erdoğan Effendi?" Akdemir asked.

"Demet and I live in Izmir. We operate a small fleet of five fishing vessels. The boats' engines break down and ultimately wear out. The war boosted the price I can get for my catch, but it's impossible to keep machinery running forever. I've nursed two of the older motors along well beyond their useful lives. Trieste is one of the few European ports not under wartime blockade. *Mashallah*, I've been able to purchase serviceable engines at a good price. I'm taking them back to Turkey."

"Isn't it unusual to take one's wife abroad in wartime?"

"Not for me, Effendi. Demet's a shrewder negotiator than I. I see you're also traveling with a female companion, much younger than mine. How old are you, Hanım?"

"Eighteen, Sir."

"What are you doing in Trieste?"

"General Akdemir was with a military mission in Switzerland and kindly agreed to take me to Istanbul. My fiancé's at Gallipoli."

"Ahh," the man clicked his tongue in a tsk-tsk sound. "That's a dangerous place. Each time I read a paper, there's news of more killings. *Inshallah*, your man is safe and well. I'm impressed that you're traveling in the company of a pasha."

"Not quite, Erdoğan Effendi," Akdemir said, "although I thank you for the compliment. I'm only a brigadier. I need at least one more star on my epaulets to be called a pasha."

"You'll be traveling to Izmir by ship?"

"Yes. My superiors want me to return by sea, via an Ottoman vessel."

"That can only be the *Mustafa Fazil Pasha*. *Inshallah*, it will make it as far as Izmir. At least we'll have the pleasure of one another's company on board."

"Bad?" the general asked.

"Let's walk along the quay. You can see for yourself."

They left the café and walked half the distance back to the bars. A square, sooty steamship of indeterminate age sat under a series of lights. "The *Mustafa Fazil Pasha*," Balikjioğlu remarked. "Pride of the Ottoman merchant fleet. A thirty-five year old rust bucket, one of the early steamers. Ordinarily we'd have taken a modern Austrian Lloyd ship plying the same route, but it's wartime and our government insists we travel under the Ottoman flag."

"I've never been on any ship before. It will all be new to me," Halide remarked.

General Akdemir winked at Halide and said, "*Inshallah* we'll get there."

Next morning, they boarded the Ottoman vessel. Captain Rahmit, having been apprised that a brigadier general was to travel on his ship, was especially solicitous toward Akdemir and his companions. He assigned them the most luxurious accommodations on board, but even those rooms were musty and smelled of oil and mildew.

The ship stayed close to the shoreline. They were always in sight of the mountainous lands of Slovenia, Croatia, Montenegro, and Albania as the ship steamed down the eastern Adriatic. "Everything you see was once part of the Ottoman Empire," Akdemir told Halide. "Now, there are so many petty kingdoms one never knows who's at war with whom."

They entered the narrow strait of Corfu, passed through a series of gulfs and inland passages, and headed across the Aegean toward their destination. "I wish we had time to stop at a Greek island," Akdemir sighed. "You'd see buildings so bright they nearly blind you. They're whitewashed to reflect the heat of the sun. Once, many years ago, before Greece tore itself away from the Empire, my wife and I visited these islands. Each one's a paradise, a pearl in the midst of a wine dark sea. Warm, lovely, boardwalks along the sea. Fresh fish and shepherd's salad. Friendly people and entrancing music. Now it looks like we'll be at war with our Greek brothers."

There was a sudden high pitched squeal, followed by a loud clanking noise. After a few moments, there was a loud *WHUM-UMP!* from below. Then silence. The ship slowed to a crawl.

General Akdemir excused himself, rose, and headed toward the captain's deck. He returned a few minutes later, his face reflecting unhappiness. "My friends," he said, "it seems the *Mustafa Fazil Pasha* has cracked a piston, destroying one main cylinder and severely damaging another. The ship will have to put in at the nearest port. The captain radioed the Greek government to allow us to land at Samos. Unfortunately, repairs may take the better part of three weeks. We could be on Samos for a month clearing customs."

"No!" Halide turned pale. "I've got to get to Metin, now!"

"I'm sorry, Halide," Akdemir replied. "There's nothing anyone can do. The *Mustafa Fazil Pasha* was ancient when they sent it out. They couldn't spare another vessel because of the war effort."

The girl excused herself and ran down the deck toward her stateroom.

"Ah," Balıkjioğlu said. "I understand the poor child's feelings. It won't help when we have to deal with Greek customs. There's no love lost between government officials of our two nations. Even though the Turkish coast is only a few miles away, the Greeks will hold any Ottoman vessel as a war trophy from the time we drop anchor in the harbor."

"Would it help if Halide holds a Swiss passport?"

"Not likely. She's a foreigner. Even if the Greeks let some of us go, the Turks wouldn't let a Greek vessel from Samos land at a Turkish harbor."

"Can't anything be done?"

"I didn't say that," replied Balıkjioğlu, a mischievous twinkle in his eye. "How well do you get on with the captain?"

"What do you mean?"

"At the rate this tub is traveling, we won't reach Samos until late tonight. If there's one thing the Greeks like, it's a good party. No one from Samos will be anxious to offload this ship until tomorrow afternoon. This ship has several large lifeboats, which are of no use to us, but I saw one of those new tubular life rafts on the upper deck. It's light enough for us to manage and could hold us all. Perhaps you might persuade your captain that the military would be quite appreciative if one of their high-ranking officers were not detained in a Greek port."

The captain was sympathetic to Akdemir's request. "Of course, General, you may use our ship's radio to contact your headquarters in Izmir, but I'm responsible for the lives of every passenger aboard this ship. How could I explain the loss of a life raft?"

"Captain," Akdemir said quietly, "I am going to ask to you to excuse yourself for a very few minutes, because the message I send is classified as a military secret, and you would not want to disclose to our Greek hosts that you are party to such information. When you return, I'll take leave of your quarters. You'll find five hundred lira, more than enough money to purchase three life rafts, in the cabinet above your bed. I regret if some desperate person, fearing Greek reprisals for an imagined crime, caused the raft to disappear during the night, before we officially made port in Samos. You will, of course, provide me with detailed instructions on how to lower the boat?"

"Of course, General," the captain said, smiling broadly. He rubbed his hands together. "If the Turkish military needs a sacrifice from me for the war effort, who am I to protest? But these are expensive rafts. Seven hundred fifty."

"Not a penny over six, you scoundrel."

"*Mashallah.*"

Late that night, General Akdemir knocked on Halide's door. She opened it slowly, her eyes red from crying. She was shaking.

"Come," he said. "You can cry later. We've no time for that now. Pack only what you absolutely need, no more than will fill a small satchel." They met the Balıkjioğlus near the raft.

"Is there room for everything?" Erdoğan asked.

"Absolutely. You're sure you know these waters?"

"Perfectly, General. It's less than fifteen miles across the strait."

"We can't count on Demet or the girl to row. We're in trouble unless the tides are just right."

"Not to worry, General. We brought three engines with us from Trieste. One of them, much smaller than the others, was designed for emergencies."

"You fishermen are a shrewd lot. How exact can you be about where we'll land?"

"Why?"

"Surely you don't intend to walk to Izmir from Dilek. My aide will need to know where and when."

"Ah!" Balıkjioğlu returned the general's compliment. "You soldiers are a clever lot."

They lowered the raft into the Strait of Samos. The two men rowed in silence until they'd cleared the harbor area. When Samos' dim lights disappeared off the port side of the raft, Balıkjioğlu started the small outboard motor. He kept the engine running at a whisper as they headed slowly east. They could just make out one or two lights in the distance. The Turkish coast. It would be a three hour trip if all went well.

Halide dozed in the bow of the small raft. She awoke to the sight of a searchlight combing the waves. "Cut the motor," Akdemir whispered. "This far in, it must be Ottomans."

They heard the roar of a powerful engine approaching. They were a stationary target, with no hope of outrunning the other vessel. An amplified voice, speaking Turkish, peremptorily commanded, "State your name, destination and intentions."

"Turkish fishermen out of Dilek."

"Impossible! We've just come from Dilek. No one reports a small boat having left there in several hours. State your name, please."

"Akdemir."

They heard a shuffling in the larger boat. The spotlight shone directly on the general. "It's him, all right! *Hosh geldiniz*, General! It's about time, sir!"

"Lieutenant Tellat?"

"Evet, Effendi! Follow us, sir, the car is waiting."

"*Chok, chok teshekkür ederim,* my friend. Thank you so much! That's my aide-de-camp," the general explained to the others. They followed the coast guard boat into a small gulf and arrived just as the sun was coming over the horizon. The landfall was extraordinary. Kuşadası, Bird Island, was connected by causeway to the mainland, dominated by the ruin of a large, rock fortress.

"Five hundred years ago, this was home to the Barbarossa brothers, the most feared pirates that ever sailed the Mediterranean," Akdemir said. "They were Greek converts to Islam who pillaged the coasts of

Spain and Italy, attacked the ships of all Christian nations, and sold passengers and crews into slavery in Algiers. The French Emperor, Charles the Fifth, personally led an expedition against Tunis in 1530. He liberated thousands of Christian slaves and killed one of the brothers. Unluckily for the Christians, the remaining brother was appointed Grand Admiral by Sultan Süleyman the Lawgiver. The surviving Barbarossa was so effective that within ten years the Mediterranean was an Ottoman lake."

When they made port, Tellat, a swarthy young man of twenty-five, turned to his superior. "General, I know you were planning to land at Izmir and take the train back to Istanbul, but headquarters received a new car from Germany. I suggested there'd be no better way to test it than to retrieve you. Besides, I know how you love mechanical things. I think you're going to enjoy this one."

He led them to a flattened area, a hundred yards away from the landing. There, gleaming in the morning sun, was an elegant black Mercedes saloon, the only automobile in sight. Akdemir let out an involuntary whistle of appreciation at the impressive machine and ran his hand gently over the hood.

"Mr. Balıkjioğlu," Tellat said, formally. "Thank you for bringing our general back to the motherland. The coast guard radioed that they offloaded the engines you left on board the *Mustafa Fazil Pasha*. They'll be shipped direct to Izmir by army transport and will probably arrive before we do. We'll start north tomorrow morning."

Halide was uncharacteristically silent during the drive along the miles of white beach shoreline. She seemed tense, but there was no undue alarm when she failed to appear for dinner. The company assumed she'd fallen asleep in her room. They decided to let her rest until morning.

10

"Halide, time to get up!"

"Go away." The voice inside the door was muffled, harsh.

"I beg your pardon?"

"I said go away. Leave me be."

"Halide? Do you know who I am?"

"Yes, I do, General Akdemir. Now please leave me alone and go away."

With an effort, Akdemir curbed his impatience. This was totally unlike the cheerful young woman. "Are you all right?"

"No, General, I'm not all right. I'm not all right at all. Now will you please go away and leave me alone."

"Halide, there are three other people waiting to get started for Izmir. They would like to leave within the hour, since we'll be driving most of the day."

"Then let them go, General. I just want to be left alone. I don't want to talk to anyone. I want to go home." He heard barely concealed sobbing.

"Please, Halide," he said, gently. "May I come in for a little while?"

After several seconds, he heard shuffling toward the door. The latch opened. Halide's face was tear-splotched, her eyes swollen. When she saw him, Halide burst into a new round of sobs. The general stood quietly until the crying subsided.

"Would you like to talk?"

The girl sat on her unmade bed, clasping and unclasping her hands. General Akdemir pulled up a chair and sat next to her. After a while, she started speaking, haltingly at first. Then the words came out in a torrent.

"All my life, I've been brilliant, ugly Halide Orhan. That poor little thing with the humpback. 'What a shame, poor dear. If only she wasn't misshapen.' Do you think I haven't heard the hushed whispers when I walk by? Do you think I'm such an idiot I don't feel when they touch my hump? That I don't look in the mirror and say, 'Why can't I look like any other normal girl?'

"Once, just once in my life, I'd like somebody to look at me and say, 'She's rather ordinary but not unattractive.' Finally, a man falls in love with me. A good man. A man who wants me for *me*. Then he's hauled off to war in a country I'm supposed to care about because he was born there and because my father's Turkish. Like a fool, I follow him to this Godforsaken place.

"Well, I'm sick of it all! I'm sick of being everybody's good little girl! I don't know why I came here in the first place. If I weren't a lady, I'd use words I've heard that would shock you, General! I'm angry. I'm tired. I've had diarrhea the whole night. I'm filthy because there's no bidet here. I don't know how I'm supposed keep myself clean. To top it all off, my monthly curse arrived last night. I want to go home! I don't want to be here at all, I want to be with my Papa!"

She started crying again, sobs wracking her small body. The general stood up, covered her with a blanket, and sat with her until she fell into exhausted sleep. He left the room, silently closing the door.

He told Lieutenant Tellat and the Balıkjioğlus that Mlle. Orhan was feeling ill, but this should not delay their return to Izmir. "Lieutenant," he said to his subordinate. "Please arrange transportation to Izmir for the Balıkjioğlus. I'm sure by tomorrow Halide will feel better. Perhaps we should visit *Meryemana*. Under the circumstances, I'm certain our high command won't begrudge me the extra day."

"Of course, General." Lieutenant Tellat saluted and was gone in an instant.

Next morning, Halide was still withdrawn, but she'd slept and eaten a little of the rice and broth Akdemir had brought her the night before. After breakfast, Tellat brought the Mercedes around to the front of the hotel. They headed inland, through hillsides lush with grapes and tobacco. An hour later, they turned onto a narrow, gravel road and climbed into the hills.

When they came to a wooded area, Tellat shut off the motor and they got out of the car. With the exception of wind whistling gently through the cedars and the flutter of an occasional bird, there was almost total silence. The general beckoned Halide to follow him. They entered a clearing, where she saw a small brick-and-stone structure of surpassing simplicity. The view of the Aegean and Samos in the distance was breathtaking. Outside the courtyard, Halide heard the soft sounds of running water. Something stirred within her. She walked inside the tiny chapel. It was no larger than her bedroom back in Paris. There were two large candles at the entryway and two more in a small alcove at the feet of a black marble statue of the Virgin Mary.

As she looked around, Halide saw several crutches, pieces of clothing and a few framed, yellowing letters written in different languages. She closed her eyes and felt warm inside. A soft breeze caressed the back of her neck. She felt the tension within her dissolve.

Halide had no idea how long she remained in the chapel, nor could she later recall exactly what happened there. Time didn't matter in such a place. When she opened her eyes and looked at the Blessed Virgin, she wondered if she were imagining things. The Virgin seemed to be smiling at her.

At length, she walked outside and found a small fountain in the courtyard. Its water was channeled toward a pool some yards away. Halide dipped her hand into the water, brought it to her lips, and kissed her fingers. She dipped into the water again, and touched her eyelids. A third time, she placed her fingers in the water and touched her heart. She whispered, "Thank You."

She turned and walked back down the path, to where she knew the general and his aide would be waiting. She was at peace. No matter what happened, everything would be all right.

They continued north through the green, hilly countryside. Halide, lulled by the uniformity of the landscape and the throaty purr of the Mercedes, fell into deep slumber in the back seat of the car. When she awoke, some hours later, she smiled and said, "I'm sorry. I really am. I've acted like a spoiled little brat the last two days, but I really am so appreciative of everything you've done."

"No matter," he said. "I'm sure what you said had been waiting to come out for several years."

"All the poison seemed to drain out back there."

"*Meryemana*? I've been told unexplained things happen there."

"What do you mean?"

"After the prophet Jesus was crucified, his mother, Mary, came to Ephesus. It's not hard to believe she'd stay in this area. Ephesus had a quarter of a million people back then. It was the third largest city in the Roman empire. About a hundred years ago, a German nun, Catherine Emmerich, had a vision that Mary's last home was here. When archaeologists and Roman Catholic scholars explored her claim, they found the ruins and foundations of a place that conformed to what Sister Catherine had seen in her dream. It's been a holy place for centuries, something akin to your shrine of Lourdes. The crutches and letters of thanks in the chapel aren't meant to impress tourists. They represent the gratitude of people who've been healed there."

"I know. It *is* a healing place," she said quietly.

11

Halide's first sight of Izmir was of green hills surrounding a perfect, crescent-shaped bay. Palm trees lined Birinji Kordon, the main street which ran along the waterfront. Immediately behind the city rose Mount Pagos. *Kadife Kale*, an imposing, white fortress from ancient times, crowned its summit. Izmir's harbor was as busy as Trieste's, but the land was much softer. Halide saw crates marked "Tobacco," "Figs," "Apricots" and "Silk," their destinations stenciled neatly on the sides.

Unknown to General Akdemir, Halide had formulated a plan that would have stunned her chaperon. It had come to her while she was at *Meryemana*. At first, it had seemed so implausible as to be absurd, but the more she thought about it, the more she realized it could be done. The Balıkjioğlus had shown themselves to be compassionate. It just might work.

The following morning, General Akdemir looked apologetic as he greeted his charge at breakfast. "Halide, I'm afraid you'll have to spend your first day in Izmir without me. I must attend a military briefing at division headquarters. Lieutenant Tellat will be at your disposal. He knows some of the most interesting areas in Izmir."

"That's all right, General," Halide remarked, with a dramatic sigh. "Much as I long for your company, I'll try to survive the day without you. Perhaps Lieutenant Tellat might drive me to visit the Balıkjioğlus."

"What a wonderful idea!" he said, obviously relieved.

The plan was starting out much better than she'd anticipated.

Erdoğan Balıkjioğlu had been very modest indeed about his "small" fishing fleet. Two of his five boats, the *Yolju* and the *Chabuk,* were large, modern vessels that dwarfed the nearby wooden caiques. When Halide and Lieutenant Tellat arrived, he was installing the new engines. He invited them both to come to his home for the noon meal. Halide accepted immediately. Tellat apologized, explaining he'd promised to retrieve General Akdemir.

"I understand, Lieutenant. Why don't you and General Akdemir join us for an early supper later this afternoon?"

"I see no reason why not. In any event, allow me to drive you to your home, Mr. Balıkjioğlu, so I'll know where it is when I return."

During lunch, Halide quickly explained to her friends exactly why she'd sought them out. "You're really serious?" Erdoğan asked, amazed.

"I am, but I need your help. Father gave me five hundred francs. I'd be pleased to pay you for your trouble."

"I won't hear of any such thing!" Demet said sharply. "When it comes to young lovers, money is never important, right Erdoğan?"

"Yes, my love." He grinned sheepishly.

"Now," Demet continued, delighting in the plan and becoming part of it. "My cousin Yetkil has a farm near Dikili."

By the time the general and his aide arrived, the plan was in place.

Three hours north of Izmir, the road again met the sea at Chandarla Bay. Halide asked, "Could we stop here for lunch? It's so lovely."

"I know just the place," Akdemir said. "A small fishing village, Aliağa, not far away. The freshest fish you'll ever taste." The entourage caused quite a stir when they drove into town. Villagers had never seen an automobile like the Mercedes. Everyone from the *muhtar* down to the poorest peasant came round to stare in rapt amazement. With a warmth and hospitality Halide had never experienced in France, villagers insisted that she, Akdemir, and Tellat accompany them to a white stucco garden restaurant, trimmed with dark green vines, which overlooked the sea. They were served *meze* – tidbits of every imaginable variety, grape leaves, eggplant, spinach, stuffed with a mixture of rice, currants, and pine kernels – and thin, doughy pastries stuffed with white cheese, ground meat, chopped fish, or rice.

A fisherman carried two small red fish, still thrashing gamely, toward the restaurant. Halide nudged her escort to get his attention. "*Barbünya,* mullet," he said. "Wait 'til you see how it's served."

Several minutes later, an attentive waiter brought a fresh, steaming, hot loaf of bread. A sharp, crackling sound caught Halide's attention. Three more men approached their table, each bearing a large, hot ceramic tile, with a generous serving of flaky, white fish sizzling on top.

"Your mullet, Mademoiselle," Akdemir said, and smiled. "Freshly baked alongside the bread, and served on the same tiles that were in the oven."

After they enjoyed the last of their dessert, Halide said, "General Akdemir, thanks to you, I've traveled a thousand miles without so much as a broken fingernail. Might I strain our friendship by asking one more small favor?"

"Anything you want."

"Would it be very wicked of me if I asked to stay in a small village like this one, overnight? I'd like to get to know the real Turkey."

"I don't see why not. There are fine lodgings at Chandarla, just up the road. We can start for Balıkesir in the morning. Whether we spend the night on the Aegean or inland makes little difference. Let's finish our tea and have a leisurely stroll through Aliağa."

The waiter, who'd listened to this exchange, recognized Halide from the description circulated by Yetkil, Demet Balıkjioğlu's cousin. By the time Akdemir, Halide, and Tellat arrived at their destination that evening, Yetkil's old hay wagon was halfway between Dikili and Chandarla.

"Halide, get up! We must be off if we're to make Balıkesir by nightfall." The general's tone became ever more exasperated. Children had been so much more predictable when he was growing up. He pounded on the door with increasing force. "Halide!" he called again. No response. Now he was worried. He asked the innkeeper to open Halide's door.

"But, General, when a young lady wants to sleep in, she mustn't be disturbed."

"I've been banging on her door for fifteen minutes."

"Very well. Follow me." The hosteler shrugged his shoulders and went down the hall with his master key.

"Halide!" General Akdemir called another time. Nothing. He nodded to the innkeeper. The two walked into the room and stared in amazement. The bedclothes had not been turned back. The room was empty. Not a stitch of clothing. No indication anyone had even been in the room.

"General, there's a letter by the nightstand. I can't read but perhaps you might."

Dear General Akdemir:

How can I ever thank you for all you've done for me? Whatever I could say would never be enough. I thank you so much for being there in my hour of greatest need.

When you read this, you may feel I've betrayed your trust. I sincerely hope not, because I will consider you my friend as long as I live. When I started my journey I had no idea where I'd end up. I intended to go to Istanbul to meet Metin's parents, to be so much nearer to him than Paris. That's why your coming into my life was such a miracle.

*I don't mean to repay your kindness by deceit. It's just that it's no longer enough for me to be **near** Metin. I must be **with** him. You see, General, I fear he may not survive Gelibolu – so many young men have not – and if I didn't see him, I'd never forgive myself. Call me a silly woman if you will. It's not that I have any premonition of his death. It's just a realistic appraisal of what could happen at the battlefront.*

When I left France, I had no such plan. The idea came to me at Meryemana, and I thought, "Why not? What have I got to lose?" And so, my dear, dear General Omer Akdemir, I'm asking you the greatest favor of all. Pray for me. Pray that I make it safely to Gelibolu. Pray that I'll be able to see my Metin.

You may be angry and frustrated with me when you finish reading this letter. I know you believe I'll never make it to Gelibolu. But when one wants something as badly as I do, anything is possible. Your wife is one of the luckiest women in the world. Inshallah I will meet her and your children some day. Be of good health and courage my friend.

With fondest love, Halide

When Akdemir finished reading the letter, he whispered, "May Allah protect you, my child." Then he called his lieutenant and showed him the letter.

"Shall we comb the countryside, General?"

"To what avail, Tellat? You know village Turks."

"What should I do?"

"Make arrangements at the highest level to protect the girl if she's spotted. No one is to interfere with her passage. Find some way I can get a telephone connection to the front. Get me Mustafa Kemal. One more thing."

"Yes, General."

I want to speak with Erdoğan Balıkjioğlu down in Izmir. I have a hunch he's involved in this up to his bushy eyebrows! Lieutenant, we are going to make sure that little snippet gets to Gelibolu in one piece!"

12

At the moment General Akdemir was reading her letter, Halide was having serious second thoughts about the wisdom of her enterprise. She was buried in hay. The wooden wheels of the clumsy cart squealed and complained at every turn. There wasn't a part of her that wasn't sore. It had all started so easily. Within ten minutes of checking in to the small hotel in Chandarla, a young man had helped carry her bags to her room. Once inside the room, he'd turned to her and said, "One hour after the sun goes down tonight, Yetkil will be here."

She could hardly contain her excitement at dinner, but had managed polite conversation. Neither General Akdemir nor Lieutenant Tellat objected to her turning in early. Less than five minutes after she'd completed her letter to General Akdemir, there'd been a knock on her door.

If anyone had told her to choose someone who fulfilled her idea of what a Turkish peasant would look like, it would have been Yetkil. The man was as short as she, with a large barrel chest. The coat he was wearing was much too tight for him. What tufts of gray and white hair she could see under his peasant cap stood out from his head in all directions. Under bushy eyebrows and a bushier moustache, he had a most engaging smile. "My sister, Demet, says you wanted a ride to Dikili, yes?"

"Yes, Mister...?"

"Yetkil. Take your bags and follow me."

Now it was nine hours later. She felt a sharp jolt as the cart finally came to a halt. "Time to get out!" Yetkil called, cheerily.

A very dirty girl smelling of hay and dried manure, her hair matted with straw, her eyes bleary from lack of sleep, shook herself and emerged from the cart, just in time to look into the laughing faces of ten women of various ages. The largest of the women stepped forward. "Hello. My name is Fetiha. I am Yetkil's wife. My sister-in-law says I'm to get you ready by tonight. First we'll get you a good bath and breakfast. Then we'll deal with the problem."

For the second time in as many days, Halide was struck by the warmth of Turkish villagers, moved by their willingness to help a stranger. After breakfast, Halide found herself at the center of a social gathering of a dozen women. Fetiha studiously measured Halide for clothes. "We must make a new outfit for you. The little lump in your back is not a bad thing, but we must disguise it for travel. Our *muhtar* – the village headman – can get new shoes for you, but we must measure your feet."

After the noon meal, the women gathered together again. "Try this outfit on," Fetiha said.

As one of the women held it out, Halide stared dumbfounded. It was a sloppy, outrageously large Turkish army uniform, the kind she'd seen enlisted men wearing in Izmir, heavily padded in numerous places. "Surely you don't expect me to wear that?"

"You're not going to a village dance. You're going to the battlefield at Gelibolu. How welcome do you think you'd be if you suddenly appeared at the height of battle dressed for a party? The general who brought you this far will alert everyone within a hundred miles of Gelibolu that you're trying to get there. How far do you think you'd make it, before you were turned back to Istanbul or arrested as a lunatic?"

"But, Madame!"

"Enough talk. Try it on, please." She did.

"Where are the shoes?" Fetiha asked a wizened older woman, the *muhtar's* wife. The woman handed Halide a large, heavy pair of high-top military shoes. Halide obediently put the brogans on over thick white socks. When she was fully attired, the women almost collapsed in giggles. Even Halide laughed when she looked in the mirror and saw a very short, round soldier, wearing an ill-fitting Turkish military uniform, who looked very much as if "he" wished "he" were someplace else – any place else.

After the women had left, Halide asked Fetiha, "Do you really think it will work?"

"Why not? Just keep your mouth shut 'til you get to Gelibolu. Most Turks can't read anyway. Hand them this card and look as stupid as you can." She gave Halide a small, white piece of cardboard on which were written the words "Gelibolu" and "Gallipoli," the first in Arabic script, the second in Roman letters.

At midnight, the small quay was deserted. Halide saw lights offshore flash on and off, three times, the prearranged signal. She got into a small rowboat, blew a kiss to Yetkil and Fetiha, and sat quietly during the half hour trip out to the *Chabuk*. Once aboard, her reunion with Erdoğan was emotional and heartfelt. She knew he was risking his life and his fortune. What could she possibly say to such a man?

The following morning, he brought Halide hot tea, warm rolls, rose petal jam, feta cheese and olives. After she finished, he showed her about the boat. "The vessel was built to house eight men in comfort. On this journey, we've only got three plus you. We're carrying extra fuel tanks. We'll need them. By tonight we'll be north of Samothraki. Thereafter, we'll stay outside Turkish waters 'til the last part of the trip. I doubt we'll be disturbed by anyone while we're in Greek waters."

Balıkjioğlu took Halide to the upper deck, where he kept his current charts. "Up here," he said, moving his finger north, "is the entrance to the Dardanelles. On the east is Chanakkale, ancient Troy. The Gelibolu peninsula guards the straits. The entire area is under siege. The British have blockaded the west coast from Cape Helles to Bulair. We'll make landfall at Enez, just this side of the Greek frontier, for refueling. Then, we'll make our way as far east as safety permits. We'll drop you off somewhere along this coast, under cover of night, and you'll be on your own. Turkish army convoys continually travel from the Greek border to Gelibolu. Keep your mouth shut and point to the card Fetiha gave you. Sooner or later you'll get to the front."

As they headed east along the Turkish coastline, Erdoğan cut the engines to one quarter speed. The vessel could not be heard from a distance of a hundred yards.

Halide had hardly fallen asleep when the night exploded in light. She heard the shrill blast of two horns, followed by a megaphone-amplified voice. "*Chabuk,* this is Turkish Coast Guard ship *Giresun.* What are you doing in these waters?"

Balıkjioğlu, stifled a smile, picked up his own megaphone and answered, "*Giresun,* this is *Chabuk* out of Izmir, fishing vessel, most recently out of Enez for minor repairs."

"You received no approval to enter these waters. Permission to board and check for contraband?"

"Allah!" Balıkjioğlu swore in a voice loud enough for Halide to hear, as she came up the stairs from her sleeping quarters. "What can we do? The ship is armed. It could blast us out of the water in seconds. I should have let you off when we had the chance at the border. Forgive me, Halide." He spoke into the megaphone. "Permission granted, *Giresun*."

Within moments, the gunboat pulled aside the *Chabuk* and secured lines. A stern-looking Turkish officer came aboard and saluted Balıkjioğlu. "Captain Hassan, *Giresun*. Permission to inspect?"

"Of course," Erdoğan said, resignedly.

"A small crew for being so far from home," he remarked.

Captain Hassan continued his cursory inspection of the *Chabuk*. "Please have all crew stand to attention, Captain Balıkjioğlu."

Hassan's eyes narrowed as he looked at Halide. "Well, well, well. A Turkish soldier among you? He seems to fit the description we were given at headquarters. A spy or a deserter from the front, perhaps?"

"No, Captain Hassan," answered Balıkjioğlu quickly.

"We'll have to see. Identity papers, son," he said, addressing Halide.

She fumbled in the pockets of the uniform and brought out the piece of cardboard. "Gelibolu," Hassan read. "Are you supposed to be there?" Halide nodded.

"Captain Balıkjioğlu, I don't know what this is all about. I'm going to take this young fellow with me until we can straighten it out." He took Halide by the arm and led her onto the *Giresun*. "You're free to go, Captain, but I'd be careful if I were you. You're a long way from home to be out at night." Halide did not see the wink and smile the two men exchanged.

By morning, the *Giresun* made port at the northeast corner of the Gulf of Saros. A stocky major approached Captain Hassan. "We've got an unexpected visitor from Turkish General Staff, a brigadier no less, who's taken over the commandant's office. I've been ordered to bring in anyone within a five mile radius of Kadiköy fortress."

"Looking for spies or deserters, no doubt," Hassan said. "All I've got to offer is this runt I picked up off that fishing boat last night. He can't even speak. When I ask him anything, all he does is take out some card that has 'Gelibolu' printed on it. Useless village idiot if you ask me."

"Maybe so, Hassan, but orders are orders."

"You can have him, so far as I'm concerned."

The major escorted Halide to the commandant's office at Kadiköy, the nearest Turkish outpost, some two miles inland. When he knocked on the door, Halide heard a muffled voice. "Come in, Major." As they entered, all Halide could see was the back of the commandant's chair. The visitor's back was to them. He was looking out the window toward the distant sea.

"General," the major said, "You said if we found anyone who matched the description you gave us, we were to bring him in for questioning. *Giresun* picked this one up on a fishing boat last night. On your orders, I've brought him here now."

"Very good, Major. You're dismissed." The major saluted the back of the chair, did an about-face, and left the room, closing the door behind him. The dignitary turned and faced Halide.

"Wouldn't you say he's done very well indeed, private?"

Halide stared, speechless, as she found herself looking straight into smiling eyes of Brigadier General Omer Akdemir.

13

"You can't stop me, General. I'll get to him somehow."

"Relax, young lady," he replied, chuckling. "You did a remarkable job getting this far. Far be it from me to frustrate a love that's gone to this extreme."

"How did you...?"

"Find out about your adventure?"

"No. I know you read the letter. I figured you'd eventually get in touch with Erdoğan. I'm curious how you got here so fast?"

"Tellat knows the territory very well. When you're a general, it takes no great effort to commandeer a fast boat. The run from Karabiga to Sharköy only took three hours."

"What if I'd have landed elsewhere?"

"I alerted all the border checkpoints. We knew you'd have to come in from the sea. The Dardanelles and the Gelibolu peninsula are hemmed in by our enemies. You had only a thirty mile area in which to land. And Erdoğan was entirely cooperative."

"You mean he knew?"

"Let's say he wasn't as surprised as he may have let on."

"What happens now?"

"You made it almost as far as your destination. You wanted to see Sub-Lieutenant Metin Ermenek, did you not? Major," he called out the door, "this is not the spy I thought. Call the transport pool and arrange to have him taken promptly to Sari Bair, 57th Regiment."

That afternoon, Halide arrived at Colonel Mustafa Kemal's headquarters. There had been a two week lull in the battle. The commander nodded to the new arrival and said, "Sit in the next office until someone comes to process you in." As soon as the new soldier left his office, Kemal was on the line to Kadiköy. "She made it safely, Omer. We'll take care of it from here."

"Mustafa, despite what anyone says, you're an old romantic at heart."

"Don't push things, General," Kemal growled into the phone. "You wouldn't want anyone to think I've gone soft."

Ten minutes later, Mustafa Kemal summoned Sub-lieutenant Ermenek into his office. "Lieutenant," the colonel said, without preamble. "I can't spare you from the front during this battle, but I must meet with Von Sanders this evening. Sit watch at headquarters tonight. I doubt it'll be necessary for you to stay awake. I don't anticipate any action. There's a new recruit from the village waiting in the building. Counsel him on what life's like at Gelibolu and place him in an appropriate regiment."

"But Sir, isn't that a bit unusual? We've got sergeants and corporals to handle that kind of work."

"Lieutenant," the colonel said sharply. "Every Turkish soldier carries the blood of our nation into this battle. Every day on this Allah-forsaken battlefield could be his last. This recruit, like any other, is entitled to the dignity of knowing that he's a worthy man, that his officers care for him enough to acknowledge his existence. Every so often, you single one out for special treatment. Spend half an hour or so thanking him and telling him how much our motherland appreciates his sacrifice. You'd be surprised how fast word gets around among the troops and how much it raises morale. So please do me a favor with this one, all right?"

"Yes, Sir. I'm sorry I raised the question, Colonel." Ermenek saluted smartly, turned, and left the office. Mustafa Kemal had a hard time suppressing his laughter.

Sub-lieutenant Ermenek returned to headquarters with mixed feelings that evening. On the one hand, he looked forward to a real shower, an acceptably soft bed, and some time away from the dusty, deadly battlefield. On the other hand, speaking to these naïve, wide-eyed innocents from the steppes of Anatolia was never easy. They were usually poorly trained, illiterate bumpkins, with little comprehension of why they'd been sent so far from home. Ah, well, he thought. At least I'll finally have a chance to write Halide. It had been so long. In the heat of battle, he simply hadn't had the chance. What if she'd given up on him? It would serve him right. It had been two months since he'd written. He reached into his breast pocket and extracted her most recent letter. Halide expressed how much she loved him, how much she missed him, how she would wait forever.

Ermenek spent the first few minutes giving the recruit the basic lecture about how he was preserving the right of all Ottomans to live in peace, how his government had never asked to start this war, and how he might expect hard work and little glory. The recruit said nothing, but nodded from time to time. Metin could not fathom whether the soldier understood half of what he was saying. Something about the way the youngster looked at him unnerved the sub-lieutenant. The shape and color of the eyes, perhaps? He thought back to Halide's eyes. This was one of the smallest soldiers he'd ever seen. Almost as tiny as Halide. *Grab hold of yourself, Ermenek. You're cracking up. Keep your mind on your duty. This is a battlefield. People die if they lose their concentration.*

"And so, Private, that's really all I have to tell you," he concluded. "Do you have any questions?"

The soldier looked directly at Metin. The face crinkled into a smile – a *Halide smile.* "Just one. Why haven't you written to me in eight weeks?"

"What did you say?"

"You heard me, Sub-lieutenant Ermenek. Your future bride wants to know why you've ignored her."

"Oh, my God! Halide?" Metin went white, then blushed, then simply stared.

"The same."

"How in the name of heaven did you get here?"

"It's a long, long story. Shall I tell you now, or after we've had a chance to eat something?"

Dinner was simple. Each of them picked at their food. Neither was hungry except for the other. Halide told Metin of her journey from beginning to end. His eyes widened at each revelation. Halide's eyes glowed with the vision of her man.

By the time Halide finished her tale, it was dark. The battle front, five miles away, was silent.

"What happens now?" Metin asked.

"Do you still love me?"

"More than my own life. More than I'll ever be able to prove to you."

They kissed, with infinite tenderness, then with startlingly powerful emotion. When they broke at last, she said, "Darling, this may not be the right time to say such a thing, but how long has it been since you've bathed?"

"I'm sorry," he began, then noticed she was laughing gaily. "Seriously, angel, I'd intended to bathe tonight. This is the only building within twenty miles with a private shower. Would you mind horribly if I did?"

"Only if there's room for both of us. Someone has to scrub your back."

Metin looked shocked. She gazed directly into his eyes and smiled sweetly.

"But we're not married yet," he mumbled, weakly.

"In Allah's eyes and mine, we are. Isn't that enough?"

"You know what might happen?"

"I know exactly what *will* happen, my love. And I'm ready for it."

Her body was soft, milky white. When she emerged from the shower, she stood proudly before him. Her small breasts were beautifully formed. "Be gentle, darling. It's the first time."

"For me, too," he said. His voice sounded choked.

"It's all right, my darling. It'll be fine."

And it was.

14

The following day, Allied forces raced Turkish troops to the peninsula's highest point. The Ottomans beat the English by twenty-five minutes. Kitchener's troops retreated halfway back to the sea. Shortly after sunrise, there was a soft knock at the headquarters building door. Metin, used to responding to the slightest sound, came instantly awake. Gently, he extracted himself from Halide's arms. She moaned once, turned over, and continued sleeping. He opened the door.

"Lieutenant," an orderly said. "Colonel's orders, Sir. Every man is needed at the front immediately."

"Thank you, Corporal."

He looked back at the sleeping figure of the woman who'd risked so much to come to his side and smiled as he thought back to the night before. He would never have imagined her so passionate. It had been so wonderful. For an instant, he daydreamed about their life in the years ahead. It would be so soon, so soon. He dressed quietly, blew her a silent kiss, and left the building.

Outside headquarters, a tall captain in combat gear bellowed orders as a hundred men raggedly assembled. Two sergeants were rounding up the ill-kempt, poorly-clothed recruits into a motley formation, two abreast. "Ermenek!" the captain shouted above the din. "Make sure the men have filled their canteens! We head out in ten minutes. Bring up the rear. No laggards!"

"Yes, Sir!" Metin snapped back, automatically. He ordered the four men nearest him to carry wooden buckets from a trough to the center of the crowd. Men jostled one another for position.

At the captain's signal, Metin and the non-commissioned officers gathered around him. "What's the battle plan, Captain?" Ermenek asked.

"There is no battle plan." The captain shrugged his shoulders helplessly. "The enemy has unleashed an all-out effort to take the ridge. Our orders are to hold it at all costs."

Metin was shocked. "You mean these men are nothing but cannon-fodder?"

"My orders were to put together any company I could find and do it quickly. How many of these boys have seen action?"

"None, Sir," one of the sergeants replied. "We've got one outdated rifle for every three of 'em. What in blazes are we supposed to do?"

"Colonel says we go to the top of the ridge and Allah will provide."

"Which means?"

"We take rifles from the hands of dead men."

Metin felt a tight grabbing in his bowels. Two months ago, he'd survived a major battle. He'd been lucky to come back alive. Allah only gave so much good fortune.

"What do I tell the men, Captain?" the sergeant asked.

"The truth, Sergeant. They'll get weapons once we get to the front. How's the ammunition?"

"Forty, maybe fifty rounds for each weapon."

"Grenades?"

"A couple hundred at most, Captain."

"*Bohk!* Mustafa Kemal's orders are like last time. Once we're out of bullets, we stay there with bayonets and spades. No retreat."

"How do you know these boys won't turn and run when the time comes?"

"If anyone turns and runs we shoot him. If we don't, *we* face a firing squad."

The troops totaled one hundred fifty men. They traveled light. A single canteen of water, hard tack, a spade, which doubled as a truncheon, a hand grenade and, for every third man, a rifle of indeterminate age. They marched in surprisingly orderly fashion to the front lines. Metin heard the whistle of shells coming ever closer. The sky was cloudless. Three hours before the sun reached its zenith, the heat was already blistering.

The path that had been hacked through the canyons below Tekke Tepe, narrowed. The troops now trudged single file. A few scrub trees grew, none capable of providing shade against the brilliant sun. The soldiers were still well below the ridge line. The pounding of artillery reverberated through the narrow valley like kettledrums.

Metin, who trailed the last soldiers, saw only the backs of their heads. Perhaps that was best, since he knew that in most instances he'd be looking into the faces of death.

Just before the final ascent, the captain called a halt. He stood on a ledge, ten feet above his troops and addressed them. "Men, you are here today because it is Allah's will." There was an angry grumbling. They were here because they'd been unable to escape the government's dragnet as it dropped over their villages, and they knew it. The captain waited for the noise to die down, then continued. "We are fighting for the life of our country. Many of you may not return. Those will be among the blessed whom Allah calls to His kingdom. You are fighting an enemy who'd carry off your wives and your sisters, who'd happily make eunuchs or cuckolds of you all, and who'd force you to watch as they performed indignities upon your children. Ours is a holy war. Each of you is a piece of the whole, a thread in the glorious carpet of Islam. The Christians have shown over the centuries what they will do if they conquer. We're not trying to capture their lands. They want to dismember ours. I've told you Allah will provide arms for you who don't have them. When you get to Tekke Tepe ridge, you'll see bodies of your dead comrades, whose souls are in Allah's arms. Their shattered earthly bodies will be handing you weapons with which to preserve the heart of the motherland. Take them. Fight as they would have fought! Fight for Türkiye! *Inshallah*, we will prevail over the heathen!"

Metin could not tell what effect these words had on the soldiers. Their mouths remained closed, their eyes betrayed no emotion. The captain resumed his place at the head of the column. The troops followed him doggedly up the ravine.

Halide was disappointed to awaken alone in the narrow bed. She glanced down at her nude body and smiled. Everything she'd gone through to get here was worth it. Soon this battle would be over and Metin would be hers. They'd have children, of course, and work together to bring a better life to this land.

Gunfire and mortar shells burst nearby, startling her out of her reverie. My God, she thought, there's got to be a way I can help right now. Less than an hour later, Halide, dressed in the same 'army' uniform she'd worn to the front, but without a cap, approached the field infirmary. In answer to the startled look of a captain who was acting as the chief administrator of the place, Halide said simply, "I want to help. Any way I can."

"But you're a woman! This is a battle front."

"Florence Nightingale was a woman, too."

The captain scratched his head, then assigned her to the infirmary.

As they reached the top of the hill, Metin thought for an instant of deserting. But an officer could not turn and run. That would condemn him to death as surely as enemy bullets. There were no trees on the bald ridge. The earth was dry, rocky, hard as concrete. He'd have to dig a trench or use those already in place, sharing a shallow four-by-six foot depression with dead men. Other companies gathered to his right and left. Together, three thousand men slowly, silently approached the top of Tekke Tepe.

Sun glinted off the distant sea. Smoke from artillery fire rose from the ground below. Metin had been here before. Once in place, he was no better than the lowest private, a single human being reduced to a frightened supplicant for another night of life. Below, four huge ships loomed just offshore. Every few moments, there was a bright orange-yellow explosion of light from each, followed by a loud whistle and a thunderous crash. Metin lurched against something hard and momentarily lost his balance.

He looked down and shuddered. The corpse of a Turkish soldier in full uniform lay face up, his lower remains chewed into ground meat by a combination of shell fire and the feet of Ottoman troops who'd simply walked over the body on their way to battle. The soles of the dead man's shoes had large holes, filled in with cardboard. Part of a bloody foot projected from a tear at the bottom of the shoe. The threadbare uniform had probably been requisitioned from an earlier corpse. The pathetic body spoke of poverty. Poverty of luck, poverty of years, poverty of blessings. The dead soldier was nineteen at most. Metin continued forward.

A shell whistled over his head. He dropped to his stomach immediately, clawing the earth for purchase. There was a small slit-trench, fifty feet to his right. He scurried, crab-like, into its protective safety. Moments later, two other soldiers crowded into the small hole with him. The three of them said nothing, but began digging at the rock-hard earth with bare hands, grasping for pebbles, sticks, loose earth, anything they could find to build minuscule mounds in front of them. Metin noticed that depressions all about him were filled with soldiers, living and dead. Each trench had small barricades of the type he'd been erecting, on the side facing the enemy.

A ground squirrel leapt atop the battlement directly in front of him. For a moment, it eyed the three humans, then scampered up the hill and over the far side of the ridge.

"Where are you from, Officer?"

"Istanbul," Metin said automatically, then turned to the man who'd asked the question. "What about you, Private?" Metin was, at most, a year older than the man.

"Hozat."

"Where's that?"

"East. You got a girl, officer?"

"Yes." Metin flushed, thinking of the night before. "You?"

"No, sir. My father said when I get back, there'll be one waiting."

"Shhh!" The third man could have been a twin of the boy from Hozat. "Your talking'll give away our position." All three realized the idiocy of the remark immediately and it cut the tension.

"You been in battle before, Officer?" the third man whispered.

"Yes."

"Is it always like this, Sir?"

"What do you mean?" Metin asked. He noticed a rank odor from the man's direction.

"Sir, when those first bullets whizzed over, I crapped my pants." He started shaking.

"Don't worry about it," Metin replied. "Happens to everyone in battle."

"It ever happened to you, Sir?"

"Most likely will."

A shell screamed over the trench and exploded fifty feet behind them with a loud *WHOOOMP-PPHH.* A second later, a shower of sand and pebbles rained down.

"Oh, Allah, Allah, Allah!" the third man wailed. "I crapped again. Oh, mama, mama, mama! I want to go home."

Metin and the youngster from Hozat tried to calm the man down. "That's all right. It'll be all right. You're still here. You'll be fine."

Another shell crashed twenty feet to their left. Before either of them could stop him, the third man leaped out of the trench and ran to his right.

"Get down!" Metin shouted.

There was the crack of a rifle. Their companion stopped running, spun around and screamed, "My eye! Allah, I've been hit! My eye! My eye! Allah-h-h-h!" He fell to the ground, clutching his head. Metin saw blood running down the man's face, through his fingers. Mad with pain, he was striking his head over and over against the earth.

There was another rifle shot, this time much closer. Metin glanced over to the right and saw that one of the sergeants had shot the fellow dead.

The storm of noise deafened him. The Turks gave as well as they got. Suddenly Metin heard a thunderous boom behind him. He involuntarily looked back. Turkish heavy artillery had been wheeled into place. Death belched from the bowels of Ottoman cannon onto the enemy below. As his eyes returned to battle scene, Metin felt sheer panic. The enemy was moving inch by murderous inch up the hill toward the Ottoman position. Turkish fire intensified. The enemy crumbled like so many trees felled by a woodman's axe. Allied artillery bombarded their positions from left and right. The hills crawled with English, Australians, New Zealanders. Where in Allah's name were they all coming from?

"*Bohk!*" the man beside him cursed. "No more rounds." Metin realized he'd been firing automatically. The barrel of his gun was so hot it burned when he touched it.

"I'm out of ammo, Lieutenant," a voice next to him said. "You got any to spare?" Metin was about to toss some to his trench-mate when he realized he had only six rounds left.

"No, I've got none."

"What'll we do if they attack, Sir? Should I fix my bayonet."

"No," Metin responded, surprised at how calm he sounded. "It'll only stick inside the ribs and get messed up with a lot of other stuff. You'd have to kick the enemy back to pull it out of him. By that time, the next one'll be in the hole. Use your spade. Jab the enemy and keep him at bay. Or crack it down between his neck and his shoulders and try to chop him in two." He stopped, realizing the cruelty of his words. He, Metin Ermenek, a would-be doctor, a man whose destiny was to save lives, not take them. How dare he talk like this?

Then another part of him took over. He had to talk like this and act like this. It was the only way he'd survive this hell. Forget that the enemy were human beings just like him. Ignore that they ate and defecated, that each was someone's son, brother, lover, husband. They'd come to this land, *his* land. If he didn't kill them, they'd kill him.

Suddenly everything was silent. Heavy dust settled over the battlefield. The sun was at its zenith. God, he was thirsty and sleepy. He felt his bladder would explode. He unbuttoned his pants and relieved himself in the trench. Steam rose as liquid hit the ground and evaporated immediately. Strange. It reminded him of the way his breath had come out in little puffs of steam when it was winter in Paris and he and Halide had walked down the *Boul' Miche* together.

After a moment, he looked to his left. The fellow from Hozat was sound asleep, sitting bolt upright, his back against the front of the trench, his useless rifle clutched in his arms. Metin felt a tingling in his right leg. He'd been leaning to the side since the firing stopped and his leg had fallen asleep. He tried wiggling his toes. Jagged bolts of feeling coursed up the leg. He stretched and unstretched it, relieved when the tingling stopped.

"Lunch time," he heard from a hole ten yards away. Good idea, he thought. The meal was hard biscuit and goat cheese, which he washed down with brackish, warm water from his steel canteen. It was the best lunch he could remember.

For the next hour, the battlefield slept. An unspoken truce had been declared. Metin faded in and out of a fitful slumber. He was back in Paris. He was out on the steppe. Sheep danced before his eyes. The sun beat blood-red holes in his lids and it was painful to keep them closed, but more painful to open them and face the dry, cordite-smelling dust.

When the shelling began again, it was not as loud and threatening as it had been earlier in the day. Metin was thankful. He looked down the hill and saw that the enemy had not advanced in the last two hours.

All around him, the field was littered with bodies, from the top of the ridge down the hill to the sea.

A brisk breeze came up. The stench of blood and powder filled him with a strange excitement. God, he'd survived! He'd survived! Praise Allah, he'd live to fight another day and then another and another until this war was over and he'd go home. Home to Halide. Home to happiness.

He was out of ammunition. There was a body less than fifteen feet away holding a gun out to him. Metin waited for the next lull in the fighting. No sense taking a risk in the midst of the rampant fire.

Inexplicably, the sounds of battle stopped all at once. The hill was silent for the hundredth time that day. The beast called war was taking a break before devouring more fine young men. Moving as slowly and quietly as he dared, Metin extracted himself from the trench. He'd just reached the man's hand and placed his own on the gun when the grenade exploded. Metin instinctively tried to jump out of the way. But he had no legs left to do so.

Throughout the day, Halide volunteered for the meanest labor, bringing and removing bedpans, disposing of old bandages, changing dressings, raking hard-packed earth floor made slippery by the blood and other bodily fluids of dying soldiers.

She was attending her hundredth battle casualty of the day when Turhan approached her. "Halide," he said. "Please come here. I need to talk to you."

"In a moment, Turhan," she said, automatically. "As soon as I finish bandaging this corporal."

"Halide!" the voice was sharper. She looked into his eyes. She did not want to see what she saw there, pleaded silently with those eyes that the words wouldn't come. When he opened his mouth he said, "Metin is dying, Halide. I'm so sorry."

"No." she said softly. "It's not true. He won't die. You'll see. I'll save him. I'll give him life."

"Halide! Please don't be a fool. The man is dying. Pull yourself together."

"Turhan, I will stay by my man, no matter what. He will live. Now, please bring him in here so I might care for him."

The field infirmary reeked of carbolic, ether, sweat, urine and excrement. Halide ignored the overpowering smell. She sat holding Metin's hand. "How do you feel now, darling?"

"Not so bad. But I have such incredible pains in my feet."

Halide couldn't bring herself to tell him he'd lost both of his feet. That he'd lost his legs from just above the knees. Metin looked ghastly, yellow, with strain lines in his face. Death was working on him from inside. His eyes were already beginning to show it.

No, he won't die, Halide tried to convince herself. *Twelve hours ago he lay with me, inside me. He'll be whole again. They make prosthetics in Paris. The best in the world. He's going to be all right.*

"You'll feel better soon, my darling. Sleep for a while." She bathed his brow with cool water. Metin closed his eyes.

Halide was shocked when she looked down at his face. His features had become softer, paler. He was moving in and out of her world. "You'll be going home soon, my darling," she said softly. "To Istanbul, to your mama and papa." She held his face gently in her hands, trying to bring it back into her world. Metin's hands had taken on a waxy look. His fingers were so delicate for a man. There were faint burn marks from the heat of the rifle earlier in the day. His nails were so neatly trimmed. He groaned in his sleep.

"Turhan!" she called sharply to the orderly. "Get him a dose of morphine."

The young man who'd been working by her side the entire day returned moments later. "Colonel'd have me court-martialed if he knew. I took this out of the hospital commander's bag."

Halide administered the injection smoothly, surprised at how steady her hand was. She was suspended between her world and Metin's, and she could not let him go.

Some hours later, Metin awoke. The command doctor passed by his bed and nodded. Metin looked at the medical officer. "I've lost my legs, haven't I?"

Halide choked. He stared into her eyes. "It might have been much worse," she said. "You'll still father our sons. You'll be going home soon."

"You think so?"

"Yes, darling."

He hesitated a moment, then signaled her to bend toward him. "I won't be going home, Halide," he said quietly. "I love you so much. But I won't be going home."

"Don't talk like that, Metin. Colonel's sent for a carriage. In three days, four at the most, you'll start to mend. You must eat, my angel, so you can get back your strength."

Metin stared, uncomprehending, at a plate of lamb stew and soft, white bread placed before him. He turned from the food. "I dreamt of bringing a better life to this land."

"And you shall, my darling. They make such splendid artificial limbs in Paris nowadays. They attach them right to your muscles, so you can walk and get around. You'll see. And they'll always make improvements as the years pass."

Metin lay still. His skin was translucent. He turned his head away from her. He slept again. When he awoke, his face was so pale it looked like chalk. Halide sat where she'd been when he'd fallen asleep, gently wiping his brow with a cloth and cool water. Her hand was trembling. She felt choked.

"Halide?" His voice was a soft croak, but to her it felt like a feather caressing her soul. She bent close to him.

"Yes, my darling?"

"Tell papa I died a brave man."

"Don't talk like that," she scolded, but there was no force in her voice. "Your father's the best doctor in the Empire. We'll have you in University Hospital before you know it. You'll be all right."

Metin's face lay in shadow. "No, Halide," he said. He breathed lightly. Tears started to roll down his cheeks. An hour passed. He said nothing. He wept. He looked into her eyes. She saw what she didn't want to see. "I love you, Halide. You were my whole life." Her tears joined his, her soul joined his. She tried, God, how she tried, to hold onto him just a little longer.

Metin's life slipped slowly, quietly away. His eyes remained bound to hers, his heart locked with hers until the last possible instant. And then he was gone.

Turhan, watched as Halide sat silently, her hand holding one that no longer squeezed back. The tears continued to roll down her cheeks. Finally he approached her.

"Come, Halide," he said, as gently as he could. "You must not stay longer. He's no longer with us."

"No, Turhan," she said. "It's not true. *IT'S NOT TRUE!* This is a nightmare, isn't it? Tell me it's not true. *TELL ME IT'S NOT TRUE!*" Halide screamed from deep within her soul, a shrieking, keening wail, extracted from the bowels of hell. The battlefield fell silent as she screamed over and over, giving voice to the lament of every woman who ever lost a man to the cancer of war. For fully ten minutes, her agonized shrieking continued until her throat was raw and the sound that erupted was a ragged moan.

Turhan waited for the racking sobs to stop. Then he held her tightly and said, in the same gentle voice with which he'd pulled her from Metin. "I'm sorry. Truly, truly I'm sorry. Metin's dead. He was my friend, too. I grieve for his soul and yours. But there are thousands of men dying and wounded on that field this instant. We must save what lives we can. For Allah's sake and Metin's, pull yourself together. Help me save the few we've got left!"

She nodded dumbly and started working again. Through a growing haze of pain and numbness, Halide bandaged the wounded, carried away their excrement, bathed their glistening foreheads, and told dying men they'd be all right, without respite, without food, without sleep, for the rest of the afternoon and all through that night.

The following evening, Colonel Mustafa Kemal wrote in his journal, "*The damned malaria and exhaustion are getting to me, but I dare not let it show. The officers and men see me as superhuman. Perhaps that's necessary if we are to survive this battle. Earlier this evening, when I was feeling particularly weak, Halide Orhan attended me. What a tragedy she's sustained. She lost her fiancé less than twenty-four hours ago. Never in my life, have I seen such courage in one so young. She must have been dying inside, yet she listened patiently to me. Because of women such as this one the Turkish nation must – the Turkish nation will – survive."*

Halide refused to eat. The battle raged on. She performed her duties as if she were a wooden doll. Turhan kept her moving. Bodies continued to pile up. By nightfall, exhausted, weakened from lack of food and sleep, she collapsed. She blamed herself for Metin's death. She cursed Allah and vowed to starve herself. Turhan continued to talk to her softly, covered her with blankets, sat by her side after they'd left the infirmary tent.

"Curse Allah," he said. "He deserves it. You didn't cause this war. You brought happiness to Metin before he died. He was fulfilled as a man. Could any woman have done more?"

On the third day after Metin's death, Halide managed to hold down some hot soup and tea. As day followed bloody day, she watched helplessly as hundreds, then thousands, of young Turkish men, clothed in rags, with old weapons and little hope, died so that the Ottoman Empire could hold on to this tiny piece of land.

15

September 1, 1915.   *Gelibolu*

Darling Papa:

Only now have I pulled myself together enough to write to you. I cannot thank Colonel Kemal enough for setting up the emergency call to Paris.

I still find it hard to believe Metin's gone. I must work for two, to accomplish what we both would have wanted. Next week, I'll be leaving Gelibolu. General Akdemir has arranged for me to meet Metin's parents in Istanbul. Their suffering has been as deep as mine. How terrible it must be for a mother who carried a child in her womb, nursed him, and saw him grow into young manhood, to lose that child at the very beginning of his adult life!

Metin died for a land that is suffering. He was proud to return and fight for it. When I first left France, I found it hard to comprehend how anyone would willingly give his life for a country. Yet, since I arrived here, I've seen something I never saw in France. The people are desperately poor, their government corrupt and inefficient. But these people open up their hearts to one another and to strangers as well. So many went out of their way to help me come to Metin. So many have comforted me since he died. The people of this land have given their love to me. One day I must return that love. Isn't it strange I can still feel that emotion?

I will suffer the loss of my Metin for the rest of my life, Papa. But I had two glorious years worth of memories some girls never have. I've been blessed by the love of two good men. Now I have only one left. You were my first.

Turhan, a boy my age, has spent more time than anyone helping me through this dreadful time. I could not have survived without him. He's as exhausted as I, but he's twice refused to take leave, even though directed to do so. He said they could court-martial him if they wanted but he would not voluntarily quit this place.

He showed me a few entries from a journal he's been keeping. He said he was determined to become "Turkey's spokesman to the world," He's already had a piece published. When he showed it to me, I had a sense of déjà vu. *Remember the story we saw in* Vatan? *Turhan wrote that article!*

He's taken on a last name, something quite rare in Anatolia. He never knew his father. His mother never paid him much attention from what I can gather. He considers himself simply a 'Son of Turkey' and has taken on that last name. If you ever read anything by someone named "Turhan Türkoğlu," you'll know you heard it first from your loving daughter.

Last week, the battle lines moved closer to the infirmary. During the morning, before we evacuated the area, I saw Kemal leading an assault. He was hit by gunfire, but he refused to go down! I was close enough that I heard his Aide de Camp shout, "Sir, you've been hit!" Kemal told the man to be quiet, lest the other officers hear. He fumbled around his chest and drew a watch from his breast pocket. His face went white when he saw that the timepiece had been shattered. "See," he told his adjutant, "here's a watch that's worth a life!"

The battle went on for ten days. The hills were afire with death and destruction. Is it really so important that thousands of men die to capture a single hill? What a tragic, meaningless waste for both sides. For humanity.

In the end, the Ottomans held the high ground. The battle was abandoned. Things settled down to the same trench warfare as before. The only difference was that a hundred thousand men who'd breathed, eaten, laughed, written letters to their sweethearts, no longer walked the face of the earth.

I multiply my grief at Metin's death by countless thousands of other young sweethearts, wives, mothers, sisters, who will shortly be receiving the same news I did. And what was really accomplished? If I sound bitter, I am. What a tragedy! What a disaster!

Oh, papa, I love you so much. I pray for your happiness each night, and it comforts me to know that you are there. I hug your spirit to my breast.

Your loving daughter, Halide

On September 9, 1915, Turhan wrote in his journal, "*Halide Orhan left Gelibolu today. We're all the less for it. She worked tirelessly at the dirtiest, most menial tasks. She always had a kind word for everyone. Halide told me Lieutenant Ermenek's spirit lives on through her. If that's so, he is blessed in memory. Allah couldn't have found a better human being to send to this forsaken hellhole… They called her the "Angel of Gelibolu" behind her back.* Inshallah *our paths may someday cross again.*"

In Gallipoli, the campaign grew static. Both sides dug in. Kemal begged permission to launch one final, massive attack to destroy the enemy. The request was denied with the curt response, "We have no forces, not even a single soldier, to waste."

Mustafa asked to be relieved of his command and returned to Istanbul. Ten days later, the British evacuated the peninsula and withdrew from Turkey without further casualties.

Each side entered the Battle for Gallipoli with half a million men. Each side suffered two hundred fifty thousand casualties. And at the end, except for the oceans of blood that soaked the earth, and the oceans of tears shed by those left behind, everything remained precisely as it had been a year before.

16

After spending the winter with Metin's family, Halide went to Paris in the spring of 1916, vowing to return "home" to Turkey as soon she completed her studies. The story of her heroism at the front had spread from Istanbul to Paris, and diplomats in both warring nations insured that her passage to France was an easy one. The city had lost its love of battle quickly. The first Zeppelin raids brought war to the French capital. News that the ancient Franz Josef of Austria had died and that Kaiser Wilhelm had decreed food rationing in Germany did not lift the city's mood. A sad, dirty war of attrition ravaged the countryside. Casualties on both sides continued to mount with no end in sight.

Turhan was released from military duty about the same time as Halide returned to the west. He took a few courses at the *müderrise,* but soon became convinced he was not cut out for university life. In the fall of that year, Turhan sought full-time employment as a reporter and submitted samples of his work to every newspaper in the Ottoman capital. Despite his confidence that it would be only a matter of days before an astute editor or publisher would discover his brilliance, weeks went by and he received no job offers. He knocked on doors again.

The response was invariably the same. The papers had all the reporters they needed. Most were trying to cut staff because of expenses and the shortage of newsprint.

Although Turhan's fortune from the caravan journey was largely intact, he knew it could not support him forever. With the deaths of the Agha Nikrat and his family, Turhan's connections to power in the capital had dissolved. He spent days observing and writing about life in the city and sent his articles to the various dailies where he'd applied for work. At night, he worked as a waiter at *Rouge et Noir*, where many of Istanbul's European community gathered to enjoy the decadent naughtiness of the vaguely sinister place.

Istanbul – the Europeans continued to call it Constantinople – was a fascinating monument to collapsing grandeur. Elegant, two-storied wooden villas owned by the nobility crept up the hills overlooking the Bosphorous, from Dolmabahche Palace north to the Black Sea. High stone walls bordering the verdant lawns and miniature forests surrounded these mansions, insuring that French, Italians, Germans, and wealthy Turks were a world apart from the teeming, crowded alleys closer to the city's center.

Ships flying the ensigns of every European nation tied up at docks alongside *Galata Saray*, the floating bridge across the Golden Horn that connected European Pera to Turkish Stamboul. As 1916 gave way to 1917, Turhan noticed more and more Russians debarking from many of the smaller vessels. Often they arrived with little more than the shirts on their backs.

One evening, when he reported to work at *Rouge et Noire*, Turhan heard a voice importuning the manager in heavily-accented Turkish. When his eyes became accustomed to the dimly-lit cavern, he saw a fellow no older than himself, in battered, ill-fitting clothing, carrying a violin case that looked more tattered than the man's outfit.

"Turhan, get this Russian fool away from me," the manager said, good-naturedly. "Look, *tovarisch*," he said, turning back to the threadbare young man. "I haven't got enough work for my people as it is. Now you're telling me I need a *violinist*?"

"Please, sir," the young man said, focusing his attention on Turhan. "I'm not asking for salary. I need food. I don't beg. I only ask that your employer allow me to play my instrument a few hours a night, even outside the door, for whatever listeners might throw."

"Turhan," the manager said, exasperated. "What do I do with this man? This town's already got more than enough Russian musicians to fill every concert hall in the Empire."

"Kivrim Effendi," Turhan said politely. "Have you listened to this one play?"

"What am I, the conductor of a symphony orchestra? How would I know if he's better or worse than any other?"

"Please, sir," the musician broke in. "Won't you just listen?"

The manager glared at Turhan, who'd failed to rid him of the interloper. During the few moments of silence, the Russian opened the battered case and took out a highly-polished, obviously old, but lovingly cared-for rosewood instrument. He lifted the instrument to his chin, plucked the four strings lightly to make sure they were in tune, and started to play.

What came out of the violin was magic. The instrument laughed, cried, and sang from its master's soul. When the violinist broke into the third movement of Tchaikovsky's violin concerto, the manager stood mesmerized. Moments after the man put the instrument down, he said, "When can you start?"

"Tonight at two in the morning."

"What kind of foolishness is this? We're open from eight at night 'til four in the morning. I expect you to play the entire time."

"I can't for at least a month."

"Why not?"

"Because of my other job."

"Your other job?"

"Yes, sir. I play piano in a bordello reserved for wealthy Europeans. They only close at two."

Within a month, Turhan and the young Russian, Sascha Brotsky, had become fast friends. Sascha was as charming a companion as he was an astounding instrumentalist. Invariably he left the *Rouge et Noir* with a woman on his arm. Young, old, it made no difference. By the hungry, glazed look in their eyes, these ladies, regardless of station, had one thing on their minds. During their days off, Sascha often suggested it would be fine with him if Turhan wanted to share his wealth of female companionship. "Some of the girls in the 'house' have been providing me with their favors. Let me tell you, they're delicious, and wonderfully proficient! If you're not interested in those fillies, there are so many luscious young women in this city I couldn't possibly bed them all. Like fresh, ripe fruit, just waiting to be plucked. Trust me, you'd be doing me a favor by taking some of them off my hands."

"I haven't had much time for that sort of thing. First school, then the war, now two jobs. I'd feel clumsy. I wouldn't know what to do."

"Don't be ridiculous, my friend. Women provide the greatest relief from all the tensions of life. Surely you wouldn't pass up a little fun."

"Tell you what, Sascha. Give me a month or so to get my life in order, and then we'll talk about it."

"Suit yourself," the Russian said. "Just let me know when, what color hair you want her to have, and how large you want her breasts to be. The mood in this city is 'live for today.' With so many soldiers at the front, we have our choice of almost any woman in the capital. And we're only young once, eh?" He punched Turhan jovially on the arm.

Turhan refused to abandon hope that he'd eventually land a job as a journalist. He continued to visit the editorial offices of every newspaper in the city – often they were little more than one-room storefronts – at least once each week.

One day, Rustem Effendi, publisher of a small, conservative newspaper, *Rahin*, said, "I may have a short-term assignment for you. Would you be interested in going to the southeast?"

"Yes, Effendi. I'm from Diyarbakır province." He tried to keep the excitement out of his voice.

"Good. The British have just appointed Colonel Lawrence as political and liaison officer to Faisal's Arab army. It doesn't take a great deal of political insight to predict it'll only be a matter of time before the Arabs demand independence. All my regular reporters are covering war stories in other parts of the empire. I need someone close to the area to get a feel for what's going on down there. It's a two month assignment. I'll pay your travel expenses plus twenty-five *kurush* for every article we print."

"But Effendi, how could I possibly live on such a sum? I'm barely getting by on the three hundred *kurush* I'm paid at *Rouge et Noir* each week."

"Do you want to get started in this business or not? You can make a fairly comfortable living being a waiter. If you want to be a reporter, you've got to starve just like the rest of us. Every week, I look at my books and wonder how I've staved off bankruptcy."

"How soon would you want me to get started, Effendi?"

"Here's an open round trip ticket. You can take the boat to Iskenderun tonight."

The Levantine coast was a rowdy, noisy, polyglot mixture of all the peoples of the Earth. Egyptians selling bolts of cotton cloth were shouted down by Chinese hawking ginseng herbs guaranteed to increase sexual performance. Greek fisherman promised the freshest fish in the Mediterranean. Persian merchants displayed piles of colorful carpets stacked higher than Turhan was tall. There seemed little, if any, order here. Coastal cities blended into each other much as houses leaned against one another. Merchants and beggars congregated in narrow alleys. Urine and feces ran down gutters in the middle of these commercial "boulevards," mingling with odors of fried fish, onions, cabbage and *khari* peppers. One shout was indistinguishable from another. Turhan was pushed and shoved anywhere he walked. No one apologized or offered any excuse for such rude behavior. The cacophonous voices blended to form a strangely harmonious mural.

"Woman, sah? Nubian. Very black, very hot. You evah been with black woman, sah? My seestah. She is virgin, sah." This from a greasy-looking brown boy of ten.

"You need a horse, perhaps, My Lord? From the sands of Arabia. Very strong, very cheap."

"Alms, patron. Dispossessed of my fortune and my feet, look here your kindliness, I have only to beg."

"Come with me, young man. I want to show you some interesting drugs, guaranteed to give you the potency of a lion. You can lie with twelve women in one night and delight them all!"

Street musicians abounded, each jangling, piping, clashing, beating to outdo the other. Music from Cairo, Baghdad, Teheran, Beirut, all the mysterious places he'd read about in an atlas at the lycée, merged noisily in this place.

Soon, Turhan found there was order in this apparent chaos. Jewel merchants, usually Jewish or Persian, sometimes Syrian, camped on the east side of Iskenderun, close to trade caravans. Brown-skinned Hindus from the East congregated in spice bazaars north of the jewelers. Even the areas on the sea were divided. Fisherman docked at the northern extremities of the harbor. South of that, an Ottoman naval station dominated the central cordon. Immediately below the comparative civility of the military station was the commercial part of the bay, where everything from soft little boys to the most potent drugs could be bought by anyone with sufficient money to spend. South of the city, toward the Syrian border, wide, white-sand beaches stretched for miles beside the warm sea.

During his first week in the city, Turhan met the naval commander, walked the city's streets and alleys, and wrote dispatches back to Istanbul. There were a large number of veiled women in the marketplace. Often, he noticed that he got hard when he saw them. In the evenings, he found it more and more difficult to push sexual thoughts from his mind. Ten days after he'd arrived in Iskenderun, he'd written three articles. There was a major army installation near Diyarbakır, two day's journey to the east. Diyarbakır. The name conjured up so many memories.

Diyarbakır was more crowded than Turhan remembered. Its main streets were now paved to accommodate motor vehicles that drove about the city. The feeling of the place had not changed in the years since he'd left. Kurdish horsemen still rode through the streets, oblivious to everything else. The central marketplace still teemed with commodities. The shouts and bargaining took him back to the time when he'd worked near these very stalls. He was happy to learn that Jalal the butcher, who'd been so kind to him, had amassed a fortune purveying meat to the army after the war started, but was disappointed that the man was in the central steppes for a month, finding a new lamb supplier for the garrison. He made a halfhearted attempt to locate his mother. When he learned from old neighbors that she'd gone "south" with a Syrian, he was satisfied he'd done his filial duty.

Earlier that morning, he'd breakfasted with the press liaison officer from Diyarbakır fortress. Shortly before noon, he returned to the center of town. He felt a buzzing lightheadedness and knew exactly why. He walked toward a neighborhood he remembered so well. Enroute, he stopped for *shish köfte*, ground lamb meatballs in pita bread, with yogurt on top. His hand trembled as he ate the roll-up sandwich. "Come on," he said to himself. "You're twenty years old, a grown man and a newspaper reporter. You're acting like a child."

When he got to the street he was looking for, he stopped. Allah! The house looked exactly as he remembered it. It had been five years. She'd probably moved. No doubt, she'd changed, most likely grown old, fat as a cow. He walked around the block. His heart was pounding. His hands were clammy. He argued with himself again. "You are Turhan Türkoğlu. You've seen death at Gelibolu and shown yourself capable of finding a job with a newspaper, something you've always wanted to do. You are on assignment from a newspaper in the capital of the Ottoman Empire. There is absolutely nothing wrong with your knocking on the door of an old friend to pay your respects."

It didn't help. He walked around the block three more times. She's probably not home anyway, he thought. The shades were drawn. It was mid-afternoon by the time Turhan got up the nerve to go to the door. Even then he hesitated. He knocked tentatively. There was no sound. He knocked again, waited another minute. Then he heard a shuffling noise and a female voice, "Yes? Who is it, please?"

Was it her voice, or not? "Türkoğlu." He used his assumed name.

"Just a moment."

The door opened. He stood speechless. Time had stood still. Gönül must be thirty-four. She was slimmer, more elegant than he remembered. Her hair was cut short, in the current style, but it was still the same blue-black color. "Yes?" she asked, no flicker of recognition in her eyes.

"Ummm, Gönül Hanım?" he stammered, feeling like an imbecile.

"I am she. How can I help you, Sir?"

"Ummm, is your husband at home?"

"What kind of prank is this? Ertuğrul died last year. That's common knowledge in Diyarbakır. What is your business, young man?" she asked, somewhat impatiently.

"Gönül Hanım, you don't remember me?"

"Should I remember you? I believe you said your name was Türkoğlu. The name means nothing to me."

"I am Turhan. Don't you remember?"

She looked at him carefully. Her eyes widened with a dawning recognition. "Turhan? *Turhan*? Allah be praised, it's you! My God, it's been five years." She smiled warmly. "Come in, come in, Turhan! Allah, you've grown! I mean, you're a man!"

As Turhan entered the house, he noticed that many of the old pieces of furniture were gone. The house had an airy, lighter feel than he remembered. "Now sit down and tell me what's become of you," she said. "I heard Ibrahim died of heart failure three months after you joined his caravan. It was kind and most generous of you to send so much money back to me. I tried to get in touch with you, but when the caravan came through Diyarbakır, Alkimi told me you'd gone to Istanbul. I was surprised you never tried to reach me, but I hoped I'd be a memory you'd look back on with pleasure."

"After Ibrahim died, I was fortunate enough to attend the lycée in Istanbul. I enlisted in the medical corps and served at Gelibolu. While I was there, I started writing and I never stopped."

"What are you doing back in Diyarbakır? I thought you wanted to see the world."

"I've been sent here on assignment for a short time. I'm told the war's shifted to the southeast and there's a big military buildup along the Syrian frontier. My home's in Istanbul."

"Well, my young lion," she said. It looks like you're doing what you set out to do in life."

"And you, Hanım Effendi? You're even more beautiful than I remembered."

"You flatter an old woman, kind sir. The boy I knew has become quite the charmer. Ertuğrul died last year. He was a good man. You never met him, which was certainly for the best. He left me quite prosperous. When he passed on, his mercantile empire had grown. He taught me well. I'm still involved in the business. Whenever there's a wealthy widow, there are always men about. It's only now that I'm allowed to seek social company again. In fact, a widower merchant has asked me to dine with him this evening. What about you, 'little lion?' No doubt you've conquered the hearts, and what's between the legs, of a hundred women between here and Istanbul."

Turhan blushed deeply. "Did I strike a raw nerve?" Gönül asked. "Surely you've not gone the other way?"

"No, Gönül Hanım, it's not that at all."

"What, then?"

"It's simply that with everything that's gone on in my life I – that is – I haven't had the time or learned how to approach a woman."

Gönül laughed delightedly, a wonderful, musical, sensuous laugh. "I find that hard to believe." They sat in amiable silence for several moments.

Gönül glanced at a wrist watch she was wearing, then said, "Excuse me for a few moments, Turhan. I promised I'd telephone my widower friend about what time he should pick me up for dinner this evening. I'll only be a few minutes. Make yourself at home, unless you're in a hurry to go somewhere."

"No, that's fine," he replied. "I've got a week before I return to Istanbul."

Gönül went into the kitchen and returned with a bowl filled with apples, oranges and grapes. Then, she disappeared into another part of the house. Turhan got up, stretched, and looked at the books in Gönül's bookcase. Her tastes, as evidenced by what he saw, were wide-ranging, everything from histories of the Ottoman Empire to scientific journals. He became so engrossed in thumbing through a book on the American War of Independence that he did not hear Gönül return.

His first indication of her presence was a strong, musky fragrance that struck a long dormant nerve. When he turned to face her, he saw she'd changed into a silk robe of the Chinese style now popular in Turkey. "All done, young lion," she said, her voice husky with the smokiness he remembered from so long ago.

"I wouldn't want to keep you from your dinner engagement," he said, his words coming with difficulty.

"Oh, you won't." She walked over to the front door, locked it, and walked back toward him. She gazed directly at him, her eyes very bright. She loosened the belt on the robe and let it drop to the floor. She wore nothing underneath the silky outfit. Her breasts thrust forth, as youthful and inviting as he remembered them.

"Turhan," she said. "We're now going to prove you possess all the charm you'll ever need, as well as everything else necessary to follow through on that charm. And you are going to bring a very randy woman a great deal of pleasure. Ah, I see our friend remembers what he's supposed to do," she said, loosening his pants and pulling them down below his knees. She kneeled, and whispered, "Now let's see if *you* remember as well." She lowered his undershorts and caressed his member with her tongue. "Mmmmm," she said, her eyelids growing heavy, as her tongue darted all over him and she started sucking.

There was no way he could hold back. No way he wanted to. In a remarkably short time, he exploded with a ferocity which surprised them both. "Whew!" she said. "I think you work just fine. Now, let's see if you can satisfy both of us." He obediently followed the beautiful woman into her boudoir.

"What about your dinner date?" he asked. "You said I wouldn't keep you from it."

"You won't. I canceled it." She looked at him lustfully. "Besides, I have my own ideas of what I want for dinner this evening."

When Turhan returned to Istanbul, he suffered two immediate disappointments. *Rahin* had gone bankrupt, leaving Turhan without the five hundred *kurush* he'd been counting on. And when he returned to *Rouge et Noir*, he learned that his friend Sascha was no longer there.

"Packed up and left," the manager said. "Gave me two days' notice. I'll miss the little Russian. He was friendly enough, and the women certainly seem upset he's gone."

"Any word as to where he went, Kivrim Bey?"

"America. Strangest thing you ever saw. One evening he was playing up a storm – that Tchaikovsky number in fact. Big, fat man, about forty came in, asked me if I had a contract with Brotsky. I shrugged. He handed me six hundred lira to tide me over 'til I could find another violinist. He said America would pay a fortune to hear the fellow. Next thing I knew, Brotsky was gone. At least I've got one of my two most popular employees back. Did you discover anything of interest while you were gone?"

Turhan nodded inscrutably, hiding a secret smile.

"Ah well, no mind. I'm glad to have you back. Now if only you could learn to play the violin and speak with a Russian accent, everything would be just fine."

HUGO N. GERSTL COLLECTION

See below some of Pangæa Publishing Group's
bestsellers by the same author:

Do not miss them on your shelf!

For Hugo N. Gerstl's complete novels list and descriptions,
go to www.HugoGerstl.com

PANGÆA PUBLISHING GROUP
25579 Carmel Knolls Drive
Carmel, CA 93923
Email: info@pangaeapublishing.com

Printed in Great Britain
by Amazon